# The Odyssey of Orion

## Exile

## By

## Drew Jeffers

# Contents

# Dedication

For Lexi and Macie. Without the two of you, this would not have been so fulfilling or even possible. I love you with everything I have.

# Acknowledgments

When I think of all the people who made this book possible, I must first recognize the woman who introduced me to the beauty of story and literature, my mother. We are far from the days spent reading and conversing over stories that moved us, but now they feel much nearer. Writing this novel has been a surreal experience. It has allowed me to feel that same wonder; a wonder that I hope this story returns to her. Thank you for a life full of love, L.J. Let's go on another adventure together.

As I was writing, a little voice in my head was always there. A critic on my shoulder, if you will. This was Jason Webb's voice. Though he was perhaps my most critical teacher, his impression is long-lasting. It inspired a drive to write deliberately, in detail, with depth. It makes humility habitual. It reminds me every day that great writing is not the product of talent alone. It is a continuous dive into the depth of thought. Cheers to you, sir. Sit back, relax, and take a dive with me for old time's sake.

Meaghan and Brett, beloved parents of my loving wife, who have been eagerly awaiting the release of this novel. They have not only called out to the world and shared my story with everyone they know, they are the example and counsel I turn to in times of doubt. They are the caliber of parent everyone should aspire to be. I do, every day. Thank you for your love, support, and now, it is storytime.

My beautiful Lexi and sweet Macie, for whom this first book is dedicated. No man is complete without his wife, and no family is complete without children, so it is needless to say that I could not have felt fulfilled by accomplishing this lifelong dream if it had not been for the both of you. Every difficulty and every doubt faded in your smiles, and every beautiful moment was magnified by your perfect love. I love you both with everything I have.

# About the Author

# Prologue

At the edge of the known universe lies a cosmos unknown to all others, one that is distinguished by its two greatest forces, which impact everything within. At the crown of its spiraling structure is the largest and brightest star in existence, which casts light upon everything caught in its pull. The inhabitants of this system call it Atlas, so named for its constant pull of every world, moon, and star against the influence of the Kashii Maelstrom, a black hole spanning beneath the entire expanse of this system.

Closest to the great star of Atlas lie the oldest civilized worlds of the system: Japra, Goll, Hetra, Comra, Serpeno, Olum, Kosh, Polla, Zorum, and Tetra. One chancellor from each of these worlds sits upon the High Council to represent their people and help their counterparts keep order throughout their allied worlds. Since the council's formation, these ten chancellors have maintained the longest peace amongst intelligent species in all of known history.

Between the great star Atlas and the Kashii Maelstrom lie the Worlds of Limbo, systems of worlds caught between the gravitational pull of Atlas and the Maelstrom. Over the millennium, many of these worlds have been split into oblivion, living on only in the memories of the remaining worlds and those which are fortunate enough not to be caught between such unstoppable powers. Fleeing the threat of their planet's destruction, many inhabitants of Limbo abandoned their homes and sought asylum elsewhere. Now, the remaining worlds caught in Limbo are mostly abandoned, allocated by the high council to only be used for their resources. This way, the rest of the alliance can thrive without suffering through such an armageddon. This mass exodus was seen as a great triumph to the chancellors' subjects, followed by decades of admiration and glory for their heroic legislation and efforts to aid the common good. However, too many forgot that in this delicate system of worlds, there are greater dangers than the pull of gravity.

Holding the most horrific of these dangers are six worlds, which are caught in the slow, endless spiral of the Kashii Maelstrom. To all others, these are known as the Underworlds. They are Phobus, Cronum, Eris, Styxus, Demos, and Thraxus. These doomed worlds are the dwelling of the most dangerous creatures and beings in the cosmos. Murderers, terrorists, monsters, and criminals make their way there with virtually no interference from the high council because they are unwilling to risk entering a realm from which they would likely never return. Any unfortunate soul who is lost or caught in the grasp of the Maelstrom and marooned on one of these six dark worlds will inevitably die, whether it is by the hands of a monster or another dangerous mystery that lurks among the Underworlds.

The tale that follows began far from where one might expect it to; beyond the great forces at the center of this system and amid its countless unknown worlds. Its origin was a small planet that would be the birthplace of the greatest tragedy and the greatest legend of the cosmos; Archon Prime. It was here that the high council had its first encounter with the most infamous species in all of existence: humans.

They arrived on Archon Prime as refugees, searching the expanse of the universe aboard solar spaceships for a world they could call their own, and they found it there, on the first world orbiting around the bright dwarf star Archon. It paled compared to the planets surrounding Atlas, yet it was the first one they had discovered that they could call their own, covered with mountains and forests growing out of rich black soil, temperate climates and seasons. When they arrived, the humans rejoiced, believing they had found paradise.

Their presence was soon discovered with great distrust by the High Council, and the moment it was, the head of the High Council, Rax Jafar of Japra, immediately set out to investigate their intentions, for humans were considered notorious creatures, only known for their inclination to violence. They were seen by all others as the most selfish and destructive species, more of a pestilence than an intelligence.

When Rax Jafar arrived, he was greeted graciously by the new settlement. Yet, as he inspected the small planet's new residents, he sensed those amongst them who resented his authority. He offered them trade and commerce, resources in exchange for their help in building more solar spaceships for the rest of the alliance. As a safeguard for their new contract, a detachment of soldiers from the worlds of Atlas was sent to ensure their compliance with the laws of the alliance, and should they abide by them, they would be welcomed with open arms and protected from any that would do them harm. The humans agreed to those terms, and Rax Jafar left, still skeptical of their ability to keep their end of the bargain.

One year following that day, his greatest fears were realized when a small group of men attacked a Serpen soldier and killed him, claiming that they felt threatened by their armed presence, and thus began the first war in the history of the alliance; known as the Crisis of Archon Prime. Rax Jafar and the other chancellors immediately sent their armies to the tiny world, intent on driving the violent species out of their system. It was a bloody and horrible conflict. Children were ripped from the hands of their mothers and fathers by the high council's soldiers and imprisoned in camps as deterrents from further violence. Many brave sons and fathers fought to their dying breath to win their sovereignty and save their families, but after three years, more than half of the human population had been slaughtered, and victory for the High Council seemed inevitable, until one man rose amongst the others, a warrior named Rom Castus.

Rom rallied every able-bodied man and woman to his cause and freed the imprisoned children one by one, returning them to their families. When the final camp was routed, he was unanimously chosen by the people to be the first King of Archon Prime, and in the years that followed, he rebuilt their army into an organized and formidable fighting force. Their efforts were valiant and felt throughout the alliance. Though they did not immediately overwhelm the High Council's army, they were able to extend the conflict into a war that lasted ten bloody years.

At the end of this gruesome decade, the weary Rax Jafar withdrew his troops, unable to end the conflict and tired of fending off his displeased political counterparts on the High Council, who had already pulled their own troops back. Immediately after, he resigned his seat and was succeeded by his son, Jula Jafar, who declared Archon Prime a sovereign world, banishing them from ever setting foot on any world in the Atlas Alliance.

For the humans, this was their first great victory. They had won their freedom, and once the last of the High Council's armies had left their world, they began to rebuild their civilization. They erected their capital, Luma City, upon the final battleground and enjoyed many years of peace and prosperity, but just as Rax Jafar had always known, this peace among the humans would not last forever.

Soon, after years of fortifying their city, army, and impressive fleet of ships, the small planet's resources had been diminished, and a great drought plagued their planet, killing off their once abundant livestock and agriculture until all that remained was a dying world, swept in the whirlwinds of black sand that slowly consumed everything in its path. The once-wealthy aristocrats immediately turned to exploit the poor and, in their greed, ignited a civil war.

The once-adored King Rom was now despised by nearly every member of the working class. Many claimed that he had orchestrated the divide of their resources in favor of himself and those closest to him. Despite the allegations, he offered no official response to his people's demands or made any move to end the conflict.

Then, one night, as he slept soundly in his high chamber, his people attempted to lay siege to the palace and make him answer for the crimes he was accused of. His soldiers did everything they could, but even they could not stand against the people, and they broke into the palace.

However, what the rioters found waiting for them on the other side of the great palace door was not their tyrant king but something much worse. At the end of the great hall in the palace stood a cloaked warrior, clad head to toe in black armor and armed with only one sword. Thinking he was just another soldier, the rioters attacked him with full force.

They all met their end, every last one of them. The mysterious warrior was unlike any other they had encountered; he was faster, stronger, and perfect in every single way a warrior could be. He single-handedly quelled the entire uprising in one bloody night, then once they were all dead at his feet, he vanished without a trace.

Some say he was a mercenary from the Kashii Maelstrom, hired by the king to end the civil war. Others say that he was his personal bodyguard, but the truth remained unknown for five long years as the state of the planet continued to decline into endless squalor. The once prosperous city was now in shambles, only a few of their ships remained, and those who once prided themselves on their wealth were quickly ruined, forced to tend the ever-dying fields. Darkness clouded the skies, and their once-green world became a dark and deathly wasteland.

Then, on the fifth anniversary of the siege to the palace, a great and awful light struck down from the heavens. It almost felt like an enormous flash of lightning at the front of the palace. It vanished just as quickly as it had appeared, and at the point of impact appeared a strange and horrifying machine, with the mysterious warrior who defended the king five years prior standing upon it. The people cowered in fear, certain that he had returned by the king's command to execute them all so that he might survive. To their surprise, he made no such move against them. Instead, he walked past them silently, with his sword in his hand, into the palace and slaughtered everyone within.

When the sounds of bloodshed within had finally ended, a man was sent inside by the rest of the inhabitants of the city to investigate. When he opened the great doors, hot blood poured out onto the steps of the palace. Every tile of the stone floor was painted with the blood of their remaining soldiers. Their bodies were dismembered, decapitated, and their faces were frozen with lifeless terror. The man pressed past their corpses, cautiously seeking the mysterious warrior. He found him in the high chamber, with the king's head in his hand, silently looking out over the city, "Who are you?" the man asked.

The dark figure did not turn to face the frightened man but softly answered, "I am Oberon, and this world is now mine."

# Chapter One: Eighteen Years Later

The bright star Archon rose over the horizon of Archon Prime. Its rays lightened the shade of the dark clouds hanging in the sky, washing away the blackness of the night. This wave of grey rose over the crumbling remains of Luma City. It crept its way onto the shining fences of razors surrounding its perimeter, then into the black stone structures and dwellings within. The people slowly awoke as another day began. They rose from their beds, stoked their hearths, and prepared their morning meals. As the smoke from their fireplaces rose, it added yet another layer of smell and shadows to their squalor. Outside the door of each dwelling stood a fearsome sentry android with blazing red eyes, armed with a sharpened sword, waiting to escort its assigned family of human slaves to work as soon as they emerged from their dwellings. The moment the slaves stepped into the dismal streets, the sentries would sound off with the same instruction, in the same commanding and monotone voice as their counterparts, "Report to your station."

The people obeyed these mechanical warriors without protest. Some would tread towards the fence surrounding the city to repair any gaps in the fence or damage caused by the torrential sandstorms that would bash against the city. Others reported to the ration house at the center of the city, where they would package foul-smelling sludge and filthy water to be distributed to each family at the middle and the end of every day. As the weeks dragged on, the people's portions diminished more and more in size, even though there was enough to more than double what was given out. Years ago, some found the courage to raid the ration house, but they soon learned that resistance came with a more frightening price than starvation.

Most of the men residing in the city were marched outside its perimeter to a large field where they grew black agro, the primary ingredient in their daily rations. It was a seed as large as a man's fist and black as tar. Before the people of Luma City were slaves, the black agro was used to feed their Archonian cattle, grazing mammals that produced sweet milk and yielded delicious meat from every muscle; but since the drought, all the herds had wasted away in the black dust, along with every plant they once grazed upon.

The remainder of the slaves worked within the Regent's dark tower, which was built over the foundation of King Rom's palace after it was destroyed. All those who worked outside its walls considered themselves to be more fortunate than they were, for the mysterious warrior who had enslaved them was a living nightmare to every single one of them.

Nearly every slave who worked within the dark tower rarely ever saw the Regent, but his deeds had sparked countless horrific rumors among them. Some heard that he would have the slaves who resisted his mechanical sentries arrested and brought before him, offering them freedom if they could best him in combat. Others believed that he tortured those who resisted simply because he enjoyed it. One young and particularly unfortunate slave, the Regent's personal aide, was the only one able to confirm which, if any, of these horrors were true. Whenever asked, his answer to those questions was always the same: "Please," he would say, "don't make me tell you."

It led everyone to take everything they heard of their master as truth, no matter how grievous it was.

The Regent's personal aide was no older than eighteen, with long, unruly blonde hair and a face that projected kindness and sincerity to everyone. No one ever had the impression that he would lie to them, including the Regent himself.

His daily duties were very simple, he was to act as the Regent's informant and emissary, keeping him apprised of everything he heard among the people. He was also responsible for delegating the workers and sentries according to the 'needs of the people.' He was never sent to tend the field, the fence, or work in the ration house, but all who knew him understood that their hardest day was easier than one day in his position, a position that forced him to face their murderous Regent every single day.

He began that particular day in his usual manner as the rest of the people began theirs. When the Archon star rose and the sentry who stood outside his mother's home ushered him to his post, he stepped quickly across the black gravel streets with his favorite scarlet poncho blowing in the dry wind. He avoided the gaze of everyone he passed until he reached the front doors of his master's dark tower. He pushed one of the doors slightly ajar, then strode quickly across the black marble floor and took the long staircase at the back of the great hall to a small, elegant elevator shaft. He pressed the first button on the panel, and the elevator began to rise to the top of the tower. As it ascended, he took three long deep breaths to calm his nerves. Once the doors of the elevator slowly slid open, he stepped into the Regent's chambers and immediately fell to his knees with his head bowed, "I am here, master," he announced,

"Come," the Regent said.

He obeyed, stood up to his feet, and cautiously walked towards his master, who was standing on his balcony, looking down upon the dark city. He was clad in the same black suit of armor and cloak he had worn every day since he returned to the planet. It was covered in countless scratches, blemishes, and small stains of dried blood between its grooves. His cloak was as black as night, tattered and torn at the edges, with the hood pulled over his horrifying mask, which had a strange set of black, fanged jawbones crudely attached over the mouth.

"Yes, master?" the Regent's aid said nervously,

"Look down there," the Regent said, "Tell me what you see."

He looked out into the city and promptly answered, "I see your city, sir."

"Look again. There is something within the city that requires our attention."

He looked again and nervously replied, "Your people, sir?"

The Regent nodded his head slowly and turned around, "I see people who should already be dead, young Rowan, and yet they are not."

Rowan lowered his eyes, avoiding his horrifying gaze, and wrung his hands nervously behind his back, "I-I'm afraid I don't understand, master."

"My sentries have reported rumors amongst the people that there is a hunter living outside the city who has provided additional food to the people. What do you know of this?"

"Nothing, sir," he answered, "Is there any proof that these rumors might be true?"

The Regent brushed past Rowan to the corner of his chamber. Rowan followed him, and his heart dropped as he spotted a scrawny young boy covered in bruises with a large gash on his forehead. The boy shrieked in terror as the Regent grabbed him by the throat and dragged him out from the corner into the center of the chamber.

"This boy," the Regent said, "Was seen talking to this hunter, then taking a parcel of meat he received from him back to his family."

"The family has been arrested, then?"

"Executed," the Regent growled, "This one will suffer the same fate. However, we must make an example of him,"

"Perhaps there's another way."

"No," the Regent snapped, "This hunter must become nothing more than a cautionary tale, and you will ensure that is so."

Rowan bowed his head, "Yes, master."

"I want the city gathered in front of the tower in one hour."

"It will be done, my lord," Rowan said, turning away as he heard the boy cry out, "Please! Tell the hunter we need him! Someone has to save us!"

His cries were quickly silenced with a metallic ringing and the sound of breaking flesh. Rowan dared not look back, but he felt his stomach churn as the sound of the little boy's head hitting the floor echoed in his ears. He quickly stepped into the elevator and frantically pressed the button until the elevator doors finally shut.

He collapsed to his knees and began to shake. He tried to breathe and calm himself down, but he just panted harder, and his heart beat faster. He did not realize the elevator had reached the great hall until the doors slid open once again. He scrambled back to his feet and breathed as deeply and slowly as possible. He walked deliberately, feigning normalcy as much as he could, but everyone noticed that his pace was much more urgent than usual.

He approached one of the sentries, "The Regent wants everyone gathered here in one hour, see to it."

The machine nodded at his demands, and then Rowan made his way back out into the city, informing the rest of the sentries at each post of their master's wishes.

Before half an hour had passed, every slave was ordered to stop their tasks, and the sentries herded them back onto the gravel streets, directing them to the steps of the dark tower. They were all forced to their knees, and those who responded too slowly had their heads pushed to the ground by forceful, metal hands. Rowan kept his head down, forcing himself not to watch these cruelties. Once the entire population was assembled, he took his usual place at the front of the crowd, kneeling as the rest of them did, with the crown of his head buried in the black gravel.

When the final seconds of the hour had expired, the Regent emerged through the great black doors of his tower, carrying a severed head in his hand. He walked silently and slowly until he reached the top of the steps,

"Look at what your defiance has led to!" he cried out, casting the cold head into the crowd, watching it land in front of Rowan's hands.

Rowan's hands began to shake as the Regent continued his address.

"This boy was found conspiring with a hunter! Smuggling food into the city! He praised him as a savior, even though such disorder sentenced him and his entire family to death!"

Rowan heard the sounds of women and children crying. He even felt tears begin to well up in his own eyes, but he dared not show such emotions before the Regent. He clenched his fists and pushed his head deeper into the gravel, forcing a distraction of pain upon himself to keep from crying out in fury.

"If there are any among you who have any knowledge of who or where this hunter is, you will inform me at once! Any further conspiracy with this hunter will be punishable by the same fate!" With those final words, the Regent turned around and walked back into the tower, and the great doors slammed shut behind him.

"Return to your dwellings," the sentries commanded in unison.

The people immediately scurried away, moving as quickly as they could, leaving the head of the child untouched, kicking pieces of gravel onto it in their frightened haste. Rowan was the only one among them to resemble composure. As he turned to walk away, he stopped and looked down at the boy's face. He had the same shade of hair he did and a thick layer of freckles on his now ghostly pale face.

"I'm so sorry," Rowan whispered tearfully. He turned away and made his way back to his mother's home.

Their dwelling was one that everyone in the city knew. His mother kept the black stone as free of dust as she could and hung their old family crest above the doorway, a red banner with a sword in front of a star. Rowan shook his head as he glanced up at the now-tattered and beaten banner.

"Look at us now," he grumbled to himself.

He stepped into the black stone house and shut their creaky door behind him. "I'm back, Mother," he said,

A scrawny woman with curly blonde hair and a red shawl wrapped over her shoulders rushed over and threw her arms around him,

"Oh, Rowan!" she groaned, "I was so worried. Are you alright?"

"I'm fine. Are you alright?"

"Yes, yes, I'm fine. What happened?"

Rowan shook his head, and tears began to freely fall down his face, "I don't know," he shuddered, "I thought we were being careful. I was sure that there wouldn't be any sentries when I told him where to go," he buried his tearful face in his mother's shoulder and sobbed.

She ran her fingers through his flowing blonde hair, "It's not your fault," she soothed, "He's been doubling his patrols and tightening security ever since they started cutting our rations again."

Rowan backed up his head, "I have to go and tell him before we get someone else killed."

His mother's eyes opened wide as she glared at her son, "Absolutely not!" she hissed,

"Mother, I don't have a choice! He has to know. We have to do something before someone else gets hurt."

His mother scoffed, "People get hurt every day, Rowan. Do you want to end up just like your father? Dead in the street trying to make a stand against this monster? Don't you remember that is how you ended up as the Regent's pet?"

"I know!" Rowan shouted,

His mother jumped as his harsh words filled the walls of the house. She fell silent and looked tearfully at her son,

"Please," she begged, "I can't lose you too. I can't lose my baby boy."

"You'll never lose me," Rowan sighed, "But there are others who are losing everything and everyone they have, and if someone doesn't do something, he is going to kill us all."

His mother stepped away and wiped tears out of her eyes, "You sound just like him, you know," she trembled. Rowan could not find any words to respond, he reached for his mother's hand, but she pulled it away, "You can't leave now," she said, "Just wait until nightfall for me, alright?"

"Alright," Rowan sighed as she walked away, silently crying as she shut the curtain around her bed and lay down facing the black stone wall.

Rowan walked over to his bed and pulled out a folded leather bag from underneath it. He unfurled it and began packing it with the other items he had hidden under his bed. He packed another tunic, a canteen, a small lantern, and a knife. Then he shoved his packed bag underneath his bed and tended their fire, patiently waiting as the end of the dreary day passed on, silently watching as his mother drifted into an uneasy sleep.

Once the Archon star began to dip into the dark horizon, and the city had fallen into an eerie silence, Rowan rose from his spot in front of the hearth, moved to the center of their home, and pulled back a corner of a large mat resting on the floor. Beneath it was a small metal hatch. He grabbed his bag from underneath his bed and took one last look at his mother before he unlocked the hatch, climbed inside, and quietly shut it behind him.

Once he was inside, he turned on his small lantern, and it began to glow with a bright orange light. The lantern revealed the small wooden ladder he had placed inside of the shaft, descending into the old sewer system beneath the city. He climbed down the ladder until his feet touched down the floor of the old tunnel. He held the lantern up, looked down both sides of the passage, ensuring that he was alone, then turned to his right and began running as fast as he could.

The tunnel ran for many miles, stretching far beyond the city limits and out into the barren forest resting at the foot of the nearby mountains. At the end of the tunnel was another ladder leading to another hatch identical to the one hidden beneath Rowan's home. Once Rowan reached it, he climbed up and peeked out beneath the lid of the second hatch, ensuring that the sentry patrols had moved back to the city. All he saw were dead trees with bare limbs and a thin layer of fog that was drifting down from the nearest mountaintop. He sighed with relief, clambered out, and silently shut the hatch behind him, then directed himself towards the peak of the mountain in front of him.

The mountain was a place held in the highest reverence amongst the people of Luma city. It was the sanctuary that protected their forefathers from the onslaught of the High Council's armies. It was where they assembled themselves to reclaim their freedom. Rowan often wondered what it would have been like to live on the mountain, how peaceful it must be to be free, undisturbed by the violence and cruelty of other men. His mind was cleared every time he came here. It made him feel like he was finally free from the Regent, even if it was for just a few hours at a time.

He brushed past the low-hanging limbs and dead undergrowth until he found the well-trodden trail leading toward the mountain. From there, he picked up his pace once again. He ran as quickly as he could through the fog, hoping that the rabid nocturnal predators that lurked within the forest would not pick up his scent.

Since the beginning of the drought, the entire ecosystem of the planet had crumbled. All the wild creatures that once freely roamed the forest were hunted to the brink of extinction by every predator, but none more than the Vyper Hounds; packs of venomous, four-legged creatures that stalked through the mountains. They were the most dangerous creatures lurking in the forest and had become so rabid that now, they would just as easily kill a human as they would anything else. Rowan knew that if he was to make the end of his journey before they came out to hunt, he would have to arrive at his destination before the star sank below the horizon. He was running out of time.

He sprinted through the fog until he had made it all the way up the winding trail, to the foot of the mountain. Once he finally saw the peak, he paused for a moment to catch his breath.

He wiped the sweat off of his brow, but then he felt his heart stop as he heard a shrieking howl no more than ten feet away from him. He turned to where it sounded from and saw a Vyper Hound, growling as it slowly walked towards him.

It had dark eyes and a scrawny body beneath a thin layer of shiny black skin clinging tightly to its bones. It hissed and clicked as it blocked the path in front of him. He frantically reached for the knife in his bag. When he retrieved it, he held the blade out to the vicious creature, attempting to frighten it back into the woods.

It did not move, and four more of its pack emerged to stand beside it, all growling with dripping jaws as they glared at him ravenously. He stood his ground, intent on showing them that he had no fear, hoping they would sense his demeanor, but they simply did not care. They began closing in around him.

Then, a sharp, whistling sound broke through the air. A small part of the fog suddenly parted, and an arrow landed at the feet of the Vyper Hounds. Rowan smiled, for the creatures knew just as well as he did how much danger they were in. They immediately took off back into the forest, yelping in terror.

"I was wondering if you saw me coming," Rowan called out. A voice answered from further up the summit, as the hooded figure it belonged to revealed himself from behind a large rock along the trail.

"You're hard to miss when you wear that stupid poncho," he said.

"It's a family heirloom, and it's still better than yours," Rowan quipped, "Come down here."

He watched as the hooded figure slid down the mountainside, then came running up to him. Rowan held his arms out and embraced him as he ran into his arms with a warm laugh. "It's so good to see you," he said.

"It's good to see you too, Orion," Rowan sighed.

Orion pulled the hood off of his head and revealed his head of long, curly black hair, glowing blue eyes, and his warm smile, which glowed under Rowan's lamplight.

"What are you doing here?" he asked, "I thought you wanted me to start delivering the meat to the city?"

"That's why I'm here," Rowan said, "We shouldn't talk in the open. Let's get up to the cave." Orion nodded and held his hand out to the trail in front of him.

The two ran up the trail in silence, constantly looking over their shoulders for anything lurking around the mountain. They ran until they came to a large cave embedded into the peak of the mountaintop. Rowan smiled as he saw the warm light of a fire flickering from within. He ducked his head and entered first, with Orion following behind him with one last cautious look around before he stepped inside.

Rowan dropped his bag and took a good look at his friend with a smile. He was wearing an old blue tunic, a worn, dirty pair of boots, and his dark blue poncho. He still had the same old leather quiver slung over his back, full of arrows and a steel recurve bow with beautiful spiraling engravings and a leather-bound grip.

"I see you haven't changed much since the last time I saw you," Rowan observed.

"I've been busy," Orion replied,

"Hunting?"

Orion paused, "Yes… but not today,"

"Oh. I'm so sorry. I forgot today was-"

"It's alright," Orion finished, "It's got to be hard to keep track of everyone that we lose now."

"But it's your parents. I should have remembered,"

"I finished their headstone today, and I know they're at peace. I'm sure that they wouldn't have wanted us to grieve for too long over them,"

"They still deserve to be remembered for what they did," Rowan said.

Orion looked at his friend and shook his head, then turned to the small fire burning at the center of the cave with a crudely cut piece of meat roasting on a spit above it.

"Are you hungry?"

"Starving," Rowan said.

Orion nodded, picked up a spit hanging over the fire, and handed it to his friend, who began to chomp away at the juicy meat pierced upon it.

"What is this?" Rowan moaned,

"If I told you, you probably wouldn't eat it," Orion replied.

Rowan stopped chomping and glared at Orion, "Alright, now I really want to know."

"It's a specific kind of rodent."

"Leech rat?"

"Leech rat."

Rowan stared in disbelief at the hunk of meat and sniffed it, "I'm not proud of this, but I'm still going to eat it."

Orion chuckled and smiled at his friend as he lowered himself onto the ground beside the fire, smiling as he watched his friend eat what must have been his biggest meal in weeks.

Once Rowan had his fill, he passed the spit over to Orion and looked around the cave while his friend slowly and quietly ate. Everything was exactly the same as it had always been. His fur bedroll was still nestled in the same corner, along with his seemingly endless reserve of arrows he made from tree limbs and claws from Vyper Hounds. He still had the same small pile of books that he had brought him so many years ago, and nothing more material than that.

"I can bring you some more books if you want," Rowan offered.

"I know you wouldn't have come here if you just wanted to bring me more books, Rowan."

Rowan sighed and pulled his long hair back in his hands, "He killed them, Orion."

"Who?"

"He killed that little boy's entire family and then cut his head off for what we did."

Orion dropped his head and sighed, "So he knows now."

Rowan nodded solemnly.

"I guess we have to stop for a while now."

"No, no, that is not what I'm saying," Rowan said,

"That's exactly what you're saying," Orion said, "If he's onto me, then it's only a matter of time before he's on to you and comes after your mother."

"This isn't just about you or me. This is about the people!"

Orion rolled his eyes and glared at Rowan, "Well, when are the people going to stand up and fight for themselves?"

"When will you start fighting for them?" Rowan demanded.

"Do you know what it's like to have to sentence them to death every day? To be the one who tells the sentries to keep cutting their rations? To cause suffering every day so that he doesn't break down my mother's door and cut her head off in her sleep?"

"You still have your mother!" Orion snapped.

"You weren't the only one who lost someone that day, Orion! We lost both of our fathers that day, and they saved our lives for a reason!"

"They died fighting a battle they were never going to win!"

"To save our lives! To set us free! How many times do we have to talk about this before you understand that it's our responsibility to finish what they started?"

"Why do you keep bringing it up?" Orion asked.

"Why are you so convinced that I'm going to help all those people who watched as they were cut down in the street?"

"They're just scared. We're all scared, Orion. They need someone to show them that we can beat him if we stand together!"

"You seem to have that covered just fine, Rowan. You keep everyone informed of his plans, and that alone should be enough for you to devise some kind of plan to take him out."

"They all don't see it that way! I have to watch my back every day because some of them believe that *I'm* trying to get them all killed. You don't know what it's like to be attacked by them, to have your mother attacked by them just because of who you are.”

“I’ve told you over and over again if you’re so scared for yourself and your mother, leave the city, come live here,”

“I won’t abandon the people,” Rowan said, “You may be too angry and stubborn to see it, but I know that these people are worth fighting for. Our freedom is worth fighting for. Your parents understood that too.”

“Enough!” Orion snapped.

“I’ve already told you I will help however, I can. I will bring whatever food I can to you, but I’m not ‘The Hunter’ from this little myth you’ve started, and I never will be. Stop giving yourself and everyone else false hope. It’s too late for that.”

Rowan shook his head and stood up. He stormed back over to the entrance of the cave.

“Wait!” Orion called.

“It’s too dangerous to go out there now. Stay here tonight, and I’ll take you back in the morning.”

Rowan stopped and sighed heavily, “What will it take for you to see it?” he asked.

“Just get some sleep,” Orion replied.

Rowan slowly paced back inside and laid himself down next to the fire while Orion tossed another log into the crackling embers and handed him a fur blanket from his bedroll. Rowan wrapped himself under the warm furs, and Orion laid himself down on his bed, looking up at the ceiling, trying to hide the tears welling in his blue eyes. As Rowan drifted into a restful sleep, Orion whispered to himself, "Mother, father…I really miss you, and I wish you were here. You would know what to do."

# Chapter Two: Banished

Orion laid on his bed all night, deep in troubled thought. His thoughts could not be torn from memories of the day that his parents and Rowan's father were killed. He rolled over and back again, feeling envious of Rowan as he slept peacefully through the night.

'I don't know how you can sleep,' he thought to himself, glaring at his friend. Then his thoughts of envy faded, 'I'm sure you wonder the same thing about me though.'

A few hours passed, and he could no longer stand the tortures of his own thoughts, so he stood up and crept outside into the fading night. The deep black sky was beginning to lighten, and he knew that the star would rise up from the horizon soon. He turned back towards the entrance of the cave but paused as he glanced to his right, down the slope of the mountain, where two smooth black stones rested on top of a small hill. Even in the dark, he could almost make out the names he had scratched on the faces of the stones. Altair and Lyra. Just the thought of those names made him pull away before tears could make it to his eyes.

He walked briskly over to where Rowan was sleeping, next to the glowing embers of the fire. He nudged his shoulder gently with the toe of his boot.

"Rowan, it's time to go back," he whispered.

Rowan moaned and muttered tiredly under his breath as he picked himself up from the dirt.

"How did you sleep?" Orion asked.

"Fine till you kicked me," Rowan moaned.

"Sorry," Orion said as he threw his quiver and bow over his shoulder. He slowly pulled the hood of his poncho over his head with a solumn stare into the brightening dawn, "We don't have much time before the sentries start waking everyone else up."

Rowan nodded and rubbed his eyes, then followed Orion out of the cave and into the brisk morning air. It was still dark, but a thin line of grey was rising up on the horizon, brightening the silhouettes of the barren forest enough for them to make out the path leading down the mountain. They walked silently, only hearing each other's feet scraping against the gravel beneath them.

A few distant coos of birds sounded out in the distance within the forest, and Rowan stopped to look for them.

"We need to keep moving," Orion said.

"Do you ever see them? The birds?" Rowan asked.

Orion nodded, "Every once in a while, like everything else, there's not much for them to eat so they don't last long."

"What do they look like?"

Orion looked at his friend's face, unsure of how to respond to his amazement at the simple sound of a bird, "You've never seen them?"

Rowan looked back at Orion and shook his head, "I've always wondered what they really looked like. I've seen pictures of birds in so many of my father's old books, but never the real thing."

Orion tapped his fingers against the grip of his bow and shuffled his feet.

'Maybe Rowan does have a point,' he thought, 'What if all this time, I really have been more fortunate than all of them? What if I could do more than just hunt for them?'

"Rowan I-"

He was not able to finish. A heavy thud shook the ground at the base of a large tree in front of them. Black dust and soil billowed as the shocking sound echoed through the dead forest. At its source stood a sentry, wearing a hood over its head with a sword sheathed on its back. It glared at both of them with its fiery red eyes, and its mechanical joints whirred as it stomped toward them.

"Run!" Rowan shouted.

Orion drew an arrow from his quiver and shot it at the android's head. It pierced through the machine's bright red eye, and it fell facedown with a loud clatter, but as it fell, two more dropped down from the treetops, identical to their fallen counterpart. They immediately drew their swords off of their backs and chased after Orion and Rowan as they sprinted down the trail.

Orion and Rowan ran with all their might, but the machines were gaining on them with ease. While they had to duck, slide beneath and tear through the low-hanging limbs, the sentries pushed through the forest without breaking their stride.

"We won't be able to outrun them!" Rowan shouted.

"Then get behind me!" Orion cried, planting his feet to face the charging androids. Rowan moved behind Orion as he drew two arrows and notched them. He held his bow out flat in front of him and released the arrows. They flew slightly apart from one another, and both found their mark, piercing through the two sentries' chest plates as they charged. The machines fell lifeless mid-stride, and the two friends resumed their sprint down the trail.

They scampered down the last slope of the mountain and approached the hatch to the sewer system, frantically throwing it open. Rowan tossed his bag down the shaft and was about to step through, but Orion grabbed his arm and stopped him.

"Wait!" he cried, "If those three saw you, then all the others in the city already know you were with me."

Rowan's mouth fell open, and his eyes began to gloss over, "I have to get my mother, get her out of there!"

"No!" Orion said, "I'll get her out, you stay here."

"She's my mother, I have to get her out! If you're coming that's fine, but I'm not going to just sit here!"

Rowan pulled his arm out of Orion's fist and slid down the ladder. Orion muttered under his breath and followed behind him, shutting the hatch over his head. When he reached the bottom of the ladder, he saw Rowan had already taken off in a desperate sprint down the tunnel.

"Rowan wait!" Orion shouted.

Rowan did not stop. He ran harder, putting more and more distance between them. Orion ran as fast as he could, doing everything he could to close the distance, but it was still too far to protect him from whatever was waiting in front of him. Then he spotted the second ladder beneath Rowan's home. It should have been a relieving sight. It was still shut, just as Rowan had left it, but Orion felt fear pulsing through his heart.

"Rowan stop!" Orion begged.

Rowan would not listen. He jumped up the ladder and threw the hatch open, climbing into his home before Orion even reached the ladder.

Orion jumped up after him and scrambled up the rungs of the ladder. He pulled himself through the hatch, then threw it shut behind him. The moment Orion looked up from the floor, his heart dropped into his stomach. The Regent was standing in the middle of the home, holding Rowan by the head on his knees, with his glistening black sword pressed against his throat.

"So, the people's savior has returned," the Regent said.

Orion slowly rose to his feet. As he did, he spotted Rowan's mother behind Oberon, lying awkwardly across the foot of the doorway, with her hair draped over her face and blood pooling beneath her.

"What did you do?" Orion demanded.

Oberon slowly looked over his shoulder, down at Rowan's motionless mother, "What did you do?" Oberon countered, "First, an entire family, and now an innocent mother is dead because of what *you* have done,"

Orion clenched his fists, "Just let him go."

"So now you presume to tell me what I am to do with my slaves?" Oberon said, "Take off your hood, I want to make sure you see what your actions have brought upon these animals." He pulled Rowan's head further back, fully exposing his throat, and pressed his blade harder to his throat until drops of blood began to drip down his neck. Orion threw his hood off of his face and drew an arrow from his quiver as fast as he could.

"STOP!" he shouted, hands quivering as he pointed the arrow at the sinister tyrant.

Oberon looked up at his face and froze. Orion kept his aim fixed on him, aiming for the dark helmet beneath his hood, and released his arrow.

Oberon whirled his sword immediately after Orion fired his arrow, cutting it in half as it flew. He pushed Rowan behind him and charged toward Orion, who reached for another arrow. Before his fingers even touched the fletchings, Oberon had already snatched his wrist and pushed him up against the wall. He raised the tip of his sword against his chin.

"It's not possible…" he whispered, staring at Orion's face from behind his sinister mask. Orion thrust his knee up into his gut, trying to push him back, but it hurt Orion far worse than it hurt him. It was as if he had tried to knee a boulder; Oberon barely flinched at his efforts. He kept his gaze fixed on Orion's face, craning his neck left and right, looking over every detail.

Orion's heart raced as he struggled against his grip. Then he realized the intensity of the Regent's curiosity, and it peaked his own. He slowed his struggling for just a moment, long enough for his bright, frantically darting eyes to stare into the eyes of the dark mask. As soon as their eyes met, the Regent struck Orion in the jaw, knocking him to the floor, and began pummeling him mercilessly; he only stopped once he was sure Orion was no longer awake.

"It's not possible…" the Regent whispered, standing over Orion as he lay still at his feet.

He whirled around on his heels and stormed out of the dwelling, calling out to two of his sentries standing outside the doorway. "Take both of them to the tower," he ordered. "Throw the traitor in the dungeon. Have the other one examined, I want to know his name, where he came from, everything!"

The sentries nodded and stepped inside. They shackled Rowan and Orion in chains and threw them over their shoulders. They carried them out before the entire city, up to the dark tower.

Every eye upon the streets followed the Regent and his men. A little boy focusing upon the sentry carrying Orion, noticed the steel bow in his hand, and tugged at his mother's cloak,

"Mother?" He asked, "Is that the hunter Rowan told us about?" His mother nodded, with tears streaking down her eyes. "Where are they going to do to him?" the boy asked.

"I don't know, come on, we have to go now," she replied,

"But he didn't do anything wrong! Why are they doing this?"

His mother dragged him away, fearfully shushing him, but he was not the only one dumbfounded by their regent's reaction. All those who watched what transpired fully expected their master to emerge with both of their heads in his hand, but he did not. Their fate was a mystery, but they were all certain that it would be a fate far worse than death.

Oberon shoved the doors of the tower open and stormed through the great hall, turning left, down a dark corridor leading to a single door. He swept his arm against it, sending it into the wall with a frightening clatter, then marched into the dimly lit room behind it. It was filled with metal tables and cabinets full of strange instruments. He threw his head left and right, searching each cabinet for one particular device, swinging his arms through the shelves, brushing those that he did not need out and onto the floor.

As the sentry carrying Orion entered the room behind him. It took a moment for Oberon to realize the android had entered, but once he did, he barked.

"Strap him down, I want a DNA and blood comparison."

The sentry obeyed. It threw Orion onto one of the tables and wrapped his chains underneath it, then resecured them. After doing so, he turned to his master,

"A comparison to what, sir?" the sentry asked.

"Me," Oberon growled.

He resumed his mad search through the instruments. Then, he found what he was looking for; a small metal tin. His hands trembled as he checked to ensure the contents he needed were inside. He cast the lid aside, pulled out a small vial, and quickly twisted the lid off. Then, he took a small knife from a nearby table, removed his glove, and pressed his thumb to the tip of the blade. Once his blood began to ooze, he held his thumb over the vial, watching the dark red droplets fall into the glass. He then handed it to his sentry and frantically shoved his hand back into his glove and watched the machine take another knife and clank towards Orion. The sentry's fist clamped onto Orion's wrist, holding it in place as it pressed the small blade to his thumb. Once Orion's sample was collected, the sentry turned to its master and retrieved his sample. Then, it moved to a small device on the table with two treys the size and shape of a coin. It poured a drop of blood from both samples onto the treys and activated a computerized device. It clicked to life and began its comparison. To the sentry, the entire process took less than one minute, to Oberon, it seemed to take ten times that long. Far beyond his capacity of patience, he took his sword and cut the sentry's head off of its metallic shoulders, then shoved its body out of the way and glared down at the device. Finally, a computerized voice sounded out from the device.

"One hundred percent match. Sample identified as Oberon Castus, a-"

Oberon slammed his fist onto the device before it could finish, furiously smashing it until its broken pieces were scattered all over the table, and blood smeared the surface of the table.

"How is this possible?" Oberon gasped.

He whirled back around and faced Orion, looking down at his face. Another sentry entered the room.

"Is everything alright sir?" it asked.

"Search our database for any matches to his face, find out who he is."

The sentry leaned over and looked down at Orion's face. As it looked upon him, its eyes flickered, and a long whirring sound buzzed from its head. It turned back to its master.

"This human is Oberon Castus," it reported. "No," Oberon said, "He is someone else."

"The sentry database has no other match. Facial recognition confirms with a one hundred percent match that he is-"

"Then we won't find anything there," Oberon grunted, "Wake him up, I'll make him tell me who he is myself."

The sentry turned to Orion and slapped him across the face with its heavy metal hand. Orion groaned, opening his eyes slowly and seeing everything around him as a blur.

"Where am I?" Orion groaned, "R-Rowan?"

"For his sake, you will answer my questions," Oberon growled. Orion's eyes shot open, and he lunged up against the chains. "Where is Rowan?" he demanded.

"He will be dead if you do not cooperate," Oberon said, clenching his fists, "What is your name?"

"Go to hell," Orion grunted.

Oberon slammed Orion's head back onto the table and gripped his throat."I will not let you die, no matter how much you beg for it until you answer,"

"You're going to kill me anyway," Orion wheezed, "What difference does it make?"

"Who are you?!" Oberon shouted.

Orion turned his head and twisted his face with fury, "No one to you."

Oberon released his throat, and Orion gasped for air, coughing as the sinister Regent paced back and forth beside the table.

"Leave us!" he commanded his sentry.

The sentry immediately turned and left the room, shutting the door behind him. As soon as the door closed, Oberon turned back to Orion, standing still with his gaze fixed upon him. He lowered his hood onto his shoulders and pulled two latches at the back of his mask. Orion looked up at him with his eyes wide open. No one had ever seen the face beneath that mask or heard his real voice. He watched as he slowly removed it with both hands and gasped at what he saw. The face beneath was nearly identical to his own.

He had the same shade of hair, but it was wild and unkempt, falling over his shoulders. They had the same blue eyes, but his were cold, and they glared down at him with the most apparent hatred he had ever seen. Everything on his face was a reflection of Orion's, just many years older. Only one thing clearly distinguished the two from eachother; along Oberon's right eye was a long scar that stretched down his cheek.

"How are you doing this?" Orion asked.

"You think this is a trick," Oberon said.

Orion shook his head in disbelief. It was as if he heard himself speak with a cold and malicious sneer. "This is some kind of projection or-"

"Or perhaps the reason for this coincidence is a secret neither of us were told," Oberon interrupted.

"Or you're just playing some sick game!"

"I assure you, this is not my doing," he said calmly. "However, if what I believe is true, and you are what I think you are, then you would be an invaluable asset to me."

A small and sinister smile shadowed his lips as he leaned on the table. Orion struggled harder against his chains but was completely restrained.

"You defeated three of my sentries," Oberon smiled. "Not an easy task,"

"I thought it was pretty easy," Orion quipped,

Oberon smiled wryly at Orion, "You're arrogant, foolish and you have no idea what it means to be a real warrior. Your talent with a bow is raw, but I can refine it,"

"I'm not interested in whatever you're offering," Orion grunted.

"Even if it could save your friend?" Oberon asked.

Orion thrashed on the table, grunting furiously as he tried to break himself free. Oberon stepped away calmly and smiled as Orion desperately fought against the chains."What I am offering you is a choice," he said, "A choice that will decide both your fate and Rowan's."

"I'm not playing this game," Orion growled, continuing to pull his arms against the restraints.

"I assure you this is no game. Your choice is this: join me and I will make you one of the finest warriors the cosmos has ever known. Do this, and perhaps I will grant Rowan a swift and painless death. Or, if it really is his life that you value so much, you will be exiled, never to return to Archon Prime, and Rowan will spend the rest of his days begging me for something as kind as death."

Orion glared up at Oberon and slowly shook his head in silent refusal.

"I'm going to kill you!"

Oberon turned his head slightly toward his left shoulder. "So you've made your choice?" he asked.

Orion's eyes glowed beneath his furrowed brow and twisted face, "I swear, no matter what happens to me, I will not rest until you are dead at my feet!" he snarled.

"Oh such promises," Oberon sneered, "But you have made your choice clear, young hunter. Rowan will remain here with me, and you will be sent to a world where you will be granted a slow and painful death at the hands of hell itself."

Orion's heart dropped into his gut. "Let him go!" he shouted, "You've done enough, let him go!"

"I've only just begun," Oberon said. Then he took his helmet in his hands, lowered it back onto his head, and threw his hood over it as he walked out of the room, shutting the door behind him. Orion continued to cry out, but it only made Oberon smile. Orion could not see his face, but he could feel the cruelty of the gesture and his intentions.

"Stop!" he begged, "Let Rowan go! You've done enough to him! Let him go!"

All Orion heard was the sound of his own voice ringing against the black walls of the tiny room. He thrashed and screamed on the table until it tipped over on its side. Orion groaned in pain as he hit the cold floor, still trying to pull himself free, but he felt what was left of his strength leaving him as guilt began to torture him.

'What have I done?' he thought, 'If it hadn't been for me, Rowan and his mother would still be alive. Who knows how many more families he will kill because of what I've done?'

He rested his head on the cold, black floor and closed his eyes. But before he got even a moment of rest, the door swung open again, and two sentries entered the room. One unsheathed his sword and cut the chains holding Orion. The other pushed him onto his stomach and bound his hands with rope.

"What are you doing? Where are you taking me?" Orion demanded.

The sentries did not reply. They simply grabbed Orion by the shoulders, stood him up to his feet, and pushed him out the door.

"What's happening?" Orion demanded,

"Keep moving," they ordered in unison.

Orion looked ahead and saw that they were leading him into the great hall of the palace, towards the dark front doors. All the slaves in the great hall looked up from what they were doing with sullen faces. Orion was confused by their sadness. He knew none of them, but they all looked at him as if he was one of their own, perhaps something more.

Their faces finally made Orion ponder what Rowan's little tale of a hunter in the mountain had done for them.

'Did I really give them hope?' he wondered. 'Or am I just something else that has been taken from them?'

Neither of those two possibilities did much for Orion, other than make his guilt swell harder within him. He turned away from all the faces of the slaves and looked ahead as the tower doors opened up, revealing something he had never seen before, sitting at the bottom of the steps.

It was a large and horrifying machine, surrounded by sentries. It was made of dark metals and shaped like a circular platform, with countless pistons and components that Orion had never seen before. As he gazed upon the machine, Oberon walked up from behind him,

"This is the doorway to infinite worlds," he said, "A power that only I possess."

"Where is Rowan?" Orion demanded.

"Don't worry," Oberon smiled, "I will take special care of him until you return to kill me."

He then nodded at one of the sentries. It stepped forward, bringing him Orion's bow and quiver. He examined every part of the bow, "Excellent workmanship," he marveled, "It would be a shame to deprive you of this."

He slung it over Orion's shoulder, then took the quiver in his hand and pulled an arrow out, dumping the rest onto the steps beside him. Then, he took one arrow in his hand and slowly slid it back into the quiver as he glared at Orion. Once he had done so, he threw the quiver over Orion's shoulder. Orion could not see it, but he knew that beneath the sinister mask was an even more sinister smile, and it made him clench his fists until they shook behind him.

Oberon stepped in front of him, facing the machine. He looked out to his mechanical warriors and raised his right arm over his head, signaling them to action.

Two sentries positioned on opposite sides of the machine pulled two great levers down to the ground. A loud and strange groan erupted from the machine, along with what appeared to be blue flames on the surface of the platform. The sound grew louder and louder until it was deafening. After a few moments, when the groaning had seemed to reach peak volume, Oberon dropped his arm, and the two sentries pulled their levers back into the upright position. A blinding beam of light shot up into the sky, tearing a hole through the grim clouds and crackling like lightning.

Smaller branches of light shot out from the main beam, spreading in all directions, crackling like the most intense storm Orion had ever seen. The slaves wandering the streets immediately took cover as the storming, branching light crackled and exploded over their heads. Orion was completely disoriented, unable to hear or see anything, as black dust and blinding wind swirled around him. Oberon, unphased by the chaotic eruption of his machine, grabbed Orion by the neck and marched him toward the light. Orion tried to pull away, but he was unable to pull himself free from Oberon's grip. He was marched up to the edge of the horrifying beam of light, and as he looked into it, he heard Oberon whisper in his ear.

"If you find a man called Chiron, tell him that I know his secret, and that it will not stop me."

Then, before Orion could say or do anything else, he was cast headfirst into the blinding light. As he passed into the light, a great boom echoed throughout the city, and a concussive blast shook the dust off of every dwelling. Then, the violent flash of light vanished, and Orion was gone.

# Chapter Three: A Stranger on a Strange World

As Orion was thrown into the light, he felt the most incredible force he had ever experienced push him up into the sky, though he could not see where he was going. All he could see around him was a spiral of blue and white light, flashing and whirling past him at a disorienting speed. His ears were assaulted by sounds he could only compare to a neverending crash of lightning and the roar of thunder. His body was thrown wildly by whatever force the machine had put upon him; it flipped and turned him in all directions, and he was powerless to stop it. After the initial upward thrust, he was entirely unsure if he was flying or falling, spinning or floating.

'He lied,' he thought franticly, 'He was never going to banish me, he just killed me.'

The disorientation seemed endless, timeless, and completely beyond his control. He closed his eyes and began to surrender himself to his seemingly inevitable doom.

Then, he heard a single boom echo around him, and the flashes of blue began to fade into the blinding white light. He shut his eyes, unsure of what was to come, bracing himself for some invisible form of agony. Then he felt his back crash hard against a solid surface, and his body became fixed to it. He felt as if gravity had tripled upon him, and he was paralyzed in place.

Then, his heart leaped out of his chest as something new filled his ears: silence. He opened his eyes and saw a dark, violet sky scattered with more stars than he had ever seen.

'Where am I?' he wondered, 'Am I dead?'

He felt his feet move and realized that he was no longer held down by whatever kept him in place. He sat himself up and looked over his new surroundings.

The violet sky and light from the stars cast a dim light over what appeared to be a strange forest full of more trees than he had ever seen. Their leaves were in full bloom on all of their branches, and it seemed that every tree was different from the one beside it. Some had a thin trunks with no branches and enormous leaves hanging from the top. Others had trunks that seemed far too wide for him to fit his arms around, with winding, twisting roots that wrapped themselves around everything at their base.

Orion felt something cold beneath his hands, and when he looked down to see what it was, his heart leaped. It was grass. Healthy, long grass, wet with dew.

'This is a dream," he thought, 'or I am just seeing what lies beyond the veil of death.'

He put his hand on his chest and, to his surprise, felt his lungs fill with air and his heart beat just as it always had. He tried to stand but realized that his hands were still bound behind his back.

'I am still alive,' he realized, 'but where am I?'

The weight of that question fell upon his shoulders with full force, pushing his heart into his stomach. He frantically shoved his bound hands beneath his legs and worked them out from under his feet. He reached back for an arrow but could not find one. He peeked over his shoulder and saw only one arrow sitting just out of reach. He scrambled to his knees and bowed his head forward until the arrow fell out of the quiver, then swept through the dark grass until his fingers found it. He took it and twirled the arrowhead downward towards his wrists, moving his wrists back and forth against it until he broke himself free from the ropes. Once he had, he took his arrow, threw it back into the quiver, and moved cautiously toward the dark forest.

He scanned every tree, searching for the tallest one he could find. He spotted one with large, low-hanging branches ahead of him, stretching up above most of the others. He sprinted towards its base, and as soon as his hands fell upon it, he began to climb up as fast as he could. He felt his heart beat faster and faster with every branch he passed, keeping his eyes fixed on the highest branch. When he finally reached it, he sat on one of the base of the limb and leaned out to survey the land.

The forest never seemed to end, everything around him appeared to be treetops, with no sign of civilization. No lights, no cities. Though he had lived apart from the city his entire life, this moment was the first time he felt truly, helplessly alone. His breath became heavy, and he felt tears begin to well in his eyes.

"Helloooo?!" he shouted, "Can anyone hear me?!"

Only the cold, humid wind blowing over the treetops answered his call. "Hellooo?!" he called.

Nothing answered.

He moved back towards the trunk and threw his back against it. He muttered, "This can't be happening. This can't be happening."

He could not help but think of Rowan. He thought of all the dreadful stories he had told him of Oberon, all the tortures he had subjected the people to, and no matter how hard he tried not to, he imagined Rowan suffering every single one of them, while he was marooned here; entirely unable to help him.

He could no longer hold back his tears. He let them fall off of his cheeks down to the forest floor. He sat silently, unable to put his mind to rest, his heart full of nothing but regret.

After what felt like several silent hours, he finally heard something; a loud crack is coming from below. He looked down excitedly, peeking between the branches, but he could not see the cause of the sound. He climbed down three branches to achieve a better vantage point. The noise repeated over and over and grew louder with each crack. It sounded like something was moving through the forest, something strong and large enough to be able to splinter branches beneath it as it stepped. He moved down even further until he was nearly at the base of the tree, and that is when he saw it.

It was a creature with a silhouette that seemed to outline a very large man. It was walking on its hind legs and moving branches out of its way with its arms as it moved through the trees. It was walking a wide perimeter around the tree Orion was perched upon, and as Orion listened closer, he realized that the large silhouette was sniffing the air around him. Orion moved back slowly. Towards the trunk of the tree, unsure of what this creature was searching for. As it circled, it came closer and closer to Orion's tree. After it circled the tree twice, Orion caught a clear glimpse of what this creature really was.

It was not a man. It stood like a man, but its entire body was covered in a dark, scaly hide. Its face was snouted, with a set of jagged fangs hanging out from its leathery jaws. Its hands were larger than any man, equipped with claws that shimmered in the night, and its long feet were as wide as the base of a smaller tree. It wore crudely cut furs around its waist and nothing else, but after seeing the thickness of its hide, Orion assumed that it needed nothing else to protect itself.

The creature made another pass around the tree and was now close enough to touch it with its enormous paws. Orion's heart pounded as he saw the creature scratching its claws along the trunk. Then, he heard it speak in a deep, growling tone.

"I smell you," it said.

Orion covered his mouth with his hand to try and muffle any sound he might be making. "You think you are safe up there, but you are not. Sooner or later, you will come down, and I will be waiting for you."

Orion kept as still as he could. He had absolutely no idea what to do. If he moved, he would give himself away.

'Just stay put,' he thought, 'It'll get tired of the hunt if it doesn't find me, then it will go away just like the vyper-hounds would.'

The creature did not seem to tire. It growled louder and started to slam its fist against the bark of the tree. Orion could feel the trunk shake from where he sat, and he could hear the wood splinter underneath its hand.

"Or maybe I should just cut this tree down and pull you out from under it!" the creature growled.

Orion's heart pulsed violently. He looked for any way he could escape. Every other tree was too far away for him to jump, and if he missed, he would fall twenty feet to the forest floor, completely defenseless against the monster.

Then, he felt his hand brush over something small. He looked down and saw that it was a small seed. He quickly grabbed it and threw it as hard as he could away from the tree.

The seed clattered against another tree in the distance, and as soon as the sound broke the air, the creature snapped his head in the direction it came from. It growled and hissed taking off in a sprint, pushing a smaller tree out of his way so forcefully it splintered and fell to the ground.

Orion knew he would not have long to make his escape. He scrambled out of the tree as fast as he could and jumped down to the forest floor as the creature furiously tore through the brush around him.

"I will find you, I know you are here!" it roared.

Orion gasped as he sprinted away from the tree, running headlong into the forest. The further he ran, the thicker it seemed to get. Branches snagged onto his poncho and clothes as he tore through them, searching for anything that could throw the monster off his trail. Then, he spotted a tree that stood out from all the others, one with vines hanging around its trunk like a thick curtain. He sprinted towards it.

As soon as he reached it, he ducked his head down to pass through the vines but immediately felt a sharp pain on top of his head and all over his face and shoulders. The vines were covered in razor-like thorns, which were digging into his skin as he moved through them.

He tried backing up, but then he heard the creature roaring in the distance. He could not turn back. He took a deep breath and pushed forward into the curtain of thorns. They grew thicker and thicker as he pressed forward, and he soon became so tangled he could not move in any direction without causing himself excruciating pain. He groaned and sucked his teeth in agony, feeling the blood from his wounds dripping down his arms and onto his hands. He kept pushing, shuffling his feet a few inches at a time, trying to spin and slide his way past the vines only to find more waiting for him, no matter which way he turned.

He grew tired of this patient approach, and dropped to his face and stomach, finding a little more freedom to move. He pulled his body forward, feeling the sting of thorns that had fallen on the ground digging into his chest and palms as he inched closer and closer to the trunk. Then, he felt something soft under his hand: grass.

He looked up and saw several feet of cold, soft grass surrounding the smooth trunk and roots of the thorny tree. He grabbed it with both of his hands and pulled the rest of his body clear of the vines. Then, he pushed himself onto his back and groaned, feeling the sting of hundreds of cuts festering all over his body. He held his hands up, and they were wet with his own blood. None of the wounds felt deep enough to threaten his life, but they were nonetheless agonizing. He could not move. He could not think. All he could do was lie there, as the pain burned all over him.

Then he heard heavy, crashing footsteps on the other side of the thorny curtain. Orion threw his hand back over his mouth and held his breath. He glanced up above him, squinting to see the large, dark silhouette of the creature pacing around the other side of the vines. It was hissing savagely, searching all over for some path through the vines, but it did not seem to be able to.

"Clever," the creature said, "I do not know how you got yourself in there, but you have not escaped me. You have earned your rest tonight, but tomorrow, the hunt begins again."

The creature stormed off, stomping back into the forest and cracking branches as it left the tree. Soon, the terrifying footsteps faded into the distance, and silence fell over the forest again. Orion sighed with relief, dropping the back of his head on the cold grass.

The pain in his cuts burned even hotter. He gripped both of his arms as tight as he could, trying to force some kind of relief upon his agony. Everything he tried failed, and the minutes passed like hours. Finally, his eyes grew too heavy, and his wounds grew numb. He fought to stay awake, fearful that the monster he had encountered would return, but soon, his surroundings slipped away, and his arms slowly drifted to his side on the cold grass.

His heart jumped out of his chest, and he threw his eyes open. He was shocked when he found himself lying on the black gravel streets of Luma City outside of Rowan's house. It was torn down, with smoke billowing out from the roof. He rose to his feet, looking at his arms and finding all his cuts had vanished.

'Was it all a dream?' he thought, walking up to the doorway of the house, seeing the old tattered banner hanging above the doorway now burned and shriveled as it waved in the harsh wind. He looked up and down the street and saw no one else there.

He rushed inside with his heart pounding. He looked all through the home but found no sign of Rowan, his mother, or any sign that they had ever lived there. The house was entirely empty.

'What happened? What has he done to them now?' he wondered frantically.

He rushed back into the street and realized the entire city was empty. The usual sounds of slaves at work were entirely absent. There were no sentries, and most strangely, there was a clear view of the sun above his head. No dismal clouds or anything else hanging above the city. Then, he heard a voice a few feet away from him,

"There's nothing left."

Orion looked to his left and saw Rowan sitting on his knees and looking down at the gravel.

"Rowan!" Orion gasped, rushing over to his friend and putting his hands on his shoulders. "What happened?" he asked.

"You left me here," Rowan sighed, "And Oberon destroyed everything else. Why didn't you stop him?"

Orion shook his head and looked worriedly at his friend, "I couldn't stop him. I'm sorry. I don't know what happened. I thought he sent me away…."

"You coward!" Rowan shouted, his voice suddenly changing tone to a frightening, unearthly tone, "He didn't have to do anything to you! You would have let him do all of this anyway! You stood by and watched for years while he's killed us one by one!"

"Rowan?" Orion gasped, unable to recognize his dearest friend as he stood up from his knees with glowing red eyes and a look of hatred on his face. "Rowan, what has he done to you?"

"Nothing," Rowan answered, "Ask yourself, Orion, what have you done to us?" Then Rowan pulled out his knife from beneath his cloak and charged towards Orion, roaring demonically and leaping up with his blade directed downward towards Orion's chest.

Orion's eyes shot open, and he found himself back beneath the thorny vines of the tree again. He lunged up as he woke and felt the air cool the sweat that had drenched his body. It seeped into his wounds and made them sting once again. He looked around him and realized that the darkness of night no longer shrouded the forest. Now, there was an eerie, red light peeking through the vines. He struggled to his feet to see where it was coming from and caught a glimpse of a small red star shining down in the distance. He could not look into it for long. It was brighter and hotter than the star over Archon Prime. He quickly realized that the air around him was thicker and more humid, and the temperature had surged to a height he had never dreamed possible. He slowly pulled his poncho off of his back, feeling a slight reprieve from the heat.

He saw his quiver and bow fall off his back as well and saw that he still had the one arrow Oberon had left him. He took it up in his hands, and another wave of helplessness washed over him. His despair seemed as inescapable as this dangerous new world. He could no longer delude himself into thinking this nightmare was just a dream. He truly was lost in an unknown and dangerous world, with nothing except his bow and that one arrow. He did not know if he should remain there or leave. Either choice seemed equally foolish. He sat on the cool grass, trying to fight back the tears, squeezing his bow in his hands like a helpless child clinging to a blanket. Then, he felt his finger run over a small scratch on his bow, one that made him recall an ordeal that he and Rowan had faced many years ago when they went out on their first hunt alone, without their fathers.

They had stalked their prey to a ravine deep in the mountains. As they followed the trail, the ground gave out from beneath them, and they fell into the ravine. They were trapped with no way out, and a pack of vyper-hounds had found them there. The hungry pack waited at the top of the gorge, unwilling to risk the dangers of entering but also unwilling to give up a slim chance that they would succeed in killing them to feed their pack.

Orion and Rowan were stuck for several days, both were injured, and Orion's bowstring snapped. They suffered through the cold nights and the unforgiving days, waiting for them to give up, but they would not. It was on the last of those exhausting, hopeless days that Rowan came to a realization.

"If we stay here," he said, "we will die, if we fight them, we might die, but we won't die in fear,"

Orion remembered feeling liberated by those words and felt the same strength they had given him. He knew that if he ventured out there, the beast would be waiting, whether or not he would survive was not a certainty, no matter the odds he was facing, but something compelled him to test those odds, something that until then was dormant inside him; something he could not fully undertand. He slowly picked himself up to his feet, threw his poncho back over his shoulders, threw his bow and quiver over his shoulders, then looked for a way back into the forest.

The curtain of vines was too thick in all directions, but when he looked up at the top of the tree, he saw a gap large enough for him to climb out of. He limped to the base of the tree, feeling sore from his unknown number of open wounds, but still pushed himself to climb. He took each limb slowly, hand by hand, step by step, until he was able to peek his head out over the top of the tree.

The forest around him was bursting with life on a scale he had never imagined. Every leaf was the deepest shade of green he had ever seen, like brush strokes of green paint on top of trunks that were all deep red and brown. Countless creatures wandered the forest, mammals, reptiles, birds, and insects, chittering and bellowing with their beautiful calls into the new daylight.

Orion looked out in awe. It was everything he had dreamt the forests would have been like before the drought on his world. But his amazement was soon replaced with fright as a quiet cracking of branches in the distance startled the creatures and sent them running deeper into the forest.

Orion quickly scrambled down the trunk of the tree and leaped down to the grass, falling onto his shoulders. He crawled across the ground, having no choice but to leave the way he came. The fallen razors were not as sharp as the ones on the vines, but they still dug into his flesh and filled his wounds with new pain. He crawled as fast as he could until he was clear of the vicious tree.

He jumped to his feet and began limping as fast as he could back into the forest, trying to put as much distance between himself and the last place the creature saw him. He found himself running along a trail of red dirt with no branches hanging in his way. It was taking him so deep into the forest that the canopy above him nearly blocked out the light of the blazing red star.

He stopped to rest, gasping for breath as he looked around, and realized that all the sounds of life had hushed. The only thing he heard was the swaying of the branches in the wind and nothing else. He did not know why, but this made him more uneasy.

He drew his arrow and notched it on his bow, then threw his hood over his head before slowly continuing down the path. He peeked around every tree he passed and constantly looked over his shoulder to the rear, feeling more and more on edge in the deafening silence.

A short while later, he saw something entirely out of place, something pale shining between a group of trees in front of him inside a small clearing of grass. He cautiously raised his bow and kept his arrow fixed upon it as he inched towards it.

As he approached, he realized that what he saw was a suit of armor propped up on a branch that had been cut down and fixed into the ground. Orion looked around the grass clearing and saw no one and nothing there.

'Why would someone leave this here? How did it get here?' he wondered.

His mind raced with more questions, but they all vanished once he considered that it might be better protected against the creature stalking him if he was wearing it. He lowered his bow and ran his hands over the armor as he examined it. It was in remarkable condition, with very few scratches, and it shimmered in the red sunlight. Orion reached up on top of the branch and took the mask down. It was smooth and much lighter than he thought it would be. It had no cuts for lenses.

"How am I supposed to see in this thing?" he whispered to himself.

He slipped it over his head and then jumped as a computerized voice spoke out from inside the helmet.

"Visor activated."

The inside of the helmet sprung to life with a clear view of Orion's surroundings. It was as if he did not even have the helmet on.

Then, Orion heard someone speak out from behind him.

"Usually one shows more respect for another man's things before he touches them."

Orion panicked. He threw the helmet off of his head and pulled his hood back over his face, then whirled behind him and saw a bearded man with long, unruly hair standing behind him with his arms folded across his chest. The man furrowed his brow and looked gravely at Orion.

"Who are you?" he demanded.

# Chapter Four: Brother of the Enemy

The stranger's dark tunic was faded and tattered at the sleeves. The heels of his leather boots were worn thin. His dark, disheveled hair had several streaks of grey, and that same grey was peppered through his entire beard. His suntanned face had a stony weariness, and his grey eyes glared calmly at Orion.

"I said, who are you?" he repeated.

Orion raised his bow and pulled his arrow back, "Stay there," he warned, "I will shoot you."

The grizzled man chuckled and stepped forward two paces, "If you were going to, you would have done it already, boy."

Orion started to slowly lift his fingers, poised to release his arrow the moment the stranger made any move against him. Despite his warning and his readiness to fire, the stranger remained entirely unimpressed by his threat. His unbroken calm made Orion question who was truly being threatened.

Then the stranger squinted his eyes and craned his neck forward. He stared inquisitively, trying to make eye contact with Orion,

"Do I know you, boy?" he asked.

Orion furrowed his brow, pulling his chin to his chest to avoid his sharp, grey eyes, "I've never seen you before," he answered, "What do you want from me?"

The grizzled man slowly paced towards Orion, craning his neck more and more as he stepped.

"There's something familiar about you, your voice…."

"Stay away from me!" Orion growled, "You're insane!"

The stranger stopped his advance, but only when he stood a few feet away from the tip of Orion's arrow. He squinted his eyes until Orion could only see their glimmer beneath his furrowed brow. Orion lost his patience, feeling his heart surge in his chest. Certain that this man was intent on doing him harm, he released his arrow.

The stranger whirled his arm the moment the arrow flew off of the drawstring, swatting it away with his forearm before it could reach his body. He deflected it with a speed and technique that was frighteningly familiar. Orion's heart stopped, and he instantly turned to run away. He had seen that same move one day ago in Rowan's house. Deflecting an arrow is no easy task, and it could not be a coincidence that this stranger and Oberon used the exact same technique to do so.

As soon as Orion turned his back, he felt the stranger tackle him from behind and climb up onto his back. Orion tucked his legs beneath him and flipped over. He swung his fist up at the stranger's jaw. Just as it was about to strike him, the stranger snatched his wrist and pinned it down to the ground, then with his other hand, he snatched the back of Orion's hood and pulled it back. The moment his grey eyes caught a clear view of Orion's face, they widened with fear, and his jaw slowly fell open. He froze, with his eyes locked upon Orion's.

"No," the stranger gasped, "It can't be."

Orion twisted his wrist free and punched the stranger in the jaw, knocking him to the ground beside him, then turned to look for his arrow. He spotted it just a few feet away. He leaped and rolled towards it, but just before he could grab it, the man jumped back on top of him. He pushed Orion back to the ground, pressing his face into the grass. Orion struggled to break free, kicking and digging the toes of his boots into the ground, but he could not push away. Then, he felt the stranger's arm slide against his throat and pull his neck back. Orion gasped and grunted, swinging his arms wildly, but the stranger's grip was too strong.

"Let me go!" he gasped.

"I don't know how you got here," the man growled, "but I am going to do what I should have done all those years ago!"

"I don't know you! Please!" Orion begged, "Please, I didn't do anything!"

"Of course, you didn't," he grunted, "the people brought it upon themselves, right?"

The man's words sounded so familiar, but Orion was too panicked to think of where he had heard them before. Everything he saw began to blur. He felt as if his neck was about to break as his furious attacker tightened his grip even more.

"You were meant to be so much more, Oberon," the man said, with his voice starting to break into sorrow, "I loved you, and you betrayed us all."

Orion's eyes shot wide open. He threw his arm back and tapped the man's leg urgently and, with all his strength, wheezed.

"I'm... not... Oberon."

The man leaned his head next to Orion's face, "What did you say?"

Orion pushed the words out of his throat as hard as he could, "I'm...not...Oberon!"

The stranger finally released his grip and scrambled away, falling onto his back as Orion rolled onto his back and gasped for air. The stranger's once furious face was now pale and frozen with a very different look of shock.

"You survived!" the stranger gasped. Orion coughed and glared up at him.

"Why did you just try to kill me?!" he wheezed.

The man stammered, "I-I'm so sorry, you look…just like someone I knew." "Oberon?" Orion grunted, "How do you know, Oberon?"

The stranger rose to his feet and brushed the dust off of his sleeves, "How did you get here? Did he send you here?"

"Answer me first!" Orion shouted. "How do you know, Oberon?"

The old man sighed and held his palms up, "You have no reason to trust me. I don't blame you for being frightened, but if you are who I think you are-"

"Who the hell do you think I am?" Orion snapped, "You act like you know anything about me, and you just tried to kill me! We just met!"

The man dropped his hands and calmly said, "Your name is Orion."

Orion blinked and shook his head.

"How could you possibly have known that?"

"I will explain everything. You have my word, but not here. Oberon may have spies in this forest, and if he sent you here, then they will most certainly be looking for you."

Orion stepped away from him.

"That's who you are," Orion gasped, "He sent you here to kill me!"

The stranger shook his head and held his arm out to him, "No, Orion, wait!"

Orion snatched up his bow and arrow and took off, running away from the clearing, and back down the trail. He sprinted back towards the tree he woke up under, hoping he would discourage the stranger from following him by hiding behind the thorns, but as he looked over his shoulder, he saw him chasing after him.

"Wait!" the stranger shouted, "It's not safe out there, Orion!"

Orion ignored his pleas, certain that his words were lies and that he was not going to rest until he captured or killed him. The tree came into view, and Orion ran so hard that his legs started to ache. Then, he felt his foot land upon something hard. As he pushed off of it, something snatched his ankle. He fell face-first onto the grass. His bow and arrow flew out of his hand, landing well beyond his reach into a patch of tall grass. Orion looked down at his foot and saw that his ankle had been trapped in a strange device. His foot had landed on a small metallic circle planted in the dirt, and his ankle was now locked in a small cuff tied to a few inches of chain. He pulled against the chain with all his might as the strange grizzled man was almost upon him.

"Don't move! Stay there!" the stranger shouted.

Orion pulled harder, but he could not break free from the trap.

Then, he heard a crash coming from the forest, as if a tree had just fallen. He heard thunderous footsteps, growing steadily louder. Orion knew what was coming and began to pull even harder, pushing against the trap with his free leg and pulling with all the weight of his body.

But the creature had already broken through the treeline. In broad daylight, it was even more frightening than before. Orion could see that his scaly hide was as black as fresh tar and that it stood at a towering eight feet tall. Its chest was wider than any man's, and its limbs were as thick as tree trunks. Its eyes were a blazing green with slitted black pupils, and as soon as it caught sight of Orion, it bellowed with a roar that shook the ground, and then it began to stomp towards him.

"There you are!" it hissed.

Orion frantically searched the ground around him for anything he could use to defend himself. He spotted a small pile of rocks at his side and quickly snatched one. He threw it as hard as he could at the monster's enormous head. The beast did not even flinch; the stone bounced off its snout and fell to the ground. Orion continued throwing stones, trying to hit its glaring green eye, but before he could hit his target, the enormous creature was upon him.

It reared its enormous hand back and let it fly into Orion's chest. The force of the blow would have sent him flying backward had he not been chained down. Immediately after feeling the air leave his lungs and the stinging pain from the monster's swinging blow, he felt his body fly back, then sharp pain around his ankle as he fell hard onto his back. Before he could draw breath again or scramble back to his feet, the monster placed its enormous black foot on top of Orion's chest. The weight of its foot alone was heavier than that of three men, and the texture of its foot was rougher than the coarsest stone.

"Puny human," the monster snarled, "Finding you was far too easy."

"Get off me!" Orion grunted.

"Such spirit," the monster mocked, "Let's see if you still have it when I tear your head from your shoulders!"

The beast closed its fist around Orion's hair and lifted him up from the ground. Orion cried out in pain, kicking at the monster's other hand as it reached to grab his body to pull him apart.

Then Orion heard the voice of the stranger, "Hey!"

The monster turned its gaze away from Orion. Its black pupils tightened, and steam blew from its nostrils as it snorted in a startle.

"Another human," the beast hissed, "My master said there would only be one," the scaly corners of his lips curled up into a cruel smile, "Now I get to kill two."

The monster dropped Orion and turned to face the grizzled man who was glaring at the beast with clenched fists.

"Do you know who I am?" the stranger growled,

"I don't care," the monster said.

"You should," the stranger said, "I am sworn by oath to protect this boy. No harm will come to him while I still breathe."

The monster placed Orion back on the ground and stomped toward the stranger. Orion sat himself up and looked at the stranger with widened eyes.

'He is going to get himself killed,' he thought, 'Why is he doing this?'

The stranger addressed the monster as if he was the larger creature, with a courage Orion had never witnessed before. The monster, much less impressed with the stranger's stand, snorted at his words.

"Do you know who I am, human?"

The corner of the stranger's lip curled up, "I don't care," he replied wryly.

The monster snorted, and hot breath steamed from its nostrils. It planted one foot back, then charged toward the stranger with dripping jaws and bared fangs. The stranger stood firm, and just as the creature reached out to grab him, he rolled out of the way. He turned as the creature charged past him, then jumped onto its back. He climbed up to its leathery shoulders, then struck the beast in the eye. It groaned and hissed in pain, shaking its head and falling to its knees.

The stranger rolled off the monster's back and plucked a large stick from the ground. He swung it onto the monster's snout. The stick snapped in half as it impacted the beast's hardened scales. It glared at the stranger with rage, then swatted him away. The stranger flew through the trees, landing several yards away, and the creature turned back towards Orion.

Orion pulled desperately against his chain as the monster came stomping toward him. It lunged at him, flying with open jaws toward' Orion's legs. Thinking quickly, Orion scrambled to the balls of his feet and rolled to the other side of the trap, away from the monster's jaws, which snapped shut upon the chain holding him in place.

The chain snapped, and Orion fell onto the ground, free from the trap. He sprung to his feet as quickly as he could, spotting his bow and arrow lying on the ground just a few feet from the creature's foot.

He dove towards his weapon, barely snagging his bow from the ground before the monster tackled him to the ground. Orion threw himself onto his back and pushed his bow against the monster's throat as it snapped its jaws at his face.

Then out of the corner of his eye, he saw the stranger come charging back toward them. He leaped back onto the monster's back and took hold of the bow from behind its head. Orion pushed with all of his might, feeling his arms shake against the beast while he narrowly dodged his enormous fists as they pounded the ground around him. The stranger planted his feet on the back of the beast's back and pulled Orion's bow against its throat with everything he had. The creature's wild thrashing and hissing began to slow, and its green eyes began to fall shut. Its arms fell limp, and then, the stranger let go of the bow, falling to the ground as the beast landed on top of Orion.

Orion frantically pushed against the beast, still feeling its hot breath blow out from its nostrils.

"It's still alive!" Orion panicked.

The stranger rushed over to Orion, grabbed him from underneath the arms, and pulled him out from under its heavy body.

"We have to go now," the stranger panted, "before more of his kind come looking for him."

"There's more?" Orion gasped.

"This is his home planet," the stranger said, "He will never admit to being defeated by a human to his kin, but we have to go before the others find us!"

"Wait, I'm not going anywhere with you!" Orion protested, "You just tried to kill me. You think I'll just forget that because of this?"

"I wasn't trying to kill you!" he shouted, "I was trying to kill Oberon!" Orion stuttered, "I-I don't understand."

The stranger put his hand on Orion's shoulder, and his grey eyes glowed as they stared into Orion's.

"I told you that I would explain everything, and I will. I can't explain here. It isn't safe. We have to go now, and you HAVE to trust me if you want to live."

Orion's mind stormed with questions.

'He saved my life, but why?' he wondered, 'Can I trust him? Do I have a choice?'

He took a deep breath, looked down at the ground, then back into the stranger's unblinking grey eyes.

"Just tell me where we're going," he said.

"There's a bunker hidden beneath the clearing where you found my armor," the man answered, "I'll answer all your questions there."

Orion looked into his eyes again, searching for any hint that he might be lying, but they blazed with something fiercer than sincerity; desperation. Orion said nothing but nodded his head in agreement with the stranger's plan.

"Alright," the grizzled man said, "Get your arrow, and no matter what you hear or see behind us, don't stop running until we get there."

Orion nodded again and sprinted to recover his arrow. Once he grabbed it, he took off after the stranger as he led him back down the red dirt trail. As they ran, Orion heard more footsteps in the forest and the crackling of fallen branches as they approached.

"Keep going, don't stop!" the stranger yelled.

Orion did as he said, running harder as they moved deeper and deeper into the forest, away from whatever was approaching. The cover of the canopy grew thicker and thicker as they ran, Orion knew they were close, and then he caught a glimpse of the shimmering armor in the distance.

The stranger rushed to his armor and pulled it off of the branch he had perched it on, scrambling to the middle of the clearing.

"Where's the bunker?" Orion asked.

The stranger did not answer. He frantically slid his hands against the surface of the grass and then froze once he found what he was looking for. He shoved his hand into the grass and started to pull something up. A small circle of the grass rose up as he lifted, and a hidden hatch was revealed. The stranger took his armor and threw it down the hatch, then looked to Orion.

"Go, get in!" he said. Orion slid into the hole in the clearing, finding a narrow ladder running down a shaft and a warm, yellow light glowing from what appeared to be a small room resting at the bottom. He looked up to the stranger as he descended. He saw him jump in after him, shutting the hatch over them and twisting a locking mechanism shut.

Orion sighed with relief and slowly climbed down the rest of the ladder. He looked into the room the shaft led to, and a strange sense of familiarity washed over him. The room was small, with a stone ceiling and walls. The warm light was coming from a small heat lamp resting on the floor in the middle of the room, and it shined upon a small collection of weapons resting upon a crate.

He saw a shining sword that had been freshly sharpened, a quiver full of arrows with a short sword lying beside it, and several other devices he had never seen before. He turned to look around the rest of the room and saw only a single bedroll and an old chest with intricate markings sitting beside it. The rest of the room was bare stone. This stranger had a purpose for everything he owned, with nothing else cluttering the space. He found himself closely relating to this stranger's methods, but this only made his curiosity swell.

"What are you doing here?" Orion asked, turning to face the grizzled man.

He sighed heavily, then answered, "I was banished here after Oberon returned to Archon Prime. When he appointed himself as Regent of the people, and had me out of the way, he killed all my men."

"You're from Archon Prime?" Orion asked.

The stranger nodded, "I was the commander of King Rom's army."

"I've never heard of you," Orion said.

"No one ever did," he said, "Rom was a glutton for glory, and the people were more than happy to give it all to him, but many good men died to win our freedom."

"You fought in the Crisis of Archon?"

The stranger nodded, then gestured for Orion to sit beside him, "There will be more than enough time for war stories later. There are explanations that I owe you for earlier."

Orion nodded and set his bow and quiver down on the ground. Then, he sat beside him, "I mistook you for Oberon, and for that, I apologize. It has been many years since I saw him last, but his face is one that I will never forget."

Orion felt his heart sink, "So, he looks like me?" he asked. The stranger nodded solemnly, "Just like you."

"I don't know how that's possible," Orion said, "When he captured me, he showed me his face, and it did look like mine, but I thought he was just trying to get in my head somehow."

The stranger shook his head again, "That is his face," "How is it that he and I look exactly alike?" Orion asked.

The stranger turned his head back towards Orion and paused, clearly weighing his words carefully.

"Because you and Oberon… are brothers," he answered.

# Chapter Five: The Tale of Two Sons

Orion scoffed at the stranger's revelation. He stood up from where he sat and took a few paces back, but when he looked back at the stranger, he was still staring at him with unbroken seriousness.

"You're insane," Orion chuckled, "I never even spoke to Oberon until the day he sent me here. There's no possible way he and I are related by blood!"

"True, you never knew him," the stranger said, "and that is the reason why you have survived to this day."

Orion shook his head, "I grew up with my parents, far away from the city. The closest thing I ever had to a brother was…."

Orion choked on the name. He felt the word stay stuck in his heart, and it brought him to the brink of tears. Seeing his hesitation, the stranger nodded.

"Rowan," he said, "Son of Gale and Helen Volture; the last royal family of Archon Prime."

Orion's eyes widened, and he slowly paced back toward the stranger. "How could you have possibly known that?" he demanded.

"Gale Volture was one of my most loyal soldiers, as was his dear friend, Altair."

"My father?" Orion asked.

"Your father," the stranger nodded, "Altair loved and cared for you, he taught you to hunt and survive in the wild, how to be strong in the cruel world you were born into, and he did it all even though you were not his child."

"That's not true," Orion said, "All I know I learned from him. No one else could have been my father."

"The truth had to be hidden from you," the stranger said softly. "For if you knew before you were ready, Oberon would have killed you, and all would be lost."

"None of this makes any sense," Orion said, "What do you mean 'all would be lost'? Archon Prime has absolutely nothing left to lose."

"Our world has lost almost everything," the stranger admitted. "But there is still hope,"

Orion scoffed again. "Hope for what? What hope could there possibly be?"

The stranger sighed heavily. He stood to his feet and turned away from Orion shaking his head.

"Perhaps I should tell you everything as it came to be," he said. "You deserve to know, and there is nothing I can do that would make it any easier to hear."

Orion shook his head, "By all means," he said wryly, "I can't wait to hear this."

The stranger looked back to Orion, and when he spoke, his voice lowered to an even more sullen tone.

"After the first war, after the last of the High Council's forces left our world, there was finally peace. Me and my men celebrated our peoples' victory and mourned the sacrifice of our fallen brothers, but our King, Rom Castus, did not mourn with us. The people raised him up, glorifying him and him alone for the victory. They only saw the deeds of one hero and not the lives lost to pay the cost of the victory. I was certain that Rom was also blind to all the blood that was spilled for him to be carried off on their shoulders. In his honor, the people killed ten great Archonian Cattle and prepared a feast. They danced in the soft black sand through the night and paid tribute to their new King. He, however, had his eye on one particular prize that night: a woman named Lyra."

Orion's face was flushed of all color as the stranger spoke the woman's name, "My mother," he said quietly, "her name was Lyra."

The stranger nodded and continued his tale.

"Lyra's heart always belonged to Altair. When Rom rallied us to take back our world, he vowed to return to her so they could be married and start a new life in a new, free world. Rom never knew this, but it would not have mattered to him even if he did.

Three days after the feast, as the people began building Luma City, Rom sent for Lyra's father and demanded that she be given to him as his bride. Her father obeyed his wishes and brought her before him. The two were wed against her wishes, and she was the first queen of Archon Prime.”

“But here was no queen of Archon Prime,” Orion said.

The stranger nodded again, “Rom refused to reveal his queen before the people until she bore him a son to carry on his legacy. She refused to consummate their marriage as long as she could, remaining loyal to Altair in secret, but Rom refused to allow her insolence to persist. He locked her away beneath his palace for three months, saying that she would grow to love him if she wanted to be set free, but she never gave in. When she was released from the dungeons, Rom came to her in the night and threatened her with her life if she would not give him a son. Not knowing what else to do, she lied to him, saying that she was barren. Rom demanded that her claim be put to the test, giving her one more day to submit to him or be executed.

Immediately after, she fled to Altair in the city. He came to me, begging for my help. My heart bled for them. I could not deny their request after everything he had sacrificed and everything she had endured for him. I met them outside the city, in a small cave hidden in a mountain looking over the city.”

Orion rubbed his face in his hands, then whispered, “Our home. That cave was where I was raised.”

The stranger's eyes glistened as he pressed on with his tale.

"Altair knew I had some skill with medicine. That is why they came to me. They could not consult the healers, for they all worked within the palace. They begged me to sterilize her so that she could not be forced to bear Rom, a son… and I did it, knowing that the child would ultimately suffer Rom's cruelty as well."

Orion felt tears begin to well within his eyes. 'Could this be true?' he wondered.

"Many tears were shed with this sacrifice," the stranger said. "I was able to do as they asked and conceal any sign that it had been done, but it still was not enough to free Lyra from Rom. She had to bid Altair farewell once again, promising that no matter what happened to her, she would always return to him, and then she returned to the palace.

She submitted to her king. Her lie had become the truth, but it only made matters worse. Rom's rage with her consumed him. After all that time, he had gone mad in his efforts to produce an heir. He tortured Lyra for her failure as a wife and continued to force himself upon her, time and time again refusing to abandon his madness."

Orion's blue eyes glazed over, and a single tear dripped down his face. The stranger's glossy eyes remained open, and though he shed no tears with his story, Orion could almost feel them fall within him.

"Altair did everything he could to care for his beloved. He would hunt through the night and bring her his quarry in secret. He would nurse her wounds and hold her through the night. They would steal what small moments they could together, even if it was as simple as one kiss under the moonlight before they had to part again. I learned of these moments through Gale, who helped Altair sneak through the palace, putting his own life on the line for his dearest friends."

A small smile washed over Orion's face, "Just like Rowan," he sighed.

"It was also through Gale that I became privy to the next development in Rom's madness. He came to me in a panic, waking me from my sleep, and told me that he did not know how but that Rom finally had a son.

I followed him to the palace, and when I entered the King's chambers, I could not believe what I saw. I saw Rom holding a newborn baby in his arms, laughing and smiling down at the baby as if it was a prize made of fine gold. He saw me and ordered me to come forward, overwhelmed with pride in his new son, and gave me the special charge of training him to be the greatest warrior our people would ever know. I refused, but this was not acceptable to him. He had gone too far to be denied his wishes ever again. He told me that if I did not do as he asked, he would kill Lyra. I had no choice but to accept. I asked where she was to ensure that she was safe for the moment, but Rom shrugged my questions off, saying that she was in recovery. He told me that it did not concern me as long as I carried out my duties."

"But if she was barren, the child could not have been hers, so who was the mother?" Orion asked.

"To this day, the answer to that question eludes me," the stranger answered. "I would ask many times as the boy grew, but I never got an answer. I was always told to continue my task, to make him perfect.

The boy was given a sword the moment he could hold one, and I trained him every day. He was my most gifted student. He pushed himself to his limits just to please his father, even though he only demanded more of him. I found myself taking pity on the boy, as did Altair and Gale. The three of us tried to give him more than his father did. We brought him books, we taught him to paint, and unbeknownst to his father, he became just as talented an artist as he was a warrior."

"How did no one know about Rom's son?" Orion asked.

The stranger's eyes glossed over even more, and a tear finally fell from the corner of his eye.

"Rom went to see Lyra one night, but when he found her, he also found Altair. Enraged, he attacked them and sent the guards and me to hunt them down as they fled from the palace into the forest. I misdirected the pursuit to help them escape, and I returned to Rome empty-handed. From that day forward, he forbade his son from ever venturing beyond the palace walls, telling him that humanity was cruel and traitorous and that only those exceptional enough to surpass them were fit to lead them.

Ever since that day, the boy's heart grew restless, and it was not long before his heart began to turn against his father. He pushed himself harder, but no longer with a desire to please. When he reached the end of his youth, he seemed motivated only by hatred for his father.

When he finally became a man, the great drought began, and the people grew restless under their corrupt King's rule. When the riots began, Rom's son came to him and demanded his birthright, the command of all our forces, so that he could quell the insurrection.

Rom refused, telling him that as long as he still lived, he would never relinquish his power.

His heart descended to depths that I could not pull it from, no matter how hard I tried. I was too late to stop him … from unleashing his wrath upon the people."

Orion leaned forward, "So that night when the people rioted and broke into the palace… when they fought against that one warrior who cut them all down, they were fighting the king's son?"

"Yes," the stranger sighed, "a boy who became a monster of my own making." "What happened to him? After that night?" Orion asked.

"Another answer I do not have. I tried to stop him before everything happened, but I failed. We fought through the palace, until he brought a wall down on top of me. When I came to, he was gone, and all but two of my men were dead."

"Gale and my father," Orion deduced.

The stranger nodded, "Gale hid his family beneath the city, fearful of what might happen to them, and Altair and Lyra did not know of what had happened until I came to them with the news."

"What did Rom do?" Orion asked.

"What any man does in his insanity," the stranger said, "He pressed on with his poisonous dream. Five years after his son's disappearance, he came to me holding another baby boy, who looked identical to his first son. I already knew what he wanted, but I was determined to end the turmoil his madness had caused once and for all.

I sent for Lyra and Altair, and I asked if they would take the child in if I brought him to them in the mountain. They agreed. Three nights later, I infiltrated the palace. I took the child from his bed and carried him up to the mountain so that he would be free from the cruelty of his father.

It did not take Rom long to discover what I had done, and as punishment for my crimes against him, I was stripped of my command and imprisoned to be executed. However, before my sentence was carried out, a great flash of light struck the palace steps, and from that terrible light emerged what I thought to be a ghost, but it was my darkest nightmare instead. The King's son returned and exacted his vengeance."

Orion ran his fingers through his hair and held a sweaty palm to his heart. "This isn't possible," he whispered,

"After he killed Rom, he found me in the dungeon. I was certain that he came to kill me as well, but he spared me. He chose to banish me here instead, calling it mercy, given out of the respect he once had for me. That is how I ended up here. I assumed that he would not rest until he had wreaked his havoc upon all of the people, and I had no way of knowing whether or not his brother survived until today."

Orion felt his heart pound in his chest. He began to frantically pace around the tiny bunker.

"This can't be true. This can't be true…" he whispered, "I wish it wasn't," the stranger said.

Orion planted his feet and shouted at the top of his lungs, "Who the hell are you?!"

"My name is Chiron," he said, "and you, Orion Castus are heir to the throne of Archon Prime."

Orion's heart stopped the moment he heard him utter his name. It forced the already tremendous weight of his tale tumbling down upon his heart as his mind raced with questions.

'Everything has been a lie,' he thought, 'Why wouldn't they tell me? Why would Oberon send me here?'

Then he stopped, his eyes widened, and he immediately looked to Chiron. "I'm your secret," he whispered,

"What?" Chiron asked.

"Before he sent me here, Oberon told me that he knew your secret and that it would not stop him."

Chiron sighed heavily and wrung his hands over his shaggy hair.

"So he knows. The time is upon us," he said, "I know that everything I have told you is far too much to bear-"

"Too much to bear?" Orion snapped, glaring at Chiron, "Everything you told me means that my entire life has been a lie! It means that everything I believed was just a part of that lie!"

"No!" Chiron said. "This makes the love Altair and Lyra gave you the truest love there is! It makes your life a success against the fiercest odds! It makes you far more important than you realize!"

"Important how?! You can't expect me to do anything about this! Even if I did, I couldn't beat him. I've tried, and nothing I did changed anything!"

Chiron sighed and turned his back to Orion. He let his chin drop down to his chest and shook his head.

"You're right," he said softly. "I can't. I did not want this life for you, and you do not deserve this, but surely there is something within you that cannot stand by while Oberon subjects innocent people to a life of suffering,"

Orion shook his head, "That doesn't mean I can do anything to stop him. I have done everything I can, I hunted what's left of the forest for what I can find, and I fed whoever I could. I tried everything I could to not just stand by!"

Chiron turned back and looked Orion in the eye, "What you have done may have helped a family that day, perhaps a little longer than that. Those are kindnesses they will not forget, but you must know, as well as I, that you have always been capable of so much more."

"What more could I have done?"

"What anyone does in the face of evil; make a stand, just as your mother and father did."

"And die the same way they did?" Orion asked. "You trained him yourself! You said Rom wanted him to be the most perfect warrior known to man! How would it end any differently with me?"

"Because I will teach you how to beat him," Chiron replied, "All that is needed of you is the willingness to learn," Orion's mouth closed, and as he looked into Chiron's eyes beneath the glisten, he saw a fiery resolve, "I was the one who made Oberon what he is. I can make you a warrior that would be more than his equal."

"He's had a lifetime of training!" Orion argued, "How are you going to-"

"I will concern myself with the how," Chiron said, "Do you have the will to learn and fight?"

Orion opened his mouth to answer but could not.

'How can he believe anyone could beat him?' he wondered, 'Why me?'

Chiron stepped forward, "There is something you have that Oberon never did, and that is how I know you can defeat him."

"What?" Orion asked.

"Something truly worth fighting for,"

Orion scowled, "What? Your redemption?"

"No. This is more than vengeance. This is about finishing what your mother and father died for, proving to the people that they can reclaim their freedom."

"You say that like anyone else will stand against him."

"They will," Chiron said, "If there is someone who can make them believe they can," Orion shook his head and turned away from Chiron.

'No one would believe in me,' he thought. He turned back to Chiron and took a gentle, deep breath, "Why me?" he asked.

Chiron's gray eyes seemed to glow with a breath of new life. "Why not you? Didn't Rowan believe in you?"

Orion felt tears fall freely from his eyes, "He did," he choked, "And it cost him everything."

Chiron placed his hand on Orion's shoulder, leaning to look into his teary eyes. "What happened to him?" he asked,

Orion wiped tears from his eyes, "Oberon found out he was helping me smuggle meat into the city. He killed his mother, banished me, and took Rowan." More tears streamed from his eyes, and his breath quivered as he spoke, "He said that Rowan would spend the rest of his life begging to die because of what I did!"

"But he is alive, Orion," Chiron said, "You can still save him."

"How? There is no way off this planet!"

Chiron ran his fingers through his wild hair, "Perhaps there is," he said quietly.

Orion's eyes widened, "What?"

"When I first arrived here, I spent many years searching for it but never found it-"

"Just tell me what it is!" Orion demanded.

"Somewhere in the jungle, very close to here, there is a city. The planet's hidden capitol. If we found it, we might be able to send out a distress transmission. That is our only hope of escape."

Orion's heart surged, "Please," he begged, "I will help you find it if you just help me get back to Archon Prime."

"And you think you would be able to save Rowan with no other consequence? Make no mistake, Orion, if you try to save your friend and do nothing else, you will condemn the rest of the people."

"I can't save them all, Chiron."

"No, but if you do not try, then you would only prove that Rowan's faith in you was misplaced."

His words plunged through Orion's heart. He felt so ill that he could no longer stand. He sat beside the lamp and pulled his long black hair behind his head, "I don't want anyone else to die," he said.

"Neither do I," Chiron said solemnly, "Too many already have, and it is time for it to end."

"So I just don't have a choice," Orion said, staring at the bunker floor.

"You always have a choice, Orion," Chiron said as he sat beside Orion. "I offer my help to you unconditionally. Long ago, I swore to your mother and father that I would protect you however I could, and I will never break that vow. Your actions and your choices are your own, but I know that you can see what you must do."

Orion and Chiron looked into each other's eyes in the complete silence Orion had ever experienced. The two were frozen in the pause, both frozen with unyielding expressions on their faces. Then, Orion's lip started to quiver.

"I just don't know if I can," he said softly,

"What is it that you fear?" Chiron asked.

Orion wrung his hands in his lap and bit his lip, "I don't want Rowan or anyone else to die for nothing."

"Is the chance for a better future nothing then?"

"No," Orion sighed. "But I would rather be the one to pay the price for it,"

Chiron nodded his head, "As would I."

Orion picked his head up, "I believe you," he said. "But I don't know if I can trust you."

"Trust comes after faith," Chiron said. "Just give me a chance to earn it."

Orion wrung his hands in his lap, taking another pause before he spoke again, "You promise that you will help me save Rowan?"

Chiron sighed slowly, "I will never make you a promise that I cannot keep, Orion. I will promise you this instead: if you let me help you and teach you what I know, I will stand with you against Oberon, and I will do everything I can to help you save Rowan and everyone else."

Orion nodded slightly, then brought his folded hands to his chin as he examined Chiron for any sign of deception. His gray eyes were frozen open. His entire body was frozen like a statue, leaning towards him with something far more profound than just desperation.

"What do you need from me in return?" Orion asked,

The corner of Chiron's stiff lip turned up. "For now, let me tend your wounds, and then we will begin."

The two stood to their feet, but Orion stopped Chiron before he could step away, "I'm really counting on you, Chiron," he said, "Rowan is too."

Chiron nodded. "The people are counting on you," he replied.

# Chapter Six: Drago's Mission

Not long after Orion and Chiron fled to the bunker, the creature woke from where he was subdued. He growled as he stood to his feet and searched his surroundings. He was alone, and his quarry had escaped him once again. With clenched, leathery fists, he stomped towards the now broken trap he had set and crushed it beneath his heavy foot, then turned back towards the forest, muttering under his breath.

"Filthy humans," he hissed, "They will pay for this."

He shoved every tree he passed out of his way, pushing some so forcefully that the trunks snapped from their roots and crashed to the ground. He huffed as he walked, with his bright green eyes blazing forward. He stomped for miles through the thick jungle until he came upon a large, flat stone resting on the ground with a circle carved upon its face. He glanced around him one last time to ensure he was not being watched before placing his large, leathery hand within the circle. As his black palm rested upon it, the outline of the circle illuminated with a bright green glow. Then the stone rumbled and slid backward, revealing a long stone staircase descending beneath the forest floor. The monster quickly stomped down the stairs and ducked his head as the hidden entrance slowly closed behind him. He made his way through a dark tunnel at the bottom of the steps. His ears were soon filled with the sounds of voices. They hissed and growled and spoke over one another. A thick cloud of smoke washed over his feet and billowed over him as he exited the tunnel.

When he emerged, he squinted through the haze and stepped into a crowd of his reptilian brethren, who shuffled past him at peak commotion. They moved shoulder to shoulder with and against one another under the light of torches posted along rows of dwellings made of piled earth and stone. The creature held to his straight path through the crowd, passing the vendors who set tents over their businesses, and subterranean hot springs, which heated and thickened the haze surrounding him.

He ducked his head and moved faster as he moved to the heart of the city, where the structures towered over the heads of the crowd and the mist they walked through. Despite his efforts, he was instantly recognized and acknowledged as he strode past his kin, just as he always was. They paled in comparison to his stature, especially when they scampered out of his way.

"General Drago," they said, bowing their heads as they fell to their knees.

He did not return their courtesies. Hemaintained his unsettling silence as he passed through the heart of the city. It was only when he approached a structure that was larger than all the others that he raised his head up, glaring at it as he approached.

It was a large fortress embedded into the far wall of the massive cavern which housed the entire city. It was built so seamlessly with the wall's natural formations that it would have been indistinguishable if it were not for the bright fires glowing from the turrets and windows. The path to the fortress stretched through two long rows of statues, monuments to their greatest warriors. Their stone eyes glared down upon him. He looked at them for a moment but quickened his step until he passed through the front archway of the fortress. The corridors of the fortress were dimly lit, twisting and turning in all directions. His shoulders brushed against their walls as he stormed through them, and he did not stop until he entered a room that was so dark that there was only enough light for him to see the dirt floor within. He marched into the dark room and slid a heavy stone door over the entrance behind him. With the darkness in the room now complete, he looked around once more to ensure he was alone, then knelt at the center of the room. He began to dig into the dirt floor until he pulled up a small, circular device.

He turned it over in his leathery palm and pressed a small switch on the back. The device sprung to life with a gentle whirr, and a small beam of light pierced through the dark. As it progressed through its functions, he placed it within the small hole he had dug and bowed his head, waiting patiently on his knees. Then, within the device's beam of light, the image of a shadowy figure appeared, hovering above the device, clad in black armor with a dark hood over his masked face.

"What is it?" the figure asked.

"Lord Oberon," Drago said, "I have found the human you spoke of."

Oberon wrung his hands behind his back, "Where is he?" he demanded.

"He…escaped. There is another human here, one who has sworn to protect him."

Oberon folded his arms over his chest. "The old man's interference does not absolve you of your failure, Drago," he snarled. "Surely the finest warrior of your kind would be capable of killing such *inferior* creatures."

"They could not have gone far, and they have no way off this planet. I will not fail you, master."

"You already have. Need I remind you of the bargain we struck? I offered you the command of my forces, and all I asked in return was the head of one helpless boy."

Drago shut his glowing green eyes in shame and bowed his head even lower. "Perhaps an alteration to our bargain will properly motivate you," Oberon sneered.

"What do you mean, my lord?" Drago asked.

"You have three nightfalls to kill this boy and the old man. Should you fail me again, I will come to Serpeno

myself. Believe me, little Drago, that would be most…
unfortunate, for your people."

Oberon's image vanished, and Drago was left alone in
the dark room, with his heart pounding in his leathery chest.
He clenched his clawed fists and snarled. He slammed his
fist into the dirt and crushed the communication device.
Then, he snapped to his feet and turned to the large flat stone
blocking the doorway. He kicked it with all his might,
shattering it and sending the pieces flying out into the narrow
corridors.

"Father!" he roared, storming back into the fortress. He
shoved his way past all the others wandering through the
halls, continuing to call out at the top of his lungs.

"Father! I must speak with you now!"

He strode to the heart of the fortress, approaching the
largest corridor which led to a doorway covered with an
ornate red curtain. He swung his clawed hand against the
curtain and it flew to the side as he entered the largest room
in the fortress. He looked first to the throne sitting at the back
of the room, then to the edges of a large round table in front
of it, but his father was not there. He moved further into the
chamber, approaching a small hot spring. It was steaming so
much that its haze was pooling over the entire floor. He
glared down into its bubbling waters and called out once
again,

"Father!"

The spring's gurgling surface boiled until its waters spilled over the edges as a slender, white creature emerged. It stood up in the center of the pool and looked up at Drago with bright green eyes as it waded to the edge of the spring, climbing gingerly out of the warm waters. Steam hovered over its wet scales as it limped to the throne and picked up a fine red robe laid on the seat. As it threw the robe over its shoulders, it rounded the table and walked with a hunched back towards Drago.

"Why have you disturbed me, my son?"

"Father," Drago said, "There are two humans on our world."

Drago's father chuckled, then broke into a wheeze that forced him to lean over the table. "Humans?" he coughed, "My son, they have no way of leaving their desolate little planet. Even if they did, they would have had to travel across the cosmos just to make it here."

"They are here father," Drago said, "I have seen it with my own eyes, and their presence is a violation of the High Council's laws."

"I am aware of our laws," his father hissed, "I was present when Chancellor Jafar took office and cast Archon Prime out from our protection!"

Drago clenched his fists, "Then I need not remind you that we cannot allow their trespass. If we do not respond, they will bring more of their filth here and incite another conflict."

Drago's father pushed himself off the table and stood as tall as he could, turning his head up as he glared at his son, "Tell me, Drago, why would I do anything about these two little humans? You make it seem as if all our kind, every mighty Serpen warrior is endangered by two meaningless primates. If they are alone here, they will perish in the jungle before nightfall."

"You make it seem as if they are just animals, father," Drago snarled, "They killed hundreds of our kind in the crisis. They are a violent race who think themselves superior to all others. We must enforce our laws and not allow their crimes to go unpunished."

"And if the High Council discovered their trespass, I would be disgraced forever! You are willing to risk what position we barely cling to, for your pride? What of the pride of our people?"

Drago stepped forward, bringing his wide chest up to his father's snout.

"You are losing political power because you cower here," he snarled, "You let the other Chancellors take what is rightfully ours!"

Drago's father wheezed and broke into another fit of coughing, falling to his knee. Drago shook his head and rolled his eyes, then knelt beside his father.

"I do not know how much longer I have, Drago," his father wheezed, "I do not have the strength to waste what time I have left with politics. I have grown… tired of it,"

"Then perhaps it is time you stepped aside," Drago snarled.

"For you?" his father scoffed, "Drago you are a mighty warrior, not a leader. Your blood lust would be the end of our people. Just leave this matter as it is; these two humans mean nothing."

Drago snorted and stood back to his feet.

"Do what you will father, but I will not let this pass."

He turned to storm out of the room but stopped as he heard his father call out before he could cross the threshold of the chamber.

"Drago! I know something is troubling you…if you have this hunt, would it bring you peace?"

Drago looked over his shoulder but did not speak. His green eyes were locked in his father's weary, desperate stare until he mustered a slight nod. His father dropped the chin of his snout into his chest and placed his pale, clawed hand over his eyes.

"Then you shall have it," he sighed.

Drago huffed steam from his nostrils and stomped back into the fortress, leaving his feeble father as he limped to his throne in silence.

Drago passed through the halls of the fortress, stopping every soldier he passed and barking orders.

"Prepare to move out!" he commanded.

The soldiers stood tall and rushed to prepare themselves in the center courtyard of the fortress. Drago followed his men there as they recovered weapons from blacksmiths, sharpened their swords, and prepared their armor.

Drago approached the oldest of the blacksmiths and ordered, "Bring me my armor!"

The blacksmith bowed his scarred snout and moved to the back of his shop. He returned to his master carrying a large black breastplate. Drago snatched it from his claws and threw it over his broad shoulders.

"And my weapon!" he snapped.

The blacksmith bowed again and recovered a bloodstained ax that was as tall as a small tree, with a wooden handle and deeply scratched blade. Drag took up his weapon and stormed toward the center of the courtyard.

The soldiers all interrupted their tasks and stood tall in eager silence, looking up at Drago as he looked out to all of them.

"Soldiers of Serpeno!" he cried, "There has been a trespass on our world that we cannot allow! Two humans have come to our world!"

The reptilian soldiers whispered amongst each other and growled at the very mention of the humans.

"These humans think themselves above the laws of our High Council! They believe, as their species does, that their crimes will go unnoticed and unpunished!"

His men hissed and grumbled with discontent as more and more crowded around Drago. "If they are not brought to justice, we leave our world vulnerable to invasion and make no mistake. They will bring their violence upon us! Remember who we are! We are Serpens! We are the fiercest warriors in the cosmos! Swords of the High Council! We are the superior species!

His men shouted in agreement, raised their fists and swords, and roared with rage blazing in their eyes.

"There will be no quarter until these insolent creatures are found, and once they are… we will rip the flesh from their bones!"

The Serpen soldiers erupted with war cries and began chanting his name, "Drago! Drago! Drago!"

"Move out!" Drago commanded, "The hunt has begun!"

The soldiers dispersed immediately, throwing chest plates over their shoulders and picking up weapons as fast as they could. They assembled themselves into formations and began running through the foggy streets of their underground city towards stairwells and tunnels leading to the surface.

Drago followed several platoons of his men up to the stairwell he had entered through. As the stone concealing the tunnel from the surface began to open, his men poured out from beneath it. They sprinted into the jungle with dripping fangs as their eyes glared through the trees and their snouts huffed the air around them. They filed out wildly in all directions until several hundred of them had poured out to the surface, and they all began slashing their blades against the thick undergrowth.

Drago strode out behind them and sealed the entrance to the city. He walked calmly out into the jungle and began to sniff the air around him, searching for the scent.

Then he looked to the sky and saw their great red sun begin to sink towards the horizon behind the canopy. The sky was painted a blazing red, and the forest steadily grew darker. He clenched his large dark fist tight around his ax and pressed onward, even more urgently than before.

# Chapter Seven: The Path to the City

Chiron climbed up the ladder of the bunker and opened the hatch just enough to peer through to the surface. Orion watched from below, seeing the vivid red light from the sky shine onto Chiron's weary face as his eyes darted back and forth.

"What do you see?" Orion asked.

Chiron did not answer. Orion could see his mouth move with silent mumblings, but then, his lips fell still, and he closed the hatch.

Orion repeated his question, "What did you see?"

"Nothing," Chiron grunted, "That's what worries me," "Do you think the creature is still out there?"

Chiron climbed down the ladder and brushed past Orion, "They'll all be hunting us now."

Orion watched Chiron as he began to rummage through his belongings, tossing what he did not need to the side. "What are these creatures?" Orion asked.

"Serpens," Chiron answered, "The natives of this world."

Orion stepped towards Chiron, "So that would mean that we are on Serpeno," he deduced.

Chiron nodded as he continued to throw his belongings behind him, "We are not welcome on this world, and if we are found, we will be executed."

"So how will we get into the city and send our message without being seen?"

Chiron stopped rummaging. He glanced back to Orion with unblinking graveness in his eyes, "We will be seen eventually. All we can ensure is that our presence is not reported to the chancellor."

Orion nodded as he took a quiet deep breath, "So if they see us, we will have to kill them."

"Unfortunately that is our only course of action," Chiron nodded, "The Serpens' hatred of humans runs deep, and if Drago has already reported to them, then they will be out for blood until they have it."

"Drago?" Orion asked, "That thing has a name?"

"The most well-known name among his people," Chiron said, "He is Chancellor Kobra's son and his named successor. He is a cunning, ruthless warrior, and he has more influence on their warriors than his own father does."

Orion folded his arms over his chest and winced as his sleeves brushed over his wounds, "So how do we fight them off? We're going to be outnumbered."

Chiron looked over to Orion's bow, "We start with picking the right weapon for the battle," Orion glanced over at his bow and shook his head as he looked back to Chiron, "We're going to need more than just that," he said.

Chiron turned back to his belongings and recovered a large quiver that was filled to its full capacity with arrows. He cradled it to his arms and held it out to Orion.

"The bow is only half of your weapon. An arrow can eliminate more than one opponent at a time. But doing so requires…imagination."

Orion shook his head again, "I might be able to kill two with one, but these are still just arrows, Chiron."

Chiron pulled three arrows from three different sections of the quiver, presenting the arrowheads, "In the proper hands, this is an arsenal that could stop an army," he said, "In this quiver, there are three different arrowheads: a white phosphorus incendiary, an electromagnetic pulse, and broadheads. Each one is designated by color."

Orion looked at the fletchings of the arrows, silently counting how many of each there were. He came to a total of fifteen white, fifteen blue, and twenty black as Chiron continued to explain, "The white phosphorus arrows have white fletchings. Their explosive will ignite on impact and the resulting flame burns at five thousand degrees. The electromagnetic pulse from the blue arrows is greatly miniaturized. However, it is still deadly and can travel to multiple opponents standing beside one another. The broadheads, which have black fletchings, should be sharp enough to make dispatching two opponents an easy task."

Chiron held the quiver out to Orion, who felt his hands tremble as he took it.

"I've only ever killed animals Chiron," he trembled.

"This is war, this is…different,"

"You have done what is necessary to survive," Chiron said, "This cannot be any different."

Orion nodded and placed the quiver down at his feet, "Do you think this will be enough to take on Drago and his warriors? I still don't like those odds."

"Neither do I," Chiron said, "Drago has already caught our scent, so it will not be long before we are tracked here. We must leave tonight."

"Tonight?"

Chiron brushed past him and picked up a sword with a worn leather-bound handle. He took a deep breath as he slid it into a scabbard and slung it over his back, then picked up a short sword and held it out to Orion.

Orion hesitated, taking a step back and reaching down to pick up the quiver, "I don't know how to use that," he said,

"You're going to need it," Chiron grunted, "And if we escape, there will be more than enough time for me to teach you how to use it properly."

"I just need my bow," Orion said, slinging the quiver over his shoulders.

"The blade is sharp and strong enough to pierce through the Serpens' hides. Does that sound like something you want to leave behind?"

Orion took the sword from Chiron with a heavy sigh and slid it into the quiver on his back. "Anything else?" he asked.

"One more thing," Chiron said. He held out a small wooden box in his hands and opened it. Orion looked inside and saw blue fabric.

"What is this?"

"Take it out," Chiron said. Orion grasped the bundled fabric. It was soft and light, and as he removed it from the box, it unfolded until it touched the floor of the bunker. As he examined it closer, Orion realized what it was.

"A cloak?"

"An heirloom," Chiron corrected, "The only thing I have left of Altair and Lyra."

Suddenly Orion felt his hands tighten on the fabric, and as his fingers traced it, he felt his thumb run across a long black hair. He plucked it and held it out to the light, and tears began to drip from the corner of his eyes.

"This was my mother's," he trembled.

Chiron nodded, "I gave it to her so that she could leave the palace without being seen. She would have wanted you to have it, especially now."

Orion threw it over his shoulders and shut the clasp around his neck. It fit him almost perfectly, falling over his shoulders and barely grazing the floor beneath him.

"There is a switch on the clasp," Chiron said, "What does it do?"

Chiron did not answer. He simply pointed to it, then waited with his hands held behind his back. Orion pressed the switch, then startled, as the fabric of the cloak began to flicker, and its colors began to change. When its pattern finally solidified, he could no longer see his shoulders. He checked again, turning around in circles, only catching glimpses of his legs and chest beneath the fabric. He looked back to Chiron, who had a warm grin on his face.

"It's incredible, isn't it?"

"What is this?" Orion gasped.

"It's all that's left of an experimental fabric that was designed for our soldiers to use as camouflage," he said.

Orion held the hem of the cloak, and his heart surged. The feeling of it washing over his back was the closest thing he had felt to his mother's hands in many years. More tears streamed down his cheek. He flipped the switch again and watched in awe as the cloak flickered back to its original dark blue color.

"These tools will serve you well," Chiron said, "But you must understand that those alone will not be enough to ensure your survival. No matter what we face, we must stand together."

Orion nodded, but Chiron was not satisfied with his response, "You do understand what this means?" Orion nodded again, but Chiron stepped forward with widened eyes, "If I tell you to hide, then that is what you must do. If I tell you to fight, you fight, and if you must abandon me to save yourself, then you must do it without question."

"I can handle myself just fine," Orion said.

Chiron folded his arms and rolled his eyes, "I don't question that, but your survival insures more than just your future, you must remember this."

Orion shook his head and turned to the ladder out of the bunker, "How will we find the city?"

Chiron sighed and gripped Orion's shoulder before he could take a step, "We won't find it by rushing blindly into a forest full of an army hunting us."

Orion brushed Chiron's hand off of his shoulder, "Well then what is your plan?" he demanded.

Chiron maintained his calm but annoyed demeanor, "Well," he sighed, "It is the Serpens' city, so why not just ask them where it is?"

Orion rolled his eyes, "I'm done wasting time," he turned and placed his hands on the rungs of the ladder, but Chiron stood still, looking around the walls of the bunker.

"I think if I was being held prisoner down here, I would say just about anything to be set free."

Orion stopped. He glanced over his shoulder and released a long sigh.

"That's a bad idea," he said, "We barely got away from Drago. What makes you think we could trap him or one of his men down here?"

Chiron smiled, "At night, Serpens can see better than any human, but they still rely primarily on their sense of smell when they hunt. It would take just one drop of blood to make them come running."

After hearing this, Orion looked over his arms and chest in a panic. He felt his chest surge as he saw beading, fresh blood in all his open cuts. He held his arms up so Chiron could see them clearly.

"Well if blood is going to be our bait, then we've already set our trap," he said.

Chiron threw his hands onto Orion's shoulders and tore his poncho off of his back. He threw it into the center of the room, then snatched the heat lamp. Orion, too confused to know which question to ask, watched as Chiron slammed the heat lamp onto his poncho, setting it ablaze.

"Get outside now!" Chiron said, "Before we are surrounded!"

Orion threw the hood of his mother's cloak over his head and activated the clasp. It shimmered and once again became invisible as he climbed up the ladder with Chiron following right behind him. Orion opened the hatch and looked out into the clearing. The deep red of the sunset had disappeared and given way to the deep violet of night. All that Orion could see was the swaying shadows of the trees and the undergrowth around the tiny clearing. He heard no thunderous footsteps, no voices, not even the chittering of the animals. If the wind had not been blowing, it would have been completely silent. He climbed out of the hatch and knelt in the cool grass, notching an arrow as he searched his surroundings. Once Chiron was out of the hatch, he threw the hatch completely open behind him, and Orion could see the smoke billowing from below rise into the night air.

"Why did you do that?" Orion asked.

"Like you said, the scent of your blood has already been caught. The smoke will cover that, and still draw their attention."

"So where will we trap them?"

"Nothing else has changed," Chiron said.

Orion looked down and saw the light from the fire glow brighter and more smoke billow up towards them.

Orion looked to Chiron shaking his head, "Chiron, whoever is trapped down there will be burned alive."

"Not if they tell us what we need to know," he said, "We're almost out of time now, move to the edge of the clearing and hide yourself."

"Chiron-"

"Move!" he barked.

Orion huffed as he ran into the brush. Chiron took off after him, and the two hid behind a cluster of low-hanging leaves. Orion looked at Chiron as he kept his eyes fixed on the bunker.

'This doesn't feel right,' Orion thought, 'We need to know where the city is, and we won't find it unless we do this, but this feels…like what Oberon would do,'

He bumped his shoulder into Chiron's, and the moment the grizzled man turned to look at him, he asked, "How does this make us any better than Oberon?"

Chiron hesitated, then looked down to the dirt beneath them, "I used to believe that through war, I could make things better; that the suffering it caused was just a price that had to be paid for a better future."

"So it's that simple? This one Serpen just has to pay so that we can have what we want? How is that justified?"

"It isn't," Chiron sighed, "It is wrong, and I don't want to do this either. After years of war, you realize that the only way to truly win a war is to end it. If we do not do this, and we never reach the city, the war will continue, and there will be no one to protect our people from Oberon's wrath."

"But there has to be another way."

Chiron glanced back into Orion's eyes, "For the time being, no," Orion opened his mouth to speak again, but Chiron held his palm up, "Someone is coming," he whispered.

Orion looked out to the entrance of the bunker and, just beyond it, spotted several small trees on the other side of the grove moving against the direction of the wind. They parted like a dark leafy curtain until the moonlight revealed the silhouette of a scaled hide. Orion immediately pulled his arrow back on the drawstring and took aim, but Chiron swatted down on the tip of his arrow.

"Do you even know what that arrow would do?" he scolded.

Orion scowled, then looked to the tip of his arrow. His stubborn confidence faded, realizing that it was not a broadhead. He slowly relaxed his arm and let the arrow rest against his bow.

"You would have killed him and started a fire that would have burned for miles," Chiron whispered, "You have to follow my lead."

Orion shook his head and grumbled, "Well if you don't want me to shoot him, what do you want me to do?"

Chiron slid to his side, directly against him. He pointed at the column of smoke rising from the bunker, "We need to act quickly while this one is still alone," he whispered, "If you shoot it or attack head on, he could call for help. You need to get behind him and push him into the bunker."

"Then what?"

"Then we go in after him and seal ourselves inside. Serpens will die if their hides dry out or if they overheat. All we need to do is outlast him once we're inside."

"And then we'll let him go?"

Chiron hesitated again, "If he cooperates."

Sensing that this was the closest the two would come to an agreement, Orion held his tongue. He pulled the hood of the cloak further over his face and activated the clasp. Once he vanished, Chiron watched the branches beside him shift as Orion's invisible shoulders brushed through them. He traced the indents in the dirt until they became footprints in the grass, slowly approaching the rear of the creeping Serpen.

The reptilian warrior sniffed the air around the column of smoke, wincing at the heat coming from the hatch, clutching his sword tighter as he circled the clearing. Orion's footsteps slid through the grass behind it, inching closer and closer to it as it made more and more passes around the hatch. Then it stopped, staring down into the bunker. It snarled curiously and lowered itself cautiously to a knee, hissing and flicking its tongue.

Orion's confidence slowly grew as he inched closer and closer to the serpen. He sensed his nervousness, and the differences between him and his commander became clearer with every step. Drago was at least double this Serpen's height and weight, and the vivid green color of its hide made him more like a large animal than a monster.

'It won't be any different than pushing an animal into a trap,' Orion thought, 'Just do it.'

He looked over to the brush Chiron was hiding behind, and through its wide leaves, he could see his grizzled face nodding up and down. When he turned back to the Serpen, he saw him leaning further over the hatch. His head was now almost entirely immersed in the smoke.

Orion slowly rose from his haunches and tackled the Serpen from behind. It screeched as it was taken by surprise. He didn't fall through. He had barely managed to keep himself on the surface by digging his clawed hands into the soft grass beside the hatch. Orion pressed his hands down onto its scaled shoulders as hard as he could, trying to keep it from writhing out of his grip, but as it began to panic, he felt his grip slipping. It flipped over. It snapped its jaws. It swung its claws at Orion's face. Orion threw his arms around its body and threw himself and the Serpen down to the ground, feeling his shoulder hit the metal edge of the hatch.

Chiron rushed across the clearing and jumped onto both of them. Orion dug his toes into the grass and began pushing with Chiron, inch by inch, until his head hung down into the smoking hatch. He pushed again, feeling his spine scrape across the edge of the hole. Then, he slipped and felt blood rush to his head as he hung upside down, looking down into the crackling fire, barely holding the screeching Serpen in his arms.

"Push me in!" he shouted, "Let him go!" Chiron argued, "Just push me in!"

The Serpen howled and kicked against Orion's chest. He jumped to the ladder and began scrambling out as Orion fell headfirst into the bunker. He crashed onto his back. Every huff of air was knocked from his lungs. He felt paralyzed as he gasped into the smoke for a breath, watching the Serpen scramble up the ladder. Chiron was standing above him on the surface, with his sword poised to strike. Orion rolled to his stomach, then heard a sharp ring of metal above him, followed by a horrible shriek. When he regained his footing, he looked up and saw a clawed hand falling down toward him.

He stepped aside, The Serpen's severed hand slapped the stone floor next to his foot. The shrieking creature was dangling from the final rung of the ladder with its remaining hand, growling at Chiron with blazing green eyes. He reached back to his quiver and pulled an arrow. He notched it, took aim, and aligned the tip of the broadhead with the meat of its scaled palm. He released it. It found its mark. The Serpen's clawed fingers let go of the ladder, and it fell down the shaft. As it fell, Chiron jumped onto the ladder and pulled the hatch shut behind them. The Serpen landed its back, Chiron slid down the ladder and jumped onto its chest as soon as it hit the floor, pressing his sword up against its leathery throat and growled.

"Tell us where your city is!"

The Serpen continued to shriek and writhe on its back.

Chiron stepped off the serpen's chest and grabbed its bleeding wrist. He dragged it to the center of the bunker, towards the heat of the fire.

"No! No! Mercy!" The Serpen begged,

"Start talking!" Chiron growled,

"Please! They will kill me!"

"We will kill you first if you don't start talking!"

Chrion pulled him closer to the fire, hovering his handless limb over a crackling flame. Orion could not bring himself to watch. He turned away, but he could not escape the wheezing and begging ringing in his ears. It tore his soul to hear it, even from a creature that wanted nothing more than to murder them both. He forced himself to reach out for Chiron's arm. He gripped his unyielding hand and begged,

"Stop, just let him speak!"

Chiron's expression was as unyielding as his grip. His gray eyes bored through Orion's soul. Though it went against every thought coursing through his head, Orion let go of his arm and stepped back. Chiron turned back to the Serpen and hunched over, whispering in its ear.

"You do not have to die here and we do not want to harm your people. All we want is to leave your planet without any more bloodshed; but if you stand in our way, I will not hesitate to let you burn."

The Serpen stopped writhing, and it looked up at Chiron with wide eyes, "U-Underground, the city is underground."

"How do we get there?" Orion asked.

"There is a river," he coughed, "Follow it to the end and it will take you to the falls, where the catacombs begin."

Chiron held his grip for a moment longer, then finally released him. The Serpen shrieked and broke for the ladder before either of them could stop them. He scrambled up the shaft, and all that Orion could hear of him was fading shrieks as it ran back into the jungle.

"Do you think he was telling the truth?" Orion asked.

"Yes," Chiron said, "But there may be a great deal more that he did not tell us."

Chiron walked past Orion and climbed up the ladder without another word, and the two returned to the surface. As they returned to the clearing, they could already hear more branches breaking in all directions, growing louder and closer with every snap and crash. Drago's army was closing in.

"Quick!" Chiron hissed, "This way!"

# Chapter Eight: Into the Forest

Orion's feet swept against the brush. His heels dug harder into the dirt of the forest floor as he and Chiron sprinted side by side past hundreds of trees. Their path twisted in every direction, and as they pushed further into the forest, the trunks of the trees grew larger, and the canopy above thickened until what pale light the moon provided them was nearly extinguished. As they were about to charge headlong into the darkest part of their path, Chiron abruptly slid to a stop behind a pair of fallen trees that had come to rest on top of one another. Orion stopped himself beside him. Chiron was peering through the small gap between the trunks of the trees.

"What is it?" Orion asked. Chiron snapped his head around, He silently pressed a finger to his lips, then pointed to the gap between the trees. Orion looked through and understood why they stopped. He slowly sank to his knee as he spotted three Serpens searching through the tall grass at the base of the trees just a few meters away. They were all armed with swords sheathed on their backs, and Orion could hear more following them in the distance.

One of the Serpens called back to his comrades, "There is no sign of them! We should push back and regroup!"

"Drago said to keep pushing north!" another hissed, "We will not pick up the trail if we double back now!"

The two glared at each other, and the one who spoke first unsheathed his sword, "Keep your snout shut and do as I say!" he growled.

"Do not forget your place, Kaa," the other snapped, "Drago is in command, not you!"

The one called Kaa snarled and raised his sword over his head to strike, but a third quickly jumped between the two and pushed Kaa to the ground.

"Enough!" he said, "One of us is already missing! Talon still hasn't returned from his reconnaissance, what do you think that means, Kaa?"

Kaa grumbled as he stood back to his feet, "That he's probably not as good of a scout as You said he was."

"He is one of our finest, unlike you. It means that the humans are close. We move forward, and you keep your snout shut!"

Kaa scoffed and shook his head as the group continued their search toward Orion and Chiron.

"If they get much closer, they'll see us," Orion whispered. Chiron maintained his silence, only responding with a nod, then he slowly started creeping backward. Orion moved to follow, but Chiron held his palm out to him, signalling for him to stay put. Orion held his arms out in disbelief and shook his head.

'Unbelievable,' he thought, 'How the hell am I supposed to trust him if he won't even tell me what's happening?'

The Serpens had almost reached the fallen trees, and Chiron had already taken off in a silent run back the way they came. Having no choice, Orion pulled the cloak around him and pressed the button on the clasp.

The Serpens moved around the tree, keeping their focus on the path in front of them without glancing backward. Orion slowly laid himself down on the ground and pressed his head to the ground, remaining as still as possible. He watched each of the Serpens' leathery feet pass by him, headed in the same direction Chiron ran. His heart began to race despite his almost certain safety. His concerns were no longer for himself but for how he would fare without Chiron,

'What if they capture him?' he wondered, 'How will I reach the river without him?'

The Serpens slowed the pace of their patrol to a long creep. He could hear the pace of his breathing grow faster and faster as horrible thoughts ran through his head.

'Without Chiron, I will never get back to Archon prime. Then what will happen to Rowan?' He clenched his fist and felt it begin to shake. He would not sit idly by while Chiron ran off like a coward. He could not let the Serpens capture his only ally, the best chance he had of escaping.

Orion threw the cloak off his shoulder, reached for an arrow, disregarding which kind of arrow he had set his fingers upon, and fired it into the back of the nearest Serpen. It whistled through the nearly silent night air and landed with a thud into the Serpen's body, and as it landed, a bright blue light flashed, and a shockwave broke the air. The entire group of Serpens cried out in pain as they all froze in place, with waves of blue electricity crackling all over their bodies.

Orion heard Chiron's voice from behind him.

"No!" he cried angrily, "Stupid boy! Now they'll all be onto us!" Orion felt shame wash over him.

"I thought-"

"There's no time now!" Chiron snapped, "Go! Run!"

Orion followed him as he bolted past the fallen trees and sprinted into a more tangled path of trees with low-hanging vines. He frantically threw his bow over his back and drew his short sword. He began to swing wildly at the vines, trying to clear the path as they pressed into nearly complete darkness.

He could hear more hissing voices in the distance behind them, rapidly approaching. He started to swing his sword faster, but as they continued to push forward, the moonlight disappeared, and he could barely see the vines in front of him. Then, just as he thought he had broken free of the vines, he took off in full stride, but his heart sank as the ground disappeared from beneath his feet.

He and Chiron fell down the side of a hill. Orion could not see where he was falling, but he felt the sting of every twig, branch, and stone bashing against his body. He could also hear Chiron grunting as he fell alongside him, just out of arm's reach.

Then, he finally felt his body come to rest on what seemed to be flat ground. He groaned as he picked himself back up and tried to shake himself from his daze.

He heard Chiron call out to him, "Orion," he whispered, "Where are you? I can't see you."

His voice was very close. "I'm here," he answered, "I can't see either," Then, he felt Chiron's rough hand take hold of his shoulder.

"Get down and stay down," he said, "Throw the cloak over us."

Orion dropped to the ground. He reached behind him and grabbed the hem of the cloak, then fumbled it over Chiron's shoulder until he had pulled it over both of them. The two laid themselves flat on the ground, and Orion pressed the clasp.

Mere seconds after he had done so, they heard a growling voice from above. "They fell down here!" the voice cried.

Another voice answered, "Where? I can't see anything. Light a torch and throw it down there!"

Orion craned his neck to peek up but felt Chiron's hand grab his head and push his face back onto the ground,

"Keep still and don't move," Chiron hissed. He did not release his grip on Orion's head and continued pressing his face to the ground as another Serpen crept to the ravine's edge with a lit torch in his hand.

The Serpen threw the torch down into the ravine, and it landed right beside Chiron. "We have to go now, or they'll see us," Orion hissed.

"Trust me. Don't move," Chiron said, "What if they come down here?"

Chiron did not respond, and he continued to hold Orion to the ground with a firm, calm hand. The Serpens at the top of the ravine were silent as they looked down. Their silence stretched the seconds and made Orion's heart race with unease. He felt his last shred of patience expire. He tried to shuffle out of Chiron's grip, despite what he said, but he could not escape his grip. He clenched his fists in frustration until they shook against the ground. All he wanted to do was push Chiron off him and escape before the Serpens found them. The notion became so tempting that it took all his will to keep his composure. He slid his hand back and grabbed

Chiron's hand, trying to pull it off him, but as he did, the Serpens finally broke their silence.

"There is nothing here," a Serpen growled, "Move along the ravine and see if they moved to the south!" The others followed his orders and left alongside him back into the jungle.

As soon as they were out of sight, Chiron finally removed his hand from Orion's head. Orion snapped to his feet and walked briskly back toward the side of the ravine.

"And where do you plan on going?" Chiron asked.

"We can't just sit here," Orion huffed, "We need to keep moving."

"And let them pick up our trail again?"

Orion whirled around and glared at Chiron. "They're hunting us. If we're going to have to fight our way to the city anyway, we might as well not run from it."

Chiron shook his head. "Now is not the time for that, Orion."

"You said we'd have to fight our way out, right? I'm willing to fight now. Why aren't you?"

"The fate of our people rests with us. We can't jeopardize that because of your impatience."

"Damn the people! They stood by while my mother and father were cut down, trying to set them free! They let Oberon take Rowan after all he's done for them! The only person worth a damn on that godforsaken planet *is* Rowan. We can't just sit here while he's running out of time."

"We are outnumbered!" Chiron snapped, "Outmatched and out of reach from any help. If you do not listen, there will be very little I can do to protect or prepare you for what is to come. Rowan and the rest of the people will be left with no hope, and there will be no one left to stand against Oberon."

Orion sighed, shook his head, and kicked a stone resting beside his foot as he turned his back to Chiron with clenched fists.

"You're angry," Chiron said calmly, "You want vengeance. You might think that you are ready now, but you have much to learn, and you cannot do this alone."

"That doesn't mean that there's nothing I can do! You said I could do more, so why won't you let me?"

"Because the people need you to be more than just a warrior. You need to survive and lead them in this fight."

"Why me? Why not you?" Orion asked.

Chiron shook his head, and his gentility began to shine beneath the warm light of the torch resting on the ground. "Because our people have a future with you, Orion. I do not know how many years I have left, and I am sure that what time I have left will not be enough to build back what we have lost."

"I don't want to lead anyone," Orion said, "I need to save my friend. He's all I have left."

"Do you think so little of yourself that you still can't see the great destiny that lies before you?"

"I don't believe in destiny. I believe you make your own way in this life."

"I never said that your destiny isn't a choice," Chiron said, stepping forward and placing his hand on Orion's shoulder, "But there are parts of our path are laid for us. When you make your stand against Oberon, the people will be watching, whether you care for them or not. An act of defiance will make them rise up behind you. They will fight beside you because they will finally have something that has been taken from them time and time again."

Orion shook his head. He did not understand how even Chiron, who he had known for only one day, could have such faith in him.

"What makes you so sure that I can be all this?" he asked.

"Because you are not your father. The fact that you hesitate to take this responsibility shows respect for the power you will be asked to command. You may not be ready or desire it, but like everything else, I will remain by your side to guide you through it. But I cannot help you if you will not let me teach you."

Orion kept his head turned away, feeling shame for his rash actions. He could bring himself to look Chiron in the eye.

"I'm sorry," he said, "I just…I have to save him. I can't lose what family I have left. If that means I have to kill Oberon, then so be it."

"The day will come when you are ready to face him. Until then, you must be patient, survive, and learn."

Orion gave a full nod and took a deep breath. He finally looked up into Chiron's eyes and patted his hand as he gently let go of his shoulder and glanced over to the crackling torch.

"Well, at least we won't have to build a fire now," Orion said.

Orion chuckled softly, and the two sat beside it, feeling its heat against their hands. "If only we had something to eat," Orion said.

Chiron raised an eyebrow and leaned to look behind Orion. He raised a finger and pointed at something. Orion turned and saw a strange bird stepping through the grass behind him. It had black feathers, four black beady eyes, and tiny legs with two clawed toes. Chiron made a strange cooing noise at the bird, and the bird responded with its own purr. Chiron held out his hand, and the bird hopped over to him as if the two were old acquaintances. It brushed up against his palm and hopped onto its fingers.

"That's lucky," Orion said.

"We're not going to eat the bird," Chiron grumbled,

Orion furrowed his brow and opened his palms upward. "We need the food."

"Yes, and this bird will bring it to us."

"Of course it will," Orion sighed, "Tell him to bring his friends, I'm sure there's one of them that you aren't fond of."

"Their meat is toxic," Chiron explained, "I found that out the hard way. However, this particular species forges strong symbiotic relationships with larger creatures."

Orion leaned forward, "So what do they do?"

"They pick berries off of trees and bring them back to the larger creatures so that they'll protect them from predators,"

"How do we get it to bring the fruit?" Orion asked.

"We don't, we wait," Chiron said.

Orion shook his head and folded his arms. Chiron cocked his head to the side and sighed, "Patience," he said, "there is a lesson to be learned here. While the easy choice is always clear, there is always another hidden behind it. You will never be able to see it without patience."

As Chiron spoke, the bird flapped its wings and fluttered to a branch above them, pecking at the tiny branches it perched itself on until it caught something in its beak. When it returned, it was holding a cluster of three small berries. Chiron held its palm out, and the bird dropped the cluster into his hand. Chiron took the first berry and gave it to the bird, then tossed the second to Orion and threw the third into his mouth.

He glanced warmly down at the bird, "Thank you, my friend," he said.

Orion ate the small berry and savored every sweet morsel of it. Then, he swallowed it, feeling the hunger churn in his stomach. "We're going to need more than just berries, Chiron."

"What makes you so sure that we can eat anything else?" Chiron grumbled, "There are so many animals here, there has to be something we can hunt."

"Every species here has elevated blood toxicity. It helps them to survive the harsh conditions, and we would die if we tried to eat any one of them."

"So you survived all these years eating berries?" Orion asked.

"After a while, you get used to it," he sighed, "One isn't enough to stop the hunger, but it's enough to keep you from starving for another day."

"What else should I know about this planet?" Orion asked.

"It's dangerous in every imaginable way, the perfect place to send someone if you want them to die. The fact that both of us were sent here by the same person makes me think that we should move forward with the assumption that there is something else at work against us."

"What do you mean?"

"It is possible that Drago is so eager to hunt us down because he has sided with Oberon."

Orion shook his head, "That's impossible. If the Serpens hate humans as much as you said they do, then Drago would never side with one."

"Unless there is a human that hates his own people more than the Serpens do,"

"But given a chance, Drago would have killed him,"

"If he could. With his machine, Oberon can travel across the cosmos faster than anyone. It is possible that he came here to recruit Drago, and no one would have been aware of it,"

"What would Drago have to gain?"

"Perhaps an opportunity to eliminate the human race once and for all, perhaps something else…"

Orion rested his head on his hands, thinking back on everything Chiron had told him. "If this is true, then maybe Oberon is building an army. The high council would never know, and he could take his forces anywhere he wanted to before anyone responded."

Chiron nodded, "His discovery of you threatens to cause rebellion among the people and end his reign. Whatever his plans are, he will have to act soon."

"You said that Oberon wanted to take the army out against the high council so that he could have revenge for what they did to us. Do you think he plans to overthrow them?"

"Perhaps," Chiron said, "I do not know how his ambitions have grown, but I am certain that he poses a grave danger to all, now more than ever."

Orion wrung his hands as he thought. He felt like a pawn in a much larger game, but perhaps Chiron was right. If Oberon's ambitions, maybe he did have a much larger part to play.

'But how do we win this?' he thought, 'If he can travel anywhere before anyone knows-' He leaned towards Chiron with widened eyes.

"Do you think the chancellor of Serpeno would hear us out if we had the chance to speak with him?"

"That is doubtful," Chiron sighed, "He does not hold much power with the council, and I do not think he would be willing to jeopardize his reputation further by talking to humans."

"Even if his son might be betraying him? Think about it, if we can turn Drago's father against him, he could call off the hunt, and if the high council knew about what Oberon is planning, they could intervene before it's too late."

"It would not be that simple, Orion," Chiron warned, "Their kind has hated us for generations, as does the High Council. They perceive us as animals. Violent animals. Do you really think that he would be persuaded to listen to one of us?"

"If it threatened the future of his people, I don't think it would matter who the warning came from."

Chiron ran his fingers through his shaggy beard and stared into the fire. After a moment, he looked over to Orion with the flickering light of the flames shining in his eyes, "Actually," he said, "You are the only person he might listen to."

Orion furrowed his brow, "Why not you?"

"Because I am not a prince."

Orion scoffed, "Just because Rom was my father does mean that I can decide that I'm a prince, and that doesn't mean what I say would mean any more to the chancellor."

"Of course not," Chiron said, "But claiming a throne is claiming responsibility for one's people and their future. Who would be a better authority to give this warning than an exiled prince seeking to liberate his people from a murderous tyrant?"

Orion turned away, shaking his head. He rested his folded arms over his knees and looked out into the walls of the dark ravine. He sat still, refusing to look back at Chiron,

'How can he keep asking this of me?' he thought, 'What does he expect of me?'

His angry thoughts were interrupted by something small repeatedly pressing against the toe of his boot. He glanced down and saw that the bird had returned with another cluster of berries in its beak. Orion moved his foot, trying to startle it so that it would fly away, but it would not budge. It looked up at him with a strange and instinctive loyalty.

'Stupid Bird…Rowan. He still never got to see the birds. Will he ever get the chance now?'

The bird hopped forward, gently placed the cluster of berries beside his boot, and hopped away. Orion picked them up, and though he could feel his stomach twist eagerly at the sight of food, he could not bring himself to eat them.

'Chiron isn't completely wrong,' he thought, 'In order for this new plan to work, we can't afford for the chancellor to not be convinced. Maybe there is a better chance he will listen to me if I play along with this story, but I can't be this great leader that Chiron thinks he sees in me. The chancellor must believe it…that's all.'

He finally turned to Chiron rubbing his face in his palms,

"You aren't wrong," he sighed, "That might be the only way to convince the chancellor to listen to us. I will…play my part, but only for this plan to work."

Chiron sighed, resting his chin against his hand, "Very well," he said, "You should get some rest while you can. I will take the first watch."

Orion nodded and curled himself on the ground, with his back facing the warmth of the dying torch, but before he could close his eyes, Chiron asked one more question.

"I'm sure that your dreams are filled with praise from your proud parents and an even prouder friend. I wonder what they would think of this plan?"

Orion rolled his eyes and let his eyelids close. He held his tongue but could not restrain his pounding heart. He was so certain about this decision before, but that confidence had vanished. It felt as if a doubtful eternity had passed before his heart finally slowed, and he was able to drift into an uneasy sleep.

# Chapter Nine: A Stranger in Need

Orion opened his eyes and realized that he was standing on the steps of the dark tower in Luma City. Everything seemed to be the same way he had left it, from the gloomy sky to the drab and crumbling dwellings. There was only one thing that seemed entirely out of place.

He heard angry voices. Human voices fast approaching from behind him. He turned in the direction of the noise and saw an angry crowd armed with whatever instruments they had, picks, makeshift clubs, and other blunt instruments. They charged towards Orion, screaming with fury burning in their eyes.

"This is our world!"

"No more!"

Orion leaped out of the way just before the mob trampled over him, but when he turned back toward them, he saw that he was not what they were after. They had crashed into the great front doors and had begun beating their tools against it, screaming as they tried to break them down.

"Face us, you coward!" They cried, "You can't kill us all!

Orion's heart sank as he watched this desperate attack. He saw so many faces he recognized. He saw the faces of the men who worked the field, the women who worked in the ration house, the fathers and mothers of families he and

Rowan had fed with their game. Then, he saw two faces that immediately brought tears to his eyes and made him so weak he fell to his knees.

He saw his father and mother, Altair and Lyra, at the back of the crowd. His father wore a long, thick coat of furs and was armed with a full quiver and his beautiful steel bow. His mother carried another quiver on her back and a small dagger in her fist. His father was firing arrows up into the palace windows until his quiver was emptied. His mother handed him the one on her back as the heavy doors began to splinter and crack open. Once the mob ahead of them finally broke through, the two marched forward behind them as they entered the palace.

Their advance was halted in place. Sentries were already waiting behind the doors, no more than three feet into the great hall. They began cutting the rioters down as they charged inside. Orion could smell the blood in the air, see heads fall from shoulders, and still, the mob pressed forward. The skirmish never moved more than a few paces forward, and several rioters began to run back to where Altair and Lyra stood.

"We can't get through!" They cried, "We need to retreat now!"

"No!" Altair shouted, "Stand your ground!"

"We're taking back our home!" Lyra cried.

Sentries began pushing through the crowd, and several charged toward Altair and Lyra. When they attacked, they were skilfully dispatched.

The two worked in perfect harmony, standing back to back, defending one another from the mechanical foes. Alongside several other survivors, they managed to keep the battle alive. They fended off multiple platoons of the mechanical warriors but were entirely unprepared for who emerged from the palace next. A shadowy cloak moved from the dark depths of the tower, and when it moved into the dim daylight, Orion recognized who it was instantly.

Oberon stepped over the bodies of fallen rioters and glided down the palace steps with his black sword drawn.

"Altair! Lyra!" a man with bright blonde hair cried, "Run!" It was Rowan's father. He swung a pick, aiming it towards Oberon's face, but Oberon caught the handle before the blade even touched his helmet. He twisted the pick out of his hands and, with one swift stroke, slit his throat.

The moment Rowan's father fell dead on the steps, Altair cried out in fury. He fired arrow after arrow at Oberon. None of them found their mark. Oberon whirled his sword in front of him so fast that he deflected every arrow before they could land. He pressed his advance, moving closer and closer towards all that remained of the riot; Altair and Lyra, the last two standing. He made it within arms reach of Altair and, with a swift kick, swept his legs out from under him, then plunged his black sword into his heart. Lyra leaped on top of Oberon's back and thrust the dagger into his shoulder. Oberon did not even wince in pain and threw her off of him. She landed on top of her fallen husband, looking up at the sinister dark warrior,

"You don't remember us?" she asked tearfully, "You don't think that we have suffered enough because of your father?"

"Living is suffering," Oberon said, "It doesn't matter who you are."

He plunged his sword through her heart, and Orion cried out in rage. He charged towards Oberon, leaping to tackle him, but as he was about to grab hold of his cloak, he passed right through him as if he was not even there. He fell onto the black gravel, holding his arm out in front of his face, expecting Oberon to turn around and strike him down. No move was made against him. When Orion looked past his extended arm, he realized Oberon had turned away. He was walking back into the palace, entirely unaware he was even there.

Orion crawled toward his mother and father and cried,

"Mom, Dad?" They did not answer. He tried to touch them, but he could not. Their bodies passed like smoke through his fingers. Then, from behind, he heard a woman calling their names.

"Altair! Lyra!" She knelt beside them and immediately tried to apply pressure to Lyra's wound. Orion recognized the woman immediately. It was Rowan's mother.

"Stay with me, Lyra," she begged.

Lyra, summoning what strength she had left, gripped her wrist and wheezed, "O-Orion. G-give him the bow,"

"No, no, no," Rowan's mother cried, "We need to get you help."

"We're gone, Hestia," Lyra wheezed, "Orion and Rowan must be strong. They must finish…what we started. Give Orion the bow and give Rowan the dagger."

"They're just boys! They need you!"

"They…will save…us," Her head fell limp on top of her beloved's chest, and Rowan's mother bowed her head in tears.

She did not have time to mourn. More squads of sentries emerged from the palace, and she knew she had to act quickly. She snatched the bow from Altair's hand and the dagger from Lyra's and ran back into the city. Orion rushed to follow her, but before he could take another step, he heard Chiron's voice.

"Wake up!" Orion felt a strange pull on his shoulder, and then everything around him faded into complete darkness.

"Wake up!" Chiron shouted. Orion jolted awake, with Chiron leaning over him, shaking his shoulders. Orion lunged up and gasped, feeling wet from the sweat beading all over his body.

"I-I saw them," Orion said, "Who?" Chiron asked

"I don't know," Orion gasped, "It was so real, it was like I was watching the day they died!"

"Watching who? Who died?"

"My parents, Altair and Lyra."

The grimness in Chiron's face deepened, but he said nothing, he just patted Orion's shoulder and stood up. As Chiron stepped away, Orion looked around and saw that the sun had already returned. The warm red light illuminated the small ravine they had fallen into. Its slopes were steep but still climbable, and the floor was covered in fallen leaves and thick grass.

"I couldn't wake you last night," Chiron grumbled, "Must have been those dreams of yours."

"I'm sorry," Orion said, rubbing his eyes.

"You can repay me now, actually," Chiron said, "I need to be sure that you can handle one of these," He pulled his sword out of its scabbard, "Come here, I'm going to show you how."

"But what about the Serpens?" Orion asked, "I'm pretty sure that will give us away."

"I climbed up and took a look around last night. They all passed by us. It will be a while before they double back. Come, get up."

Orion hesitated, then stood up, set his bow down on the ground, and stood in front of Chiron.

"Draw your sword," Chiron said.

Orion obeyed and pulled the sword out of his quiver. "I really don't even know where to begin," he said.

"First, plant your feet like mine," Chiron said, pointing down at his boots. Orion mirrored his stance after Chiron's.

"Good," Chiron said, "Now I will go slow at first, and all I want you to do is defend yourself."

Orion nodded and wrapped both hands around the hilt of his sword. Chiron glided his feet across the ground slowly, moving at a fraction of his normal speed. Orion raised his blade nervously, feeling foolish as their swords clinked gently against each other.

"This is stupid," Orion said.

"Then perhaps we should take it up a notch," Chiron said.

Before Orion could respond, Chiron whirled his blade and brought it down with full force toward Orion's shoulder. Orion reacted just in time, barely blocking his strike.

"Not bad," Chiron said, "Let's keep going."

Orion gasped as Chiron unleashed precise strikes against him, one after another, at increasing speed. Orion felt his feet fumbling beneath him as he was pushed backward.

"Don't let me push you back," Chiron grunted, "Your opponent will move you into a vulnerable position if you let them. You must hold your ground and wait for an opening to strike."

Chiron kept pushing his advance. Orion tried to stand his ground, stumbling further and further back until his heels finally pressed against a large stone resting on the ground. Chiron continued swinging his sword down upon him. He was relentless, and his strikes were now so fast that Orion closed his eyes, expecting Chiron to disarm him at any moment. He whirled his sword around his body, feeling Chiron strike it three times in succession, then again and again. He opened his eyes, realizing that there was a pattern. He was striking from the left, then from above, then to the right, and repeating the same sequence. Orion stomped his back foot and locked blades with Chiron as he brought down an overhead strike.

"I think I get it now," Orion grunted.

"Show me," Chiron said.

Orion pushed his full weight against his sword and forced Chiron back. He walked confidently towards him as Chiron resumed his sequence of strikes. Orion anticipated them perfectly, not allowing him to push him back any further.

"Not bad," Chiron said, "But surely you realize that your opponents will have more than just three moves."

Orion's eyes widened as Chiron stepped onto his front foot. He knocked Orion's blade away from his body, but just as he was about to deliver a fatal strike, Orion felt something like a reflex take hold of him. Something beyond his own conscious thought. It tightened his grip on the hilt and moved his arm into a decisive swing. His sword clanged onto Chiron's, pushing both blades to the ground and bringing both to their knees.

Chiron relaxed, then nodded approvingly, "Good reflexes. Not bad," Without another word, he stood to his feet and sheathed his sword.

"That's it?" Orion asked.

"That's it," Chiron replied, "I just wanted to make sure that you could… play your part."

Orion rolled his eyes, "No matter how you make this point, it's not going to work," he mumbled.

"I'm sure you told Rowan and your parents the same thing in your dream," he grunted, "You only said their names a hundred times."

Orion shook his head and pursed his lips, "Just tell me which way the river is," Chiron smiled wryly, then pointed down the long, stretching ravine.

"South," he replied, "The ravine's floor seems to be the path of least resistance. It should keep us clear of the Serpens while they sweep through the jungle," Orion nodded in agreement, retrieved his bow from the ground, then the two began trekking along the ravine floor.

Only one hour into their walk through the ravine, the slopes to their left and right had narrowed so greatly that they had become walls. The rich grass and moss blanketing the slopes had given way to dark red stone. The sun above them was beating down without obstruction, but soon they found relief from its merciless heat as the ravine walls grew taller and taller until they nearly closed above them. As they walked through the new rocky terrain, Orion almost forgot that the jungle was still out there. It was as if they were walking along a hidden desert or on the floor of a roofless cave.

"Have you ever come this way?" Orion asked, wiping sweat from his brow, "Not through the ravine," Chiron said, "I walked alongside it, and it took me right to the river."

"Good to know we're still on the right track," Orion said,

"We're going in the right direction," Chiron sighed, "Whether it is the best path is still uncertain."

"What makes you say that?" Orion asked nervously,

"The Serpens might be the apex predators, but there are still many other dangers we have yet to encounter,"

"You think we will find them here?"

"I'm sure that they will find us."

Orion's heart raced as he searched their narrowing surroundings and the path ahead, "That's comforting," he said.

Chiron chuckled, "It should be, you were raised in the wild, this planet should feel like a second home to you, and looking over your shoulder second nature."

"This isn't like home. This is different, it's…alive, Archon Prime is dead."

"Archon Prime isn't dead yet, Orion."

Orion shook his head, glancing down at his boots, "You haven't been there for years, Chiron. After the drought, the riots, and Oberon, there really isn't anything left, and nothing there could have prepared me for this."

"If that were true, you would not be alive now."

Orion clenched his fists, then put his hand on Chiron's shoulder, "Look, I know what you're trying to say, and it doesn't matter how many times you say it-"

"You won't listen," Chiron finished.

"No, I hear you-"

"That's not the same as listening, Orion," He brushed Orion's hand off his shoulder and furrowed his brow.

"I hear you," Orion repeated, "But you can't just make me see whatever it is that you see. You can't expect me to go to war just so you can right your wrongs."

Chiron shook his head, "You know, believing that men are selfish and vile creatures does you nothing. It only proves that the High Council and Oberon are right, that we should be banished, enslaved, and killed off like a plague. Can you look me in the eye and tell me that is what you believe?"

Orion choked on his words before they could leave his mouth. He looked Chiron in the eye, but their steely gray bored through his stubborn resolve and made him question,

'Is it?'

Chiron nodded, "That's what I thought."

The red star hung over their heads, and the heat of midday beat down upon them as they cleared the narrow walls of their path and stepped into a larger channel of the ravine. The wind echoed off the walls and rang in Orion's ears. After a while, Orion was unsure if he heard the wind or his own troubled, echoing thoughts. But one stood out more than the others. It brought him to a stop. "Do you hear that?" he asked.

Chiron peered ahead, and his eyes widened. It was a new voice. The two heard it call out at full volume.

"Come on, you bastard! Fresh meat!" it echoed across the ravine walls, whoever it belonged to, it was a human voice. Orion and Chiron looked at each other with shocked expressions, then took off in a mad dash.

"Ha ha! I'm going to put your slimy face on my wall!" the voice hollered.

"What is going on?" Orion asked.

"It sounds like this new acquaintance of ours is sampling the local wildlife," Chiron grumbled.

The pair turned a corner and saw the man the voice belonged to. He had a tall, confident build, wrapped under a long coat, with long, red-blonde hair and a neatly trimmed beard. He had a sword in hand and was tumbling around what at first seemed to be an enormous plant, but Orion realized that it was no ordinary fauna. The plant was alive.

What at first seemed to be vines were moving like long, green tentacles, twisting and sweeping all over the ravine floor, bashing against the ground as the man leaped out of their way. Sprouting from the center of the plant was a bulb as large as a boulder, and Orion saw that it had enormous fanged jaws, with a foul-smelling pink maw moaning as the strange man cackled, mocking it as he sliced at the vines,

"Come on, you dumb beast!" he cried, "I thought you, Serpens, would be more of a challenge!"

Chiron rolled his eyes and squeezed the bridge of his nose with his thumb and forefinger. Orion looked down with concern.

"Does he think he's fighting a Serpen?"

"It would seem so," Chiron groaned.

"We need to help him," Orion said.

Chiron looked wryly at Orion, "I'm surprised you're so eager to help him," he said, "He is, after all, fighting a plant. I suspect natural selection will take its course here,"

Orion rolled his eyes, "Chiron, we don't have time for this! He's probably the only other human on this planet, maybe he can help us!"

Chiron chuckled and shook his head, "Well, you better hurry before he gets himself killed."

Orion quickly pulled a blue arrow from his quiver and took aim at the bellowing plant.

He fired. The arrow flew through the ravine and struck the side of the plant's snapping green jaw. The shockwave exploded, and electricity pulsed all over the plant. It whined in pain and writhed in place.

The man snapped his head in the direction the arrow came from, and his face twisted with frustration.

"I did not ask for your help! I can take this beast on my own!"

"Stop!" Orion shouted.

The man ignored him and rushed towards the quivering plant. The effects of the arrow had worn off, and it began to angrily bring its focus back to the man attacking it.

He stabbed at the plant, and hot green fluids came pouring out of the gashes. The beast bellowed again but was able to wrap one of its winding vines around him. His arms were pinned to his sides, and the creature lifted him off of the ground, bringing him towards its snapping jaws.

"What did you say the white arrows do again?" Orion asked.

"No! Orion! That's not a good idea!" Chiron warned,

But it was too late, Orion plucked a white arrow from his quiver and took aim. The plant opened its foul jaws wide and lifted the man just above them. Orion fired. The arrow flew straight into its pink, fleshy mouth, and upon impact, a loud explosion of white fire erupted in its mouth. The plant dropped the man as the white-hot fire quickly spread all over the plant. Its green skin quickly began to crack and shrivel, and it recoiled all of its tentacles around itself as it finally fell lifeless on the ravine floor with a loud crash.

The man quickly jumped to his feet and called out to the two of them, "Hey! I said I did not need your help! Who do you think you are?"

"You're welcome!" Chiron said, "Now, who are you, and why are you here?"

"Piss off, old man! What? Is this thing part of your private garden? Because if it is, I think you forgot to take care of the weeds!"

Chiron shook his head, "Orion," he whispered, "Teach this little prick a lesson."

Orion twisted his face, "Chiron, we can't kill him."

"I don't want you to kill him," Chiron groaned, "Just kick his ass and put him in his place."

"We just need to talk to him, what good will that do?"

"I don't think he's in a talkative mood," Chiron grumbled, "Besides, this is a wonderful opportunity for you to see how persuasive you can be."

Orion tried to argue, but Chiron pushed him forward before he could speak, flicking his fingers at him with a confident smile on his face. Orion shook his head, then turned to face their new acquaintance.

"We don't want trouble," he said, "We were just trying to help."

"I said…I don't need your help!" The man raised his sword up, and Orion quickly blocked it with his bow. The man pressed the blade against him and tried to push him back, but Orion stood his ground. He pushed the man back and threw his bow aside, pulling his short sword out of his quiver. The man retaliated with a wild sweep at Orion's gut. Orion rolled out of the way and glared at his opponent.

"Stop!" Orion begged, "We're all not welcome on this planet, we can help each other if you just listen to me,"

"Piss off!" he said, "I don't need help, and you're just in my way!"

Orion dodged his attacks, not making any attempt to harm him, despite his frustration. "This must be your first fight," the man said, "Normally, when someone is trying to kill you, you try to kill them back."

"Thanks for the tip," Orion grunted.

The man charged again, but as he did, Orion pressed the clasp on his cloak and vanished. The man froze in terror. He looked all around him and spun wildly in confusion. Chiron chuckled to himself as the man cried out.

"What the hell just happened?"

Then, his feet were swept out from under him, and he fell hard onto the ground. His sword was knocked free from his hand and kicked away by something he could not see. He tried to reach for it but felt something step on his hand. Then, Orion turned the cloak off, and the man saw him standing on top of his wrist with his short sword pointed at his chin.

"Who are you, and what are you doing here?" Orion demanded.

The stranger finally took a deep breath and laid flat on his back. He looked up at Orion and said, "My name is

Ulysses Odin. I came here for my men. The Serpens are holding them as prisoners in their underground city."

"What? Where are you from?" Orion asked.

"We came from Diana City."

"Diana City?"

Chiron walked over slowly with a proud grin, "Diana City is an outlier settlement. It welcomes everyone, even humans."

"I thought humans only came from Archon Prime," Orion said.

"It is our origin, but there are rumors among the Serpens of more fortunate humans that live in hiding outside our world. This one must be one of them."

"Ah yes, thank you, sir. I knew you would understand," the man said.

"I wasn't talking to you just yet," Chiron grumbled. He looked at the stranger from head to toe, then turned back to Orion, "There are many pirate ports in Diana City. Judging by his weapon and inclination for stupidity, this one might be more trouble than he's worth, we should leave him and press on."

"Wait," Orion said, "he knew that the city is underground, maybe he knows where we can find it."

Chiron's eyebrows raised sarcastically. Clearly, his distrust in the stranger was not yet broken. "So you say you know where the city is?" he asked.

"I know that it is underground," Ulysses said, "The Serpens that took my crew came to pull a job with us and told us all about it."

"Oh, did they?" Chiron mocked.

The stranger chuckled, "You'd be surprised by what someone says when they are drunk."

"Not really," Chiron grumbled. He shook his head and walked away. Orion nodded regretfully in agreement, then removed his foot from Ulysses' wrist and followed behind Chiron, noticing that his pace was curiously slow.

He nudged his shoulder as they paced away, "What if you're wrong about him, Chiron? Whether he's a pirate or not, we need all the help we can get right now."

Chiron chuckled, "We'll see if he's worth our trouble any moment now."

"What do you mean?"

The stranger called out from behind them, "Wait!"

"Piss off,'" Chiron chirped.

"I have a ship!"

# Chapter Ten: Flight of the Vanish

Orion halted in his tracks. His heartbeat surged with hope. It was as if their quest had come to a swift and unexpected end. Chiron looked at him with a wry smile, then glanced back to Ulysses,

"Where is this ship?" he asked,

Ulysses pointed in the direction they were traveling, "It is at the end of the ravine, next to a river. I figured the entrance to the city had to be hidden somewhere near here," He pointed to the shriveled plant creature, "I stumbled upon this Serpen on my way through, so surely my hunch was right,"

"That wasn't a Serpen," Chiron said, "You nearly got yourself killed by a plant. The Serpens are intelligent reptiles who hunt in packs,"

"But the green skin, the fangs-"

Chiron rolled his eyes, "Clearly, this is your first visit to this world," he scoffed,

"I don't see how that matters," Ulysses snipped,

"It matters a great deal. It means that you are entirely out of your depth, no matter your reason for being here,"

Orion stepped between them. "That might be," he said, "But if he does have a ship, then that makes him our best chance of getting off this planet,"

Chiron turned to Ulysses, looking him over from head to toe again, "What would passage on this ship cost us? If it did exist?"

Ulysses scoffed, "It's my ship, old man. You're in no position to make demands of me, and I would need something from you in exchange for passage,"

Chiron's stony temperament vanished. He stomped towards Ulysses. As he did, Ulysses' smug smile vanished instantly, and his eyes opened wide. Chiron's face turned bright red as he snatched the lapel of Ulysses' coat and punched him in the jaw. Ulysses fell hard to the ground, and Chiron rested his weathered boot on his chest as he groaned in pain.

"Clearly, you do not know with whom you speak," Chiron growled,

Ulysses grumbled under his breath, then glared up at Chiron, "What are you talking about? You're just a crazy old man!"

"Not me," he said, "Him," He pointed behind him, directly at Orion.

"Well, please tell me," Ulysses said, struggling against Chiron's boot, "Is he some kind of famous killer-for-hire who has a thing for a bow and arrow?"

"That is Prince Orion Castus, the last surviving heir to the throne of Archon Prime. You will respect him as such, or you will face me for your insolence,"

Orion stepped forward, feeling his gut turn with Chiron's magnanimous introduction, "Stop!" he shouted, "That's enough, Chiron,"

Chiron shot one last glare down at Ulysses and begrudgingly removed his foot as he stepped back. Ulysses looked over at Orion, and fear froze on his face. He scrambled to his knees and bowed in front of Orion, pressing his forehead to the ground.

"Please, your highness," he said, "I did not know. Please forgive me. I had no idea…You don't know how honored I am to meet you,"

Orion looked over at Chiron, who kept his eyes fixed on Ulysses with an unsettling, stony glare.

"How does he know who I am?" Orion asked,

Ulysses answered, "There are not many humans in Diana City, my prince, but we have all heard the prophecy, and we all know your name,"

Chiron's brow furrowed, "What prophecy?" he asked,

Ulysses stood to his feet and looked Orion in the eye. His bright brown eyes shimmered as he spoke,

"The prophecy that foretells the return of the lost prince of our people; a warrior that will come from the world of our forefathers and travel the cosmos to unite us so that we can reclaim our home and remind all of what really lies at the heart of man,"

Orion chuckled, "Where did this prophecy come from?"

"Nicodemus," Ulysses answered. The very mention of this name made Chiron immediately turn his head,

"Who is Nicodemus?" Orion asked,

"He was one of my captains in the Crisis," Chiron said, "When Oberon returned, he took several of his men and their families and fled from Archon Prime. All these years, I thought he was dead or hidden so well he would never be found,"

"He is still alive," Ulysses said, "And he has kept us hidden, preparing for the day you returned, my prince,"

"Don't call me that," Orion grumbled, "I'm not a prince,"

"With all due respect, you do not know how much proof of your existence will mean to our people, "

Orion shook his head, "Look, I didn't even know the truth about where I came from until I was banished here. I don't know anything about being a prince, and I don't want to. I'm trying to get back to Archon Prime because Oberon has imprisoned my friend. I need to help him before it's too late,"

Ulysses hesitated, but his eyes still gleamed hopefully, "The prophecy has brought us together, Orion, I'm certain of it. We can rescue my men together, and you will need the strength of our numbers to save your friend. It is just as Nicodemus foretold, surely you can see that!”

“There is no such thing as prophecy,” Chiron said, “Even if there was, Nicodemus is just a man, like us. No one can foresee the future. He was one of my most trusted soldiers, so he must have discovered Orion’s existence and passed his hopes on to the rest of your covert,”

“But it has to be true!” Ulysses protested, “Orion, your name alone is proof that it is true!”

“What Nicodemus has told you and your people is not set in stone,” Chiron said, “Orion could unite the people to take back our world, but like you, he has much to learn, and that is a decision that only he can make. These exaggerations must be put aside,”

Ulysses shook his head, “You will see, once we save my crew and return to Diana City, you will see how the people love and respect him and that he has a divine gift,”

Orion shook his head, “We can’t do that. We need to get off this planet as soon as possible, we’ve already been here for far too long,”

The hopeful glimmer in Ulysses’ eyes vanished, and his eyes darted back and forth from Chiron to Orion. Then, his hands began to shake,

"If you don't help me, then I won't help you," he said, "I am sorry for your friend, and I understand that he is in grave danger, but so are my men. I cannot abandon them either, and it should not be so easy for you to just cast them aside. It is your duty to help your people in their hour of need,"

Orion shook his head, looking for Chiron to interject, but he had turned his stony gaze from Ulysses to him,

'Why is he looking at me like that?' he wondered, 'He can't seriously agree with him,' He sighed slowly, pursing his lips and clenching his fists, "We can't help him,"

Chiron shook his head, "Actually, we can, and it's less about helping him than saving people who are in grave danger,"

"Chiron-"

"And what is our alternative? Leave him and his men to die here, hoping someone else will help us?"

Orion shook his head and turned away. Then, Chiron placed his hand on his shoulder, "Orion, if you are going to leave his men to die, then look him in the eye and tell him," Orion turned and faced Ulysses. There was something about the way he looked at him, the way he could see his eyes begging for help, not for himself but for someone else.

'Rowan looked the same way every time he asked me to hunt for a family,' he thought. He looked away for a moment, trying not to let his breath shake, but when he turned back, he shuddered and felt his throat close. He reminded him so much of Rowan. His blonde hair, brown eyes, his sincerity. He felt guilty but could not understand why. It was the same guilt he would feel in himself each time Rowan came to him. It was undeniable. He wondered,

'If I was not here, if I was still on Archon Prime, what would Rowan ask me to do?' He took another deep breath, then, nodding his head, he looked to Ulysses,

"What happened to your crew?" he asked, "You said that Serpens took them to their city," Ulysses bit his lip, then nodded his head quietly, "Yes. Nicodemus sent us to raid a ship bound for Hetra.

He prophesied that there would be others in the city willing to help us, so we sought them out. My first mate made contact with a group of Serpens, and they agreed to help us. It seemed as if everything would proceed as Nicodemus promised. I planned to take my solar skiff and direct the operation from above while my first mate led our crew and the Serpens to steal the shipment. But something went wrong. After they returned to our ship, my first mate sent me a distress call, saying the Serpens double-crossed us. They took my crew hostage and turned the ship away from Diana City. I followed them here, to this planet, but lost the ship when the biggest burst of lightning I had ever seen came out of nowhere and threw me off course. I flew all over the planet, but there was no sign of them until today, I found the wreckage of our ship, which crashed in the jungle, but there was no sign of my men or anything else. All I had to go off of was what they told us about their city, that it was underground and that it could not be found by outsiders, so I landed here, certain that I would find some sort of tunnel beneath the surface,"

"The lightning that threw you off course," Orion said, "that was me,"

Ulysses shook his head in confusion, "You made lightning strike?"

"No, it wasn't lightning, that is how I arrived here. Oberon has a machine that can send anyone anywhere in the universe. When it does, it sends a beam of light up through the sky, then down to wherever he sends you,"

"Forgive me, sir, but that does not seem possible. The technology required to do such a thing has never been heard of. All interstellar travel still relies on solar power, how could one man have this without anyone, especially the high council, knowing it exists?"

"I don't know," Orion answered, "But we do have an idea of where the entrance to the city is,"

Ulysses' eyes widened, and the corners of his lips turned upward, "Are you saying that you will help me?" he asked,

Orion nodded, "But first, we have to come to an understanding about our arrangement,"

Ulysses bowed his head politely, "Speak your wishes, your highness,"

"I'm still not a prince," Orion said, "Working together is the best course for all of us to survive and save your men, and we will only do so if you take us back to Archon Prime,"

Ulysses nodded his head, and his face washed over with a seriousness that even Chiron seemed to appreciate,

"You intend to escape and return to face him; to free our people from Oberon,"

"To save my friend," Orion corrected, "I'm not the savior you think I am,"

"Perhaps not," Ulysses said. He looked down to the ground, muttering to himself, then turned back to Orion, "But if you are going to face Oberon, my men and I will join your fight. We grew up dreaming of returning to our home, and this is the first time in my life that I have ever thought that this dream might actually be possible,"

"We will need more than dreamers," Chiron said, "We need warriors,"

Ulysses smiled, "We have more than enough men, and we are ready to fight. We have weapons and ships; with you and Nicodemus to guide us, we could do this!"

Chiron scratched his beard and ran his fingers through it as he examined Ulysses from head to toe.

"You are eager," he said, "You have fair skills with a sword, but you are more of a pirate than a warrior,"

"With respect, when I give my word, I am bound by honor. The same goes for my men. If we strike this bargain, we will be worthy of your trust,"

Chiron opened his mouth to speak, but Orion spoke first.

"Trust is earned, not given. This will be no exception. If we help you and your men, and if what you say about them is true, then we will join forces. If it is not, we will go our separate ways,"

Ulysses bowed his head, "Thank you, my prince. I swear that you both will have a passage with us off of this planet and that should we earn your trust, we will fight with you to the end,"

Orion nodded, then turned to Chiron, who looked at him with a subtle grin.

"Well, the prince has spoken," Chiron grunted, "Come, Ulysses, let us scc this ship,"

Ulysses smiled cheerfully and began to lead them down the remainder of the ravine. He pushed ahead far enough for Chiron to whisper in Orion's ear without being heard.

"I'm impressed," he whispered, "You're finally taking some things to heart,"

"This doesn't mean that I'm going to be a prince," Orion said, "We just needed to give him enough reason to help us,"

Chiron patted Orion's back, "No matter how hard you fight it, there are things in motion that cannot be undone. When you face the covert in Diana City, they will see you just as this Ulysses does,"

Orion shook his head, "I never asked for this,"

"Believe it or not, that is why this birthright should be yours,"

They followed Ulysses through the remainder of the rocky ravine until it opened up to the bright red daylight again. Orion's heart soared as they made the final turn. A reflection shone into his eyes. A reflection from a metal surface. Ulysses' ship was real.

Seeing that he was not lying was a relief, but his solar skiff was not what Orion imagined it would be. He had never seen a ship before but had read about them many times.

He imagined that the ship would match the descriptions of massive metal hulls with towering solar sails capable of absorbing enough power to traverse the cosmos three times over. Ulysses' tiny skiff was somewhat of a disappointment to him.

It was perhaps too small to even call a ship. It had one swooping, triangular solar sail running across one side of its length. Its hull was dark and metallic but only spanned a length of what could not have been more than ten feet. Its design was aerodynamic, with a sharp bow and a stern with two large propulsion engines.

"This is your ship?" Orion asked,

"Skiff," Ulysses corrected, "A ship is much larger than this old girl, but she is as quick as they come,"

"Is there room for all of us?" Chiron asked,

"More than enough. There are four seats in the cockpit and two rows for four in the back. We can get you both and all of my men out of here as long as you don't decide to bring any pets along, old man,"

"You don't know me well enough to call me that, son," Chiron grumbled,

"Well, with respect, you don't know me well enough to call me son," Ulysses snipped, "Onboard the Vanish, you will refer to me by my given name or the humble title of captain,"

He patted the hull of the skiff as he said her name, and it intrigued Orion. "Vanish? Why do you call her that?"

"Climb aboard, your highness, and I will show you,"

Ulysses rushed to the side of the skiff and twisted a small handle counter clockwise. Steam blew out of the cracks of a rectangular panel as it lowered slowly to the ground with a whirr. The ramp led to the interior of the ship.

"Right this way," he smiled,

Chiron patted Orion on the back, letting him enter first, and followed him closely, brushing roughly past Ulysses. Once the two were aboard, Ulysses turned the handle clockwise, and the ramp retracted. He squeaked through as it shut behind him, and he made his way past Orion and Chiron to the cockpit. Orion followed him there and saw four chairs. Two were placed in front of a long curving window and a panel of controls and instruments. The other two were positioned directly behind them.

"Make yourselves comfortable," Ulysses said,

Orion sat in the front row, and Chiron directly behind him. Ulysses flopped into the pilot's chair and clicked several switches, and then the high-pitched whirr of the engines filled the air. Then, he turned to Orion with a smile,

"This," he said, "Is why it's called the vanish," he flipped a large lever on the console down, and as he did, the surface of the skiff began to ripple until it vanished, appearing entirely invisible.

Orion could not help but grin, "That's incredible," he said,

"Invisibility," Ulysses said, "One of Nicodemus's many gifts to us,"

"Do you all have technology like this in Diana City?"

"Yes, it's a standard in our armoury and fleet. We don't have much, but we make do," Orion looked around the ship in amazement, "I've never even seen a ship before,"

"Wait till you see what she can do in the air,"

"And where exactly are you planning on taking us?" Chiron grumbled, "I believe we should establish a clear destination first before we attract unwanted attention,"

Ulysses sighed and grinned, "I assure you, we will not be attracting any attention, and you can tell us where we are going once we're underway, old man,"

"I told you-"

Chiron could not finish, Ulysses had already pushed the two handles in front of him all the way forward, and the skiff took off. The force of its speed tossed both Orion and Chiron into the back of their seats, making the trees a blur around them. Orion's gut tossed and turned as he maneuvered the ship up with a rapid spin above the treetops.

Orion looked down and saw the river beneath them, "The river," he said, "Just follow the river,"

"Your wish is my command, your highness. Now, let me show you what this old girl can really do,"

Chiron leaned forward with a scowl on his face, "Will you stop-"

Ulysses accelerated again, but this time into a straight drop downward. Chiron's face slammed against the back of

Orion's chair as they flew down toward the surface of the river. Just as they were about to crash into the water, Ulysses pulled up again and steadied the skiff over the running water.

Orion looked at the river and saw that the water was not green or blue but pitch black. "Chiron, the water," he said,

Chiron rubbed his forehead and explained, "It isn't water. It's poison. Only species native to this world can drink from it,"

"What happens if you touch it?" Orion asked,

"Nothing. The poison has to be ingested to take effect, but just one drop would cause one nearly unbearable pain."

"How the hell have you survived here with no water?" Ulysses asked,

"Rain," Chiron answered, "It's the only source of water on this planet, and thankfully there has always been a lot of it,"

"This place sounds wonderful," Ulysses said, "I'll have to take the lads here again on a little getaway once this is all over,"

Chiron shook his head, "This is the worst place in the universe, Ulysses," His tone was so grave it shook Orion to the bone. "Make no mistake, on our way to the Serpen city, we face many dangers, and where we are going, I expect we will see some of the worst,"

"Where exactly are we going?" Ulysses asked nervously,

"To the end of the river," Orion said, "Over the falls, and then underground,"

Ulysses bit his lip and nodded silently, slowing to a much more cautious speed.

# Chapter Eleven: Through the Falls

The poison river ran for miles. It winded and twisted through the dense jungle, and Orion spotted countless life forms scattered at its edge, drinking from its murky black waters without consequence,

"Oberon definitely chose the right place to banish us," he said, "All these animals would watch us die drinking from the river while they just quench their thirst,"

"You two are perfect for each other," Ulysses said, "You're both far too serious. Despite its perils, this is a beautiful planet,"

"Maybe we just see things the way they are and not how we'd like them to be," Orion said,

"Well, forgive me, my prince, but some optimism wouldn't kill either of you,"

Orion leaned over with a scowl, "I really hope that you understand how serious this is. We have no idea where the city is or where your crew is being held. We don't even know what we're walking into on the way there, so we need to prepare ourselves for the worst,"

"Oh, I'm already prepared," Ulysses said, "Prepared to kick some reptilian ass, and once we get back to Diana City, I'm going to tell this fine Comran mistress all about it. She might even have a friend for you, your highness. Once you get past the fur and claws, their species is quite attractive,"

Chiron rolled his eyes, and Orion groaned quietly in disgust, "See, this is why we don't know if we can trust you, how are we supposed to know that when it really comes down to it, you aren't just going to leave us to die,"

Ulysses smiled, "Why, my prince, you think so little of me. I might indulge myself in life's little pleasures, but rest assured, I am a man of my word, nonetheless,"

Chiron leaned forward with a scowl of his own, "For the sake of what's tucked between your legs, you had better be,"

Ulysses gulped with a nervous smile, then quickly turned his attention back to flying the ship. "This river never seems to end. Are you sure the falls aren't the other way?"

"The Serpens came from the south, just keep pressing onward," Chiron said,

"Well, perhaps they took the scenic route,"

"I swear, one more quip from you and you'll be going for a swim," Chiron growled,

Orion leaned forward and pointed ahead, "Look!" He said, "Rapids. We have to be getting close,"

The three looked forward and saw the murky black waters slowly begin to pick up their pace and churn violently against the red stones in the river. Ulysses increased their speed. As they flew above the rapids, the poison beneath them churned so violently that they could see it splash against the invisible bow of the ship. As they rounded the final bend, Orion gasped silently and sank into the back of his chair. They had reached the fall.

The rapids became an eerie gray mist, so thick that they could only see the final edge of the river above them.

Chiron leaned forward, "Fly over the edge and take us down,"

Ulysses nodded and flew the skiff over the edge. The black fall descended downward like a black dagger, progressively narrowing into a large dark pool hundreds of feet below, shrouded in a haze that ran through the surrounding jungle. Ulysses looked at a small screen on the console,

"Scans say the pool should be shallow enough for us to land on, it's no more than a few inches deep,"

He slowed the skiff's speed until it hovered above the dark pool and then began a slow descent.

"How many Serpens do you think are down there, Chiron?" Orion asked,

"If this is one of the paths to their city, then there are likely far too many for us to take on for very long,"

"My instruments aren't picking anything up," Ulysses said, "We should be safe,"

"As long as we are here, we are not safe," Chiron said, "Keep your wits about you,"

"I never go anywhere without them," Ulysses snipped,

The skiff slowly set itself down on the pool and landed solidly, sending smooth ripples across the surface, with its bow pointed towards the misty fall of poison.

"How are we going to get through that?" Orion asked, "Won't we be poisoned if we breathe in the vapors too?"

Chiron nodded silently, and then Ulysses shot his hand up with his forefinger upright. "I have an idea,"

He leaped out of his chair and moved to the back of his ship, digging through the cargo netting on the walls of the hull. He retrieved three black suits with armor plates and three strange collars.

"These," he said, "are pressurized suits. We use them for spacewalks, but they should protect us from breathing in the fumes, and the armor could come in handy,"

"What are these collars?" Chiron asked,

"Helmets for the suits," he explained, "You strap them on around your necks, and when you activate it, the nanites form an airtight mask around your head,"

"Show us," Orion said,

Ulysses nodded and instantly began throwing off his clothes. He threw his coat to the side, pulled his shirt off his back, and dropped his pants with his bare buttocks pointed right at Chiron and Orion, who quickly turned away at sight.

"What's wrong, boys? Embarrassed?"

"A warning would have been nice," Orion grumbled,

"We're all men here, right? Though I can understand if you're embarrassed, not everyone in the cosmos can be as fine as I am," he slid the suit over himself and put his tunic and cloak back over his shoulders. Then he turned to face them, "Well? What do we think? Do I make this look good or what?"

"What," Chiron grumbled, "Does the damn thing work or not?"

Ulysses strapped the collar around his neck and clicked a switch. A translucent pattern formed over his head, then the pattern then washed over with a smooth, dark color, and a shining black helmet formed over his head.

Chiron turned his head to the side as he examined the armor, "Another gift from Nicodemus?" he asked,

"Yes," Ulysses said, "There are hundreds of these in our armory,"

"This design looks just like my armor but it is much more advanced. This will definitely serve us well,"

Ulysses deactivated the helmet, smiling smugly, "Well then, suit up, my friends!"

"Turn around," Chiron grumbled,

"If you insist," Ulysses laughed,

As Orion slipped the armor on, he could not believe how comfortable it was. It fit snugly against his body and allowed him to move freely with no interference from the plates, even under his tunic, quiver, and cloak. He strapped on the collar and activated his helmet, and Chiron did the same. Then, once the three of them were clad in armor, Ulysses lowered the ramp.

As he stepped into the shallow pool, Orion could not see more than a few feet in front of him. He quickly turned back to ensure he had not lost sight of the skiff and was relieved to see it standing firm. Chiron rested his hand on his shoulder and pointed his sword out in the direction the bow of the skiff was facing.

"The fall is just ahead," he said, "Just keep moving in that direction, and the mist should clear once we're through,"

Orion nodded and pressed forward cautiously, with his bow at the ready. He looked all around him, nervously drawing breath as billows of poisonous vapors blew over him. The falls were not far, but the tension he felt was just as thick as the fog around him. It was impossible to judge how much distance they were covering. He turned his focus downward, counting his paces and watching his boots splash against the black pool.

After twenty paces, he checked behind him to ensure the skiff was still there. Its smooth surface barely shone through the fog. He knew that it would only take a few more paces for it to be late to turn back,

'It's right there,' he thought, 'Maybe it's not too late to just leave while we still can,' He turned to grab Chiron but froze when he saw him. He had stopped dead in his tracks with his sword in hand. Orion immediately looked ahead and saw a dark silhouette standing in front of them. He took one more step towards it, but Chiron grabbed his shoulder to stop him. Orion looked back,

"What is it?" he asked,

Chiron pushed Orion behind him, saying nothing. Orion drew an arrow from his quiver, and Ulysses drew his sword as the dark silhouette stepped toward them. Its footsteps rumbled. Ripples washed up at the trio's ankles, and they could hear a low, growling chuckle coming toward them. The voice was unmistakable. The silhouette was Drago.

Once he was clear of the mist, he stopped and pulled his ax off of his back. His nostrils steamed with every breath as his green eyes shone through the mist. Orion slowly started to pull his drawstring tight, trying to prepare himself for Drago's imminent attack. But he stood still, with the leathery corners of his jaws turned upward, savoring their fear. With a low growl, he slowly whirled the head of his ax down and lowered it into the poisonous pool, resting his enormous hands on the handle.

"So… predictable," he said, "So…pathetic,"

Chiron stepped forward, "Drago, we know that there are human hostages in the city. We have no intention to trespass. Release them to us, and we will all leave your world with no quarrel,"

"What makes you think I would allow that?"

"Our presence in this world is forbidden, no matter the circumstance. If you keep those prisoners here, and the high council discovers what you are doing, your father and your people will be disgraced forever. If you do allow this, I give you my word that no one would ever learn of our presence here,"

Drago huffed at Chiron's offer. He picked up his ax and began to pace back and forth in front of them. The black slits of his eyes tightened to horrifying lines against a sickening green.

"You think my father's honor means anything to me? You are a fool if you think that tired old fool has any honor to lose. He wasted his life squabbling with the other chancellors for power when we could have taken what is rightfully ours!"

"Is that what Oberon promised you? Power? That's something that cannot be given, Drago,"

Drago stopped his pacing and glared at Chiron, clenching his black, clawed fists tight. "The dark lord is wise. He sees the corruption that plagues the cosmos. With my warriors and his vision, we will purge every world and restore power to its rightful owners,"

Orion stepped forward, "That won't be you," he said, "He will destroy your people!"

Drago chuckled cruelly, "We are not like your kind, boy. We are slaves to no one, and we will be here long after your kind is extinct,"

"Then why follow him?"

Drago snorted at those words, glaring at Orion with a low, rumbling growl. "Enough talk," he hissed,

More silhouettes emerged through the mist, surrounding the three of them. Ulysses and Chiron pressed their backs up against Orion's and looked outward as Drago's men began to close their circle around them.

"I count fifteen on this side," Chiron said,

"Thanks, old man, that's so comforting," Ulysses chirped,

"Just stay focused, how many on your side?"

"Fifteen," Orion answered,

Ulysses' eyes darted from left to right, "Well, if we have ten apiece, who gets the big one?" he asked,

"Stay out of his way," Chiron warned, "He'll try to draw us toward him so his men can surround us. If we take his men down first, then we can take him together,"

"I'll take him if he's too much for you, old man,"

Orion snapped his head back and glared at Ulysses, "There's no time for that! Your men won't make it if we die here, just do as he says,"

Ulysses rolled his eyes, "Fine. Your wish is my command, highness,"

Orion nodded and pulled his arrow tight. Drago unleashed a dreadful roar that shook the surface of the black pool, and the Serpens charged toward them.

Ulysses and Chiron rushed in opposite directions. Orion ran back towards the skiff. He threw his bow up onto the bow and climbed up after it. He scrambled to a knee and looked out to pick his targets. Chiron was cutting down every Serpen in front of him, but one was charging toward his back. Orion fired. His arrow pierced through the back of the Serpen's leathery head, and it fell dead, splashing behind Chiron. Ulysses' wild and furious swing of his sword cut down two at a time, but three closed in on his flanks.

"Ulysses, move!" Orion shouted,

Ulysses rolled out of the way, and Orion drew a blue arrow. He fired. The arrow hit one of the Serpens in his chest, and the shockwave knocked the others back, paralyzing them.

Drago growled, running towards Chiron with his ax over his head. He swung it down. Chiron leaped out of the way. The force of Drago's swing sent the black poison splashing in all directions. Orion pulled another blue arrow from his quiver and fired it at Drago. It landed on his shoulder, and the blue electricity crackled over his body, but he did little more than wince in pain. He turned his dark head to Orion and began stomping towards the skiff. Orion drew a white arrow and fired. It struck Drago in the chest plate, and white flames exploded all over his body. Orion could hear him groan as he fell into the pool, with a fire crackling all over his body.

Undeterred, Drago jumped to his feet. He raised his ax overhead and swung it into the bow of the skiff. It cut a long gash along the hull at Orion's feet. Ulysses heard the screech of metal and snapped his head back toward the direction it came from.

"Hey!" he shouted, running back to the skiff like a frightened mother, "Get away from my ship!" he shouted,

Drago turned and swept the back of his left hand into Ulysses' face, sending him flying backward. He splashed into the pool on his back and groaned in pain,

"Orion, kill this bastard!" he shouted,

Orion pulled two white arrows and fired them at Drago's scaly neck. They ignited, and the flames burned so hot that Orion could feel the heat through his armor. Drago groaned and rolled in the pool to extinguish the flames.

"That's it!" Ulysses shouted, "Keep at it, Orion! We'll hold off the rest of them!"

Chiron looked back, and when he saw Drago so close to Orion, he ran back, frantically shouting, "Orion, get away from him!" Orion looked over at Chiron, then at Drago, his green eyes brightening with rage. He snarled and swung his ax, again and again, leaving long gashes in the hull of the skiff. Orion could feel fear pulsing through his body as Drago attacked faster and faster. He jumped off the side of the skiff and fired one more white arrow at Drago as he fell into the pool. The arrow struck him in the arm and ignited. The flames engulfed Drago's body and cracked over the hull of the ship. It bought just enough for Orion to get back to his feet and rush towards Chiron.

More Serpens emerged from the mist, one after another, charging at them with vicious snarls as they drew their swords. Orion fired three blue arrows into small groups, dispatching nine as they ran toward them. Then he stopped, firing black arrows at any that were not in range for Chiron to cut down. He shot down ten charging warriors with precision Drago had never seen. Some were shot through the eye from at least thirty feet away. It was clear to him that this one human, the youngest of the three, was not to be underestimated.

Orion notched and fired three more black arrows all at once, and three more Serpens fell into the pool with arrows in their scaled chests.

"Switch to your sword!" Chiron grunted, "You need to save the arrows, and we can't keep this fight up for much longer,"

"So what do we do?" Orion asked,

"We have to push for the fall, if there is a tunnel behind it, we can funnel them, and you can take them all out in one shot,"

"Give the word," Orion said, slinging his bow over his shoulder and drawing his sword.

Chiron cut down one more Serpen, then yelled, "Go now!"

Orion took off running. He passed by Ulysses as he pushed a dead Serpen off of his sword,

"Come on!" he cried. Ulysses took off after him, and Chiron bolted after the both of them. What few Serpens remained gave chase to the three of them as they disappeared into the mist.

"After them!" Drago shouted, "They're heading into the tunnels!"

Orion, Chiron, and Ulysses had made it through the misty column of poison, and when it cleared, they saw an enormous cave in front of them. The roof was tall enough to stand above Oberon's Luma City tower and nearly as wide. The three ran as fast as they could into the cavern, hearing the hissing and growling of Drago's soldiers behind them.

"Orion, look up!" Chiron shouted,

Orion did as he said and saw a large group of stalactites hanging from the cave's ceiling. "Once we're clear, shoot them down!" Chiron cried,

Orion nodded and sprinted harder to get ahead of them. He planted his feet and slid to a stop. As he turned back, the Serpens were from the mist. He sheathed his sword and readied his bow with three white arrows notched on the string. He held his position, patiently waiting for the right moment to release them.

"Orion, shoot!" Ulysses yelled,

"Hold Orion, wait for the right moment!"

Orion stood firm, drawing the string tighter. The Serpens were nearly in place.

"Now, Orion!" Chiron shouted,

Orion held for just a few more moments. He slowly released his breath with both eyes open. Then, he closed them for one moment, feeling his lungs empty. He fired. The three arrows whistled into the ceiling and exploded with blinding white light. He watched as the ceiling of the cave cracked, and the first stalactite fell free. He turned and ran, hearing the Serpens cry out in panic as they were squashed under the rocks. The ground shook under the impact, and dust lifted off the floor of the cave as they ran. The cave grew darker, and more stalactites fell behind him until what little light shone through the cave vanished, and he, Chiron, and Ulysses were immersed in the thickest blackness he had ever experienced.

There was no sound, no light. Nothing but the sound of his breath. "Chiron?" Orion called,

"I'm here," he answered,

"I'm here too, thank you," Ulysses said,

Orion sighed with relief and looked all around him. "I can't see anything," he said,

Then, he saw two small lights break through the blackness right next to him. It was Chiron. He jumped as he felt a hand grab his helmet and flip a small switch, which activated two beams of light on the sides of his helmet.

"Ow!" Ulysses groaned, "That's bright," he shielded his eyes as he turned his own headlights on. The three turned behind them and saw that the entrance to the cave had been sealed off by the rockslide Orion had caused.

"There is no turning back now," Chiron said, "Whether or not the city is down here, we have to press forward,"

Ulysses shook his head and let out a long sigh, "Wonderful," he groaned.

On the other side of the rocks, Drago pounded his fist into the dark pool with a furious snarl.

"You fools!" he growled, "We will lose half the day before we reach the nearest entrance to the city!"

"Sir, what about the Leviathan?" one of his men said, "She would kill the humans before they find the city if we released her,"

Drago struck his soldier in the snout and stomped on him with his leathery foot. "Lord Oberon requires proof that the humans perish!" he snarled, "If we release the Leviathan, we would report to him empty-handed, then he will bring his machines here and slaughter your wives, your sons, your daughters, and there will be nothing left of our city!" His man writhed and gasped under his heavy foot, unable to free himself. He kept his foot upon his chest and looked up to the rest of his men.

"You cowards will get into that tunnel, and you will burn the humans out of it! There is no time for your failure!" He lifted his foot off his soldier's chest, waited just long enough for him to draw breath, then stomped down on his snout. His head was pushed under the surface of the black poison, and he squirmed even harder, desperately flailing his arms and legs. The rest of the soldiers watched in horror as their commander drowned their comrade before their eyes. Only when he had fallen lifeless did Drago remove his foot. He stepped forward and roared at his men with such force it echoed through the jungle. They jumped in fright and immediately began carrying out his orders. Drago looked up into the red sun. It had already begun its descent toward the horizon.

"There is no time," he hissed, "No time…"

# Chapter Twelve: The Caverns

Orion looked down the dark tunnel. It ran so deep that he saw the ends of his headlights disappear into the thick darkness. He kept his gaze slightly downward to light the ground in front of him. As he walked, he scanned the enormous curving walls, searching for any signs of the dangers Chiron spoke of.

Ulysses cleared his throat, "So, Chiron," he said, "What exactly can we expect to find here? Other than the Serpens?"

"Monsters," Chiron answered,

Orion and Ulysses froze, and the rocks scratched beneath their feet as they planted them. They looked to Chiron with shock,

"Wait, monsters?" Orion asked,

"Like the plant from before? What kind of monsters?" Ulysses pressed,

"I've heard the Serpens speak of a monster they keep trapped in their city. It guards their territory, and they unleash it upon anyone who trespasses. They call it The Leviathan,"

Orion gulped and asked, "What else do you know about it?"

"I only know that it is an ancient and powerful creature. The Serpens cannot fully control it, so they satisfy it… with sacrifices,"

"What kind of sacrifices?" Ulysses asked,

Chiron simply turned and stared at Ulysses. Even under the mask, Ulysses could feel Chiron's eyes stare through him. He understood that the answer he feared was the one he should take to heart. Then, Chiron spoke again, turning back towards the tunnel,

"We need to keep moving. It will not be long before something discovers us here,"

They continued down the enormous tunnel. There were no alternative routes they could take, so they had no choice but to move directly ahead, following the long, wide path in front of them as it turned and twisted downward. They walked for hours, descending deeper and deeper into the darkness until the only sound they could hear was the scratching of their own feet on the path. The almost deafening silence left Orion with no distraction from his own thoughts,

'How are we going to get out of this?' he wondered, 'Will Rowan survive long enough for us to reach the city?' There was no way to answer these questions, and that just made him all the more uneasy. He clenched his fists and pressed forward, but it was impossible to escape those thoughts until something finally broke the silence. The sound of someone coughing. Orion turned to Chiron and moved closer, and he could hear him heaving for breath beneath his helmet.

Orion touched his shoulder and whispered, "Hey, are you alright?"

Chiron nodded, "Just tired," he replied,

"Well, let's stop, rest for a moment,"

"We can't, Orion, we have to keep moving,"

Orion's feet scratched to a complete stop, and he stared firmly at his companion, "Sit down," he demanded, "We all have to make it to the city in one piece,"

Chiron looked down, sighing reluctantly as he nodded, and the two sat against the great curving wall of the cave.

"Getting tired, old man?" Ulysses snipped,

"He needs to rest," Orion said, "We've been walking for miles, sit down with us, we need to keep our strength up,"

"Or we could just keep going, and he could catch up to us after his nap,"

Orion stood to his feet and deactivated his helmet, then glared at Ulysses, "What's your problem?" he demanded,

"Nothing's wrong, your highness," he said, "My men are being held prisoner, there's probably a monster in the same tunnel we're walking through, and the old man, with all his wisdom, wants to stop now. Everything is wonderful,"

"He would have kept going if I didn't stop him," Orion said, "We'll be no good to your men or against the monster if he doesn't make it there with us,"

"We don't have time to rest," Ulysses growled, "We have to keep going,"

Orion shook his head and scoffed, "Look, I don't know why you have a problem with this, what we really don't have time for is fighting amongst ourselves. The Serpens will be coming no matter what we do, and we still don't know what else is down here. I don't know about you, but I'd rather just let him rest so he can help us fight what comes next on our terms,"

Ulysses chuckled in frustration, "Look, your highness, I'm just doing what you said, I'm looking out for the best interest of my men. I'm their captain, and it's my job to put them first,"

"You can't help your men right now," Orion said, "Trust me, I understand how hard it is not being able to help someone. My friend is being held prisoner back on Archon Prime, and I would do anything to be able to help him right now, but I can't because I'm here. If you really want to help them, then you need to be ready, and you need both of us. Sit down,"

"I'm ready now," he grumbled, "If you're the prince you're supposed to be, you'll get the old man off his ass right now and help me get this done,"

"I'm not a prince, and you are not my captain," Orion growled,

Ulysses shook his head and bit his lip, "Yeah," he sighed, "you're making that pretty clear,"

Chiron stood back to his feet and moved between them, glaring at Ulysses, "Do you have something you'd like to say to me?"

"Oh, I have plenty to say to you, old man," Ulysses said, "First, if you can't keep up, just stay out of our way. Next, how about you tell him that if he wants my men to follow him, he better start showing some spine,"

Chiron took hold of Ulysses' coat with both fists and shook him furiously, "Do not forget that it is only because of us you've made it this far. You would've been nothing but fertilizer if we didn't put an end to your stupidity! You would've been torn apart without us watching your back!"

Ulysses shook his head defiantly. He would not even look Chiron in the eye as he tried talking sense into him.

"And if you didn't have me, you'd be walking through a jungle full of reptiles with swords," he grumbled, "Maybe you two needed me more than I needed you…old man,"

Chiron pulled his fist back to strike him, but Orion caught it before he could land his punch, "Enough," he said, "None of this is helping!"

Chiron sighed and let go of Ulysses' coat. Ulysses brushed his sleeves and shook his head, "If Nicodemus could see you right now, he'd be ashamed he ever followed you,"

"And what would he say about you?" Orion asked, "You didn't finish the mission he sent you on, and your men are being held hostage, what kind of captain does that make you?"

Ulysses' face twisted with a scowl, he raised an angry finger and was just about to speak, but a strange sound broke through the quiet cave.

"What the hell was that?" Chiron said. All three of them turned into the tunnel. The sound was growing louder and clearer. It was a high-pitched screech coming from the roof of the cave ahead of them.

"The monster," Ulysses gasped. He drew his sword quickly, and the three readied themselves, scanning the roof above them. Then, they saw a snout inch into the light. Behind the snout emerged a head of the black fur with four pointed ears on its side. The creature's eyes were a sickening white, and its entire body was covered in shaggy black fur. It growled and tilted its head backward, baring its sharp fangs. Saliva dripped from its upper lip to the cave floor as it glared hungrily at them.

"Shoot it!" Ulysses whined,

Orion pulled a blue arrow and fired. It struck the beast and it crashed to the ground with the arrow stuck in its hideous snout, quivering as blue electricity flickered all over it. When it finally laid still, Orion stepped forward to see what he had shot.

Sprouting from its four arms were long membranes that looked like wings. At the tip of each of these wings were three long, clawed fingers, and it had two long, bony legs with large clawed feet. As Orion inched closer, he gagged at its foul stench and could hear the creature breathing. He stopped dead in his tracks as he looked into its' ghastly pale eyes. They were still open.

Then Orion felt a slap on his back. He jumped in a startle and heard Ulysses belt out a hearty laugh, "Well! He shouted, "So much for this legendary monster!"

The creature screeched and sprung back to life the moment those words left his mouth. Orion reached for another arrow, but the creature knocked him aside, growling as it flapped its leathery wings and snatched Ulysses' arms in its' claws. Ulysses cried out in terror as the monster beat its wings harder and carried him off down the tunnel.

"Ulysses!" Orion shouted, running after the creature, "Shoot it! Shoot it!" Ulysses begged,

Orion fired a black arrow, but it only lodged itself in the membrane of its wing. The creature squealed in pain but continued beating its wings, flying faster and faster into the tunnel. Orion and Chiron ran as fast as they could, but the creature had gained too much distance for Orion to take another shot.

Ulysses screamed in terror as the creature suddenly reared up and then dropped downward. Orion slid to a stop, and when he looked down, he saw the path end at a ledge leading into the dark. Ulysses was carried into it.

"Ulysses!" Orion shouted, looking frantically into the abyss.

He heard nothing and turned to Chiron, "We have to get down there!" "There's no way down," Chiron said,

Orion shook his head. He pulled a white arrow and shot it into the abyss. When it finally struck the bottom, the white light illuminated the chasm and revealed a shining mass that looked like some kind of nest suspended by strings attached to the sides of the cavern walls. Orion peered into the center of the nest and saw something kicking its legs like an animal stuck on its back. It was Ulysses.

Orion chuckled slightly in relief, then frantically searched to his left and right for any way to reach the nest. He traced every string holding up the strange mass and finally found one running just below the edge they stood on.

"I think I can get down to this line here," Orion said,

"No!" Chiron snapped, "I'm not going to let you die trying to save this fool!"

Orion glared at Chiron, "Right now, this fool is the only person we can save, and I'll do it with or without you,"

Chiron groaned and sighed deeply, then slapped his palms against his thighs, "I suppose you have a plan then?"

Orion looked over the entire scene, then turned back to Chiron, "If you lower me down over the edge, I'll have a better chance of catching the line. Once I'm on the line, I can make my way over and get him out,"

"What then?" Chiron asked, Orion, peered through the darkness, then froze. He saw the edges of another tunnel on the other side. He pointed across the chasm,

"The tunnel continues on the other side," he said, "We'll just take another line across to the other side,"

"Just like that?" Chiron asked,

"Just like that,"

"And if the creature comes back?" "Still working on that part,"

Orion shuffled to the edge and lowered himself onto his stomach. He swung his legs over the edge, and Chiron took hold of his wrists. He slowly lowered Orion down until the bottom of his boots were dangling just two feet above the line.

Orion looked down at the line and then back up to Chiron, "On three, let me go," "Are you sure?" Chiron said,

Orion nodded, "I trust you," he said, "It's time to trust me,"

Chiron returned with a nod and took a deep breath, "One," he said,

"Two,"

"Three,"

Chiron let Orion fall. Orion's heart sank as he dropped, seeing no sign of the bottom beneath him. Then, the translucent line flashed in front of his face. He reached up. His palm slapped the line, but he could not wrap his fingers around it. Terror gripped his heart.

To his shock, he felt his arm snap straight, and his fall ended. He looked at his hand and saw that it was stuck onto the line. He sighed with relief,

"It's some kind of web, I think," he said to Chiron,

Chiron sighed with relief, "I thought you were done for," he said,

"I'm still here. I'll swing my other hand up and help you onto the line,"

Chiron nodded and leaned over the edge with his arm outstretched. Orion swung his legs and pulled his body up as high as he could. He snatched Chiron's hand and looked up,

"Ready?" he asked,

"Ready," Chiron let himself fall free. Orion felt the weight pull him down, and the line stretched down with them. When it recoiled, Orion pulled Chiron's hand up with all his might, and Chiron slapped his palm onto the line.

"This… is… disgusting," Chiron groaned,

Orion chuckled, then swung his other hand up onto the line. He pulled his other hand off the line, feeling a sticky residue still pasted on his glove. Chiron did the same, and the two continued to climb hand over hand to the massive nest ahead.

With every passing hand, Orion could hear Ulysses' voice clearer and clearer. It was muffled, and he could see the nest shake as he continued to twist, trying to break himself free. When they finally reached the main mass, Orion reached out and stuck his hand onto the side of the nest. It was much more adhesive than the line was, and the fabric of his sleeves stuck to it with the slightest brush.

"If we do make it out of this alive," Chiron grumbled, "I'm going to kick that little prick's ass and rip his ship apart,"

Orion was the first to reach the top of the nest. He peaked over the edge and saw Ulysses lying at the center, trapped in a mass of translucent white fluid from his boots to his mouth. Ulysses saw him and let out a muffled cry for help.

"Shh!" Orion hissed, "Stay calm," Ulysses nodded,

"Is the creature still here?" Orion asked,

Ulysses shook his head no and continued to kick and struggle against the fluid.

Orion pulled himself, then Chirion, onto the nest. The surface was unstable, and it flexed with each of their footsteps. The two snuck to the center of the nest, then drew their swords and began sawing at the fluid holding Ulysses.

Their blades made some progress but quickly became stuck as the sludge thickened. It took several minutes to free just one of his legs. When they cut his arms free, Ulysses pointed at the splatter, holding his mouth shut, pleading under the muffle for them to cut it off.

"No, I think we'll keep that on, you're much more bearable that way," Chiron smirked,

Orion chuckled, but then, the horrifying screech of the creature cried out from above them.

Orion looked up and saw the creature howl as it dropped down upon them. The entire structure sank under its weight when it landed on the nest. It reared its neck back, and Orion could hear a sickening gurgle in its throat. The beast howled again, and a spray of the translucent fluid shot out from its jaws. Orion and Chiron jumped out of the way and struggled against the snaring nest to get back to their feet.

The beast reared back to spit more fluid, but Orion had regained his footing. He pulled a white arrow and fired. It hit the beast in the chest, and its fur ignited with white flame. It squealed in pain and fell onto its back. The fire quickly spread to the nest, and Orion's heart dropped as the lines supporting it began to snap.

"Hold on!" he shouted.

Chiron looked at the dying creature and saw the snapping lines, then dove face first beside Ulysses. Orion jumped after him, but the fire had spread too quickly and had reached the last line. The nest fell free.

The creature howled as it fell into the abyss, and the nest swung towards the other side of the chasm. Orion reached out desperately for anything he could get his hands on, feeling nothing but the air of the chasm against his back. Then the tip of a line swung in front of him.

He snatched it with one hand and felt his body swing with the rest of the nest, and before he could stop it, he slammed face first into the side of the abyss.

Chiron looked down but could not see him, "Orion!" he shouted,

"I'm here!" Orion answered, relieved to hear his voice,

Chiron sighed, then shook his head with a small grin, "As far as plans go, not bad!"

Orion chuckled and began climbing up towards him. Together the two finished cutting Ulysses free, and the three climbed up to the ledge together.

Ulysses laid on his back and moaned with relief, then pulled against the sludge on his face until it ripped off.

"That was the single, worst, most terrifying thing that has ever happened to me," he said, Chiron chuckled as he stepped past him,

"Not one word, old man," Ulysses grunted,

"You're welcome," Chiron grunted,

Ulysses just shook his head and heaved a heavy sigh. "Thank you," he said, "If it hadn't been for you both, I would have died,"

Orion sat beside him and deactivated his helmet, "Look," he sighed, "I'm sorry that I'm not the prince you were hoping for," Orion said, "I'm much less than what our people deserve after all these years, but that doesn't mean I don't want to help you,"

Ulysses sat up and sighed. "I am the one who must apologize," he said, "I suppose I am doing just about everything I could do to make you not trust me or my men,"

"Yes, you are," Chiron grunted as he sat beside them, "But that does not mean that we are through here,"

"I would understand if you two went on without me," he said,

"We got here together, we're getting out together," Orion said, "We are all men of our word, right?"

Ulysses nodded but turned to Orion with a wounded look, "I don't need you to take pity on me," he said, "I will still have some pride after today,"

"This isn't about your pride," Orion said, "You are the captain of a ship, the one man who is trusted by his crew to lead them. I was just surviving the best I could on my own back on Archon Prime, Chiron was alone here for years. I don't think any of us really know how to work with anyone, but we have to. Otherwise, we won't be able to save any of the people who are counting on us,"

Ulysses nodded, and Chiron looked at Orion with a grin, "Spoken like a true prince, wouldn't you say, Ulysses?"

"Indeed," Ulysses admitted.

Orion shook his head, stood up to his feet, and offered his hand to Ulysses, who took it with a grin. The trio then turned and resumed their walk into the dark tunnel.

Far behind them, the Serpens had placed the last of their explosive devices between the rocks blocking the tunnel. They scrambled back and forth amid Drago's shouting as the last edge of their red sun began to dip into the distant horizon.

"Faster!" Drago ordered, "If we are not through the rocks before the sun is down, I will kill you all myself!"

"Sir?" one of his men said from behind him, Drago whirled around and glared down at him.

"Lord Oberon is asking for a report," the Serpen said nervously, holding a communication device out in his hand.

Drago snatched the device and shoved him out of his way. He stomped away from the rest of his men and knelt in the shallow pool, then activated the device.

The shadowy image of Oberon hovered above him. "Report, Drago," he ordered,

"Master, the humans have trapped themselves in a tunnel beneath the falls. We will soon have them,"

"Do not lie to me, little Drago," Oberon growled, "If they were truly in your grasp, you would have had them by now,"

"We will have them, my lord," Drago said, bowing his head lower, "By nightfall tomorrow, I will be standing upon their corpses,"

"And I will be there to ensure that,"

Drago looked up, the dark slits in his green eyes widened, "But master, you said-"

"I do not need you to remind me of my words," Oberon growled, "I will arrive at nightfall tomorrow. What fortune befalls your people is still in your hands…little Drago."

# Chapter Thirteen: Poison

After walking for several minutes down the second tunnel, Orion started to notice a subtle blue light growing brighter as they walked. It lit the path in front of him so well that he no longer needed the headlights on his helmet. He turned them off and looked up to the ceiling.

"Chiron, look," he said, pointing upward. Chiron turned his head up. He too saw what Orion had noticed.

"Strange," he said, "I have never seen so many…any in fact, below the surface,"

Ulysses joined them, looking upward, "What are they?" he asked.

The trio gazed up at a ceiling full of blue, bioluminescent flowers. Thousands of them, in full bloom, on a thick blanket of vines covering the roof of the tunnel.

"These," Chiron said to Ulysses, "are one of the few gifts this world has to offer humans."

"What? Poisonous flowers?" Ulysses asked.

"The opposite," Chiron responded, "An extract from these can counteract just about any poison or infection I've seen. It's what I've used for medicine all these years."

"Then we should collect some," Orion said, "Your crew might be injured,"

"Yes, but how?" Ulysses asked, "I mean, I could throw my sword up there."

Chiron rolled his eyes, "There's probably a loose vine further down. Let's look for a better way to go about it that doesn't involve losing our weapons."

Ulysses shrugged and shook his head, and they continued, looking upward for anything that might give them access to the flowers. As they walked further, the possibility seemed far less likely. The vines were tight against the ceiling, with nothing hanging below the blossoms.

"They cover the entire ceiling," Orion gasped, "How many grow above ground?"

"Almost none," Chiron said, "They do not survive for more than a few days on the surface, but as you see, they thrive down here."

"I'm starting to think that everything here survives better when you can't see it."

Chiron raised an eyebrow and looked at Orion with concern, "I'm not sure what you mean by that."

Orion shook his head, "I mean, think about where Ulysses comes from. If it's true that there are more humans there, ones that Oberon may not even know about, doesn't it make more sense to leave his people out of the fight and just take our people away from Archon Prime once we have a ship? We could start over, somewhere else, somewhere where Oberon could never find us."

"Perhaps it would be the best for our people," Chiron admitted, "But the greatest danger they have ever faced would still remain. We will not win the war by simply surviving it."

"But that's what we're fighting for. The survival of our people."

"There is far more at stake than just that, Orion. Even if Oberon succeeded in destroying us, his ambition has grown far beyond just that. These Serpens are now his followers, and this realizes our worst fears."

"So you do think he does mean to make a move against the High Council."

Chiron nodded gravely, "I'm certain of it, and I suspect our people will still have a part to play in this plan. Otherwise, he would have killed them all already."

"So what do we do?" Orion asked, "Even with all the humans that are in hiding, his forces will still outnumber us."

"That depends entirely upon the conversation you will have with the Serpen chancellor."

Orion's feet scratched to a halt, "Wait," he said, "We won't need anything from their chancellor anymore, once we have Ulysses' crew, we can fight our way onto the ship and leave before they catch up to us. We don't need him to call off the hunt."

"That is no longer our plea," Chiron said, "Drago has confirmed that he is conspiring with Oberon, so now, you must try to persuade the chancellor to join our cause, to prevent his son from gaining any more influence over their people."

Orion could not help but gasp with a disbelieving scoff, "That will never happen, especially if it comes from us, we've already killed so many of his people, he would kill us the first chance he gets!"

"Those men are no longer his, they are Oberon's. If you make him see the extent of his son's treachery, he will see our good intent, and it is possible he would even join us in our fight against this threat."

Orion shook his head again, "Chiron, I gave you my word that I would play the part as much as I need to, and I trust you, but I just don't see how you can have this much faith in them, after everything that has already happened between our two worlds, how could we all of a sudden become allies?"

"A common enemy often forms unexpected alliances, Orion," Chiron said, "Take Ulysses, we have little in common with him, but still he has still proved to be a valuable ally, and if you remember, it was not I who saw this at first."

Orion could not argue. He even found himself looking with a slight warmth at Ulysses, reminded of his own growing faith in him as Chiron continued, "A wise leader must offer the same faith to all, for in the end, it is up to them to decide whether they are our friends or our enemies."

"But what about Rowan? We've already lost so much time, how can we do this and get back in time to save him?"

Chiron placed his hand on Orion's shoulder, "Ask yourself this Orion: If we do not do this, what would you really be doing for Rowan? Yes, he would get to live, but what kind of life would you leave for him? One where he is hated for what he is, hunted until he is eventually killed? Is that really what he would want? Would that really be worth the suffering he has already endured? I think he deserves better."

Orion felt his chin hit his chest and his heart race as Chiron walked away. He opened his mouth to call out to him, but Ulysses broke the silence first.

"Nothing," he called out, "There's no way to get them down," "Look closer," Chiron said.

Orion looked harder into the blanket of flowers, trying to spot anything Ulysses might have missed. Then he saw it, one loose vine held to the roof of the cave by only a tiny stem clinging to the dark rocks.

"Still nothing," Ulysses said, "It was a good thought, really, but I don't think we can waste any more time with this."

Orion pulled a black arrow from his quiver and took aim at the tiny stem. He raised the bow up and slowly let the arrow go. It struck the roof of the cave.

Ulysses lifted his palms upward and then looked at Orion, "See," he said, "Nothing."

Then, a tiny snap cracked above them, and the end of the loose vine fell free, right into Ulysses' palm. Orion smiled, and Chiron chuckled as Ulysses stared at his hand in shock.

"Well…good work," He said, "Solid group effort."

Chiron rolled his eyes with a smirk as Ulysses began carefully shaking the vine. Several glowing blossoms shook back and forth, but none of them broke free. Ulysses shook harder, but nothing dropped down.

"You're doing wonderful," Chiron said, "Keep at it,"

"That's it, I'm climbing up there," Ulysses grumbled, "Great idea, I wonder why you didn't do that first,"

Ulysses just shook his head, wrapping the vine around his foot as he leaped up and started to inch his way up. "You know, Chiron," he said as he climbed, "With a sense of humor like yours, I'm surprised we haven't found more common ground. Tell you what, once we make it to Diana City, I'll buy you a drink, get you to loosen up a bit."

"I'll settle for silence instead," Chiron said.

Once he reached the ceiling of the cave, Ulysses drew his sword and swept it up against the vine, and seven blossoms dropped down to the cave floor.

"Ha!" Ulysses cried. He held his sword proudly above him as he began to slide down the vine, and as he was about to reach the floor, he smiled smugly, "See what a remarkable team we make?" He said. He was so proud of his contribution that he did not mind where he held his blade. It swung back far enough to nick the vine holding him, and he fell from the ceiling. Orion and Chiron rushed forward as he fell hard onto his back in front of them.

"Are you alright?" Orion asked.

"Oh," he groaned, "My back, I think I broke my back."

Chiron knelt beside him and slapped his face, "Does your back still hurt?" he asked.

Ulysses held his hand to his cheek, "Well, no," he mumbled, "Now my face does. Your hands are really rough."

"Get up and help us pick these up," Chiron said.

Ulysses rolled over and slowly bent over to pick up the blooms with them. Orion looked over with a grin, "Thanks Ulysses," he said.

"Think nothing of it, my friend," he said, dusting himself off, "May I… call you my friend?"

Orion chuckled quietly, shaking his head, "Sure," he said, "It's better than you calling me a prince."

Ulysses returned his response with a smile as they handed the blooms to Chiron, who counted them and tucked them away into his tunic.

"How many men are in your crew?" Chiron asked, "Nine," he answered, "Why?"

"Each flower only holds enough medicine for one man," Chiron said, "If we find that all your men are hurt, we will not enough for all of them."

Ulysses nodded, appreciating the seriousness of what Chiron said, "Let's hope that this is enough then."

"We should pick up our pace," Orion suggested, "The Serpens can't be far behind us and this won't help them at all if they catch us."

"I agree," Chiron said,

"Aye," Ulysses replied.

Orion nodded and moved ahead, breaking into a run down the dark tunnel. They turned their headlights back on and rushed down the cavern. The ceiling above them began to sink closer and closer to their heads, and the tunnel turned far more frequently than before. The darkness deepened so much that their lights seemed to do almost nothing when pointed straight ahead, and as they ran, they began to hear a distant crash growing louder and louder behind them.

This crash was the explosions erupting from the fallen rocks as Drago's men detonated the layers of explosives they had planted. Rocks flew out into the night air all around them, and Drago stood impatiently with folded arms, awaiting his men's report.

"Are we through?" he demanded.

"Nearly, sir," one answered, "The rock is thick, we will be able to continue the pursuit shortly."

Drago snorted, and steam blew out from his black nostrils as the explosions erupted through the mist. Then, he heard one of his men cry out from the other side of the fog.

"We're through!" he shouted, "Come on, you dogs! Get after them!"

The rest of the Serpens rushed through the fall, hissing and growling eagerly, and Drago stomped behind them. After his last man, he stepped into the cavern and inhaled deeply.

"They're close," he hissed.

He walked briskly in the darkness without any need for a torch. He saw every detail of the rocky walls perfectly as if the darkness shrouding them did not exist. He caught up to the rest of his men, who were huddled against the edge of the chasm at the end of the first tunnel.

"Why have you stopped?" he growled.

"There is no way across, sir!" a Serpen answered.

"There are Arachnibat nests in the chasm!" another whined.

Drago hissed and growled, then snatched his soldier's throat and lifted him up from the ground. He struggled and wheezed, begging Drago for forgiveness. Drago did not reply. He silently moved through his men, who scurried out of his way. Drago marched, holding the choking Serpen out in front of him until he reached the edge of the chasm. The Serpen wheezed in terror as Drago clenched down on his throat. He kicked and writhed desperately as he was held over the chasm before all the others.

"Lord Oberon is coming," Drago said. The rest of the Serpens looked at each other and recoiled at Drago's mere mention of the dark lord's name. "He will arrive at the next nightfall to ensure our task is done. I can only warn you that he will be far less tolerant of your weakness than I am."

His soldiers watched as he dropped the choking Serpen into the abyss, hearing his terrified cries followed by awful screeches and sounds of gnashing teeth upon flesh.

"Sir," one Serpen said, "Perhaps we should warn the chancellor, evacuate the city?" Drago swept the back of his enormous fist upon him before he could utter another word.

"You fail to follow my orders and now you defy the dark lord?!"

"And what if we do?" another Serpen hissed, stepping forward with folded arms, "You've killed two of our own for him already, and I have a feeling it won't end there."

"Kaa," Drago hissed, "You're right. I've grown tired of you and your insolence,"

"Insolence?" Kaa said, "I fight for our people, not for you. I wanted to bring glory back to our kind, not see them slaughtered by someone who has made a pet out of you!"

Drago roared and snatched Kaa by the arm. Kaa bit down into Drago's arm and clawed furiously at him, but despite his efforts, Drago took hold of his other arm and pulled both off his body with a cruel growl. Kaa fell to the ground in front of his comrades. He hissed and screamed in pain as he flipped himself onto his stomach and tried to kick himself away from Drago, but his fearsome commander snatched him by the ankles and dragged him back. He began pummeling Kaa, bashing his heavy fists against his face, roaring as his blows shook the cave's floor. All his men could hear Kaa's skull cracking, but Drago did not stop. He bashed his fists upon his head long after he was already dead. When he finally tired, he looked upon his clawed black hands, now drenched with thick green blood. He felt them shake and tightened his fists, then glared at his men.

"All of you have a simple choice," he said, "Finish these humans or die."

His men backed away slowly and silently began searching for some way to reach the other side.

Orion could hear Drago's roar echoing through the cave behind them. He stopped, looking back for just a moment as his heart stopped, "They're in the cave," he whispered.

Chiron and Ulysses both looked back for just a moment, but there was no time for words. They ran harder, bumping their shoulders into the sides of the cave as it continued to twist their path. Then, Orion spotted something ahead, something sprouting up from the ground. He slid to a stop, and Chiron and Ulysses stopped just behind him as he looked down at the strange thing in front of them.

It was made of dark red stone like the rest of the cave, but it was hollow, and when Orion looked forward, he saw that the path in front of him was scattered with many more that looked exactly like it.

"What are these?" Ulysses asked.

"We don't have time to find out," Chiron said, "Just don't touch them and we should be fine."

Orion carefully stepped around the strange funnel and continued down the tunnel. They were easy enough to avoid. Until he lifted his head to look forward, one was dangling down from the ceiling that none of them spotted, and Orion could see his mask crack as his head struck it.

"My helmet," he said, "It's cracked."

Before they could respond, they all heard a gentle hiss come from the funnel Orion had struck. When they turned towards the sound, they saw vapor pouring out of it into the air around them. Orion gasped, but not even a moment after, he felt as if his lungs had been lit on fire, and he fell to the ground screaming in pain.

"No!" Chiron shouted. He shoved Ulysses out of the way, and more funnels began to billow with hissing vapors.

"It's poison!" Orion screamed.

"Get up!" Chiron shouted, "Keep going!"

Orion struggled to his feet, clutching his chest as they broke into a full sprint. As they ran, the tunnel became shrouded in toxic fumes, and Orion started to feel his throat close.

"Chiron, I can't breathe," he wheezed,

"Come on!" Chiron urged, "Keep going!"

"I can't."

"Yes you can, you have to!"

It took all of Orion's strength to just move one leg forward, and what strength he had left was fading fast. He felt his heart beat so hard inside his chest he thought that it would explode inside of him. Ulysses ducked down and threw Orion's other arm around him.

"Come on!" he shouted, "I can see the end of the tunnel!"

Chiron looked up and saw the steam break ahead of them, and together, he and Ulysses ran harder, but Orion was falling limp.

"Stay awake Orion," Ulysses said.

Orion felt his eyes grow heavy. He could not force even one word out of his throat. All he felt was his limp body shaking as they dragged him out past the last column of toxins, and then, nothing.

"Orion wake up!" Ulysses begged.

"Put him down, take the mask off!" Chiron said.

Once they were clear of the fumes, Ulysses dropped Orion and turned him over. He deactivated Orion's helmet, threw the collar to the side, and placed the heels of his palms on his chest. He pushed down frantically and with all his might, yelling at the top of his lungs.

"Orion, wake up!"

"Open his mouth," Chiron grunted, scrambling through his tunic for the blue flowers. He broke the stems in half and looked back up to Ulysses, "I said open his mouth!"

Ulysses lifted Orion, supporting him against his knee, and squeezed his face until his mouth opened. Chiron held the broken stems of the flowers over Orion's mouth as he squeezed it hard, ensuring as best he could that every single drop made it down his throat.

"Hold his chin up," he told Ulysses, "He needs to swallow it."

"His heart's not even beating!" Ulysses snapped, setting him back on the ground, and resumed his chest compressions. He stopped and put this ear to Orion's mouth, then cried out with worry. Then he snapped his head up.

"His arrows," he gasped, reaching for his quiver, "Wait!" Chiron said.

"We don't have time to wait," Ulysses said, pulling a blue arrow from the quiver, "Electricity should get his heart beating, and he needs it now!"

Ulysses raised the arrow, poised to stab its head into Orion's chest, but Chiron caught it as his hand swung downward.

"Stop!" he said, Ulysses looked at him with wide, desperate eyes, but Chiron had more to say.

"The arrowhead," Chiron said, "Take the arrowhead out, then do it."

Ulysses nodded quickly and began twisting the arrowhead off, finding two small metal prongs protruding from inside the shaft.

"Do you think this will work?" Ulysses asked, "I don't know but we have to try," Chiron said.

Ulysses nodded again, raised the arrow, and brought it down onto Orion's chest with all his might.

Orion's body jolted, but it did not wake him. "Again!" Chiron urged.

Ulysses struck him again, finding the same result, "It's not working!" he cried, "Stop! You have to trust me, or he's going to die!" Chiron said, "Hit him again!"

Ulysses clutched the shaft of the arrow with both hands and let out a desperate shout at the top of his lungs as he brought it down onto Orion's chest for the third time.

When it struck, Orion's eyes opened wide glowing as bright as the blue flowers. "Orion?" Ulysses gasped.

Orion did not answer, but then his entire body began to convulse and shake furiously. His head tossed and turned back and forth violently, and he groaned as if he was trapped by something they could not see.

"Is this a seizure?" Ulysses asked.

"No, no, no, I don't know!" Chiron answered, "Orion, wake up!"

# Chapter Fourteen: Trapped

Orion found himself in a room that he had never seen before. He did not know how, but it felt as if he had been there many times, as if he was drawn to it by something inside of him he could not define. The floor was covered with the same glossy black tile that covered the main hall of the dark tower in Luma City. He saw a large window looking out upon the crumbling ruins of the city.

'Am I back?' he wondered.

He tried to take a step forward towards the window but could not. He tried again but could not move. His arms were fixed behind his back. He did not feel anything binding him. Whatever was holding him was invisible, but it felt powerful.

Then, Orion felt his arms fall down to his sides. He realized that he was holding a sword with a familiar black blade, and he felt his lips move to speak; he heard himself say in a very different voice.

"Your friend is strong…stronger than I believed he would be. My followers on Serpeno have been pursuing them for two days and two nights, and still, he survives."

Orion felt his heart beat with terror. The voice with which he spoke was not his. It was Oberon's. He tried everything he could to stop himself, to move even one finger under his own power, but he could not. He felt trapped within his own body if it even was his body.

He felt himself turn around, and on the floor behind him was Rowan. He was stripped of all his clothes, with every inch of his skin torn with wounds or blotched with every shade of red, purple, and grey. His blonde hair was stained with streaks of dried blood, and the only proof that Orion could see that he was still alive was the frantic, rapid, wounded rises and falls of his chest as he lay still on the floor.

'This is just a dream,' Orion thought, 'I need to wake up,' but then he felt his lips move to speak again and heard Oberon's voice come from his mouth.

"It's strange, how I discovered he was still alive only a short while ago and I still know things about him that you did not, even after a lifetime of knowing him."

Rowan's lip quivered as he wheezed, "Y-you know nothing about him."

"You don't know how wrong you are, Rowan. I am him, and he is me; we are vessels intended for destruction on a scale the cosmos has never known. Like me, he destroys everything he touches. You are proof of this. He left you here in his place to prolong his own survival; to continue spreading his chaos to two more unfortunate souls on another world."

"He…didn't leave me," Rowan moaned.

"No? He didn't take you, and he is not coming back to save you. You are expendable to him, despite everything you have done for him in all the time that you've known him,"

Orion could not feel tears in his eyes, but he felt them in his heart. He wanted to scream and burst out from his own body to destroy Oberon for what he was doing to Rowan, but he could not.

'This can't be happening, this is a dream,' he thought.

"You sent Orion away," Rowan quivered, "You're keeping me here."

Orion felt his lips move again, "I am merely fulfilling my purpose, Rowan. I am unbiased, constant, the inevitable result of choices that others make. Your suffering is the result of Orion's choices."

"You're insane," Rowan said, struggling to sit himself up.

Orion felt his body jolt into a spinning kick, then the impact of Rowan's jaw against his heel. Rowan rolled further away on the dark floor. His arms shook as he struggled to raise his body. He coughed weakly and spat blood onto the tile.

Orion felt his body stand still once again, then his mouth spoke again, "Life as humans know it, is insanity," Oberon's voice said, "Insanity that springs from free will. I am death. Peace and order that life cannot comprehend."

"You think you're different than the rest of us," Rowan whispered, "But you're wrong. You can't be death and be alive. You're just a traitor to what you really are. You're a tragedy, Oberon, and you know it."

Orion felt his body surge down to a knee and his hand wrap around Rowan's throat. He felt every pulse of Rowan's blood as if he was holding it with his own hand.

'This is not a dream,' Orion realized, 'What is happening?' He felt Oberon's voice growl out of him again,

"You will see, whether or not you want to, I will make you see. You will be the first of your kind to see my vision, and you will carry it out…when the time comes."

Rowan looked Orion in the eye. Orion could see shimmering tears streaming down his bloody face. His face twisted with defiance, "I…will not be your slave."

Orion felt his hand throw his head down against the floor as he stood over him and pressed the tip of his sword onto his chest. Orion willed with all of his soul that Rowan's torture would end, but it did nothing. He felt his grip tighten as the tip of the sword broke Rowan's skin, and Orion felt his arm drag it across the length of his chest. Rowan groaned and cried as his blood poured out and beaded onto the floor.

'Stop!' Orion thought, 'Leave him alone!' his thoughts did nothing, no matter how his own heart bled.

Orion felt his hand finish the cut, and his body kneel beside him. Rowan shook like a wounded animal but still looked with fiery defiance in his eyes.

"No matter what you do to me, you will never own me," he said, "And Orion will avenge us."

Orion felt his fists swing down to pummel Rowan, even after he fell out of consciousness. Then, Orion's vision faded into darkness.

Then, he heard a faint voice in the darkness whisper, "I think it's over."

"Orion?" It was Chiron's voice. Orion blinked to assure himself he was awake and looked all around him but could not see anything.

"Chiron?" he said into the dark.

"I'm here," his grizzled companion said, "You had a seizure, probably a side effect of the toxins you were exposed to. It lasted for an hour."

"No, no, no, something else happened," Orion said, feeling his whole body tremble. "What do you mean?" Chiron asked.

"I-I don't know what it was, but it was not a dream," Orion answered, "I think I was seeing what Oberon was seeing, or maybe what he has seen."

Orion described everything he had seen to Ulysses and Chiron, and as he spoke, they did not make a sound, but Chiron slowly held his hand to his mouth, very deep in his own thoughts with the most serious expression Orion had ever seen upon his face.

When he had finished, Orion looked at Chiron and asked, "Chiron, is there something about me and Oberon that you did not tell me?"

Chiron shook his head, "I told you everything that I know with absolute certainty, Orion."

"'Absolute certainty'?"

Chiron nodded, "Many rumors emerged about the methods which your father used to bring about you and your brother's birth. Some said that he consorted with witches, others thought that he had the healers subject your mother to experimental treatments, some even said that you two were not even human, but none of those rumors were ever confirmed to be true."

"Are you saying that something might have been done to us?" Orion asked.

"That is all I can say based on what I know and what you have told me," Chiron said, "Nothing else would explain this."

"But it makes sense," Ulysses said, "His eyes were glowing, that couldn't have happened unless something had been done to him."

Orion felt shattered. There were no questions plaguing his heart. He felt paralyzed, replaying every dream he ever had in his head, and with each recollection, he felt his heart sink lower and lower into his chest.

"I think that whatever happened, it was done to us both," Orion said, "I think that it connects us somehow. The other night, when I dreamed about my parent's death…It was the first time I really knew what happened to them. The day that it happened, Rowan and I were hunting in the mountains and we did not know until his mother told us," Orion held his bow up in front of him, "That was the day she gave me this, and the day she gave Rowan his dagger."

"Perhaps Nicodemus has some answers," Ulysses said. Chiron rolled his eyes at the idea, but Ulysses continued, "We may differ on what to call his wisdom, but he was there right? Maybe he knows something that we don't."

"Perhaps," Chiron admitted.

Orion shook his head and groaned as he stood up, "It doesn't matter. If Oberon knows about this connection, then he wanted me to see what he is doing to Rowan. He wants me to know that he could take complete control of me and that there's nothing I can do to save Rowan. He's already won."

"Orion wait," Chiron said, "We don't fully understand what has happened to you, or if Oberon is aware of it."

"I do, Chiron. I was right from the start, no one can stand against him. Even if Rowan is still alive, there's nothing I can do to stop him from killing him. Whatever Oberon is planning, it's already happening. All we can do is escape before it's too late, start over somewhere else."

Chiron stepped forward with a furrowed brow, "What you saw should give you hope! There is still a chance to save him, to save everyone! To give them a better life by fighting back!"

"How? How am I supposed to save anyone if I'm fighting Oberon and myself?"

Chiron shook his head and sighed, "You've done nothing but fight yourself Orion. You are all that is really standing between you and your friend. If you make this choice, the only person you are really surrendering to is yourself, and you leave everyone else to suffer for it."

"They're already suffering, Chiron. But their suffering will end. I'll do everything I can to help you save Ulysses' crew and get you off this planet, but after that, I would do more harm than good. I'm sorry."

Orion pulled his hood over his head and took off down the tunnel. Ulysses looked to Chiron, hoping he had something to say, Chiron just took off after Orion without a word, shaking his head, and Ulysses followed behind silently.

Meanwhile, the Serpens had tied great lengths of rope to arrows and fired them across the chasm with crossbows. One by one, they leaped onto the lines and climbed hand over hand to the other side, all under the impatient eye of Drago, who watched over them in impatient silence.

As he usually did, he followed his last man, and when he climbed onto the other side, the Serpens resumed their chase past the glowing blue flowers and into the tunnel past it. Drago huffed and inhaled the air, feeling the scent growing stronger and stronger as he followed his men. As they approached the steaming path full of toxic funnels, Orion, Chiron, and Ulysses could hear their hisses and growls louder than ever before.

"Run!" Chiron shouted.

The three companions sprinted down the tunnel and began to see another faint light ahead of them. A warm, flickering light.

"Fire!" Ulysses shouted, "This must be the entrance to the city!"

They sprinted faster until they reached it, but what they saw was not a city. Orion slid to a stop, almost falling off the ledge of a spiral staircase made of red stone lit by torches. He could not see what it led to, but they had to take it where it led them. He turned without hesitation to his left, and Chiron, and Ulysses followed, hearing the Serpens grow louder and louder. After the first several stairs, they heard a hissing voice call out from the top of the stairs.

"There they are!" he shouted. The Serpens had found them. Orion pulled a black arrow from his quiver and turned behind them. He fired at the Serpen. The arrow struck him in the throat, and he fell off the ledge into the dark chamber below. Behind him, more and more filed past the torches and ran down the stairs after them. Orion turned back again and fired a blue arrow into the charging Serpens. Several were electrified, and their bodies fell onto the stairs, slowing the others' advance, but only for a moment. They quickly stepped over them and pressed on.

Orion, Chiron, and Ulysses reached the final leg of the stairway and found themselves standing upon a large stone circle, and at its edge, nine metal cages scattered evenly upon it. They looked around for a door, finding nothing. They were trapped. Then, a voice Orion had not heard before called out, a human voice.

Ulysses snapped his head in the direction of the voice, "Triton?" he said.

"Here!" the voice shouted. An outstretched hand shot out from one of the cages. Ulysses rushed to it, and his voice broke as he looked upon what Orion assumed was a member of his crew, "Are you alright? Where are the rest of the boys?"

"We're here captain!" a deep voice shouted from another cage, "We knew you'd find us!"

Orion and Chiron looked back and saw the Serpens file down to the circular room, laughing as they slowed from a mad dash to a confident walk. They did not attack. They stared at them with smug smiles filled with fangs. They knew just as well as Orion knew that they had been pushed into a trap.

"You nearly succeeded," a deep, growling voice said from further up the stairs.

Orion recognized its owner and watched him push past his men down the stairs until he stood in front of them.

"It seems that our hunt is at an end," Drago said, "Lay down your weapons,"

"Don't do it, Uncle!" Triton shouted, "Take them down with you!"

"Triton," Ulysses said calmly, "We will be no help to any of you if we are dead," He looked to Orion and Chiron with eyes that seemed to ask if they were sure that was what they should do. Chiron simply looked over to Orion, intending not to move until he did. Orion looked back and forth between Drago and his two companions. Chiron was about to whisper to Orion, but he had already made his choice.

Orion threw his bow down in front of him, then pulled out his sword, and placed it next to his bow. Chiron nodded and threw his sword down. Ulysses reluctantly surrendered his weapon last.

"Give us the word, sir," a Serpen said, "We will tear them apart right here."

"No," Drago said cruelly, "The dark lord would want to see this for himself," He smiled, and his blazing green eyes gleamed with pride, "Lock them up with the others. We will call Lord Oberon so that he may see the humans die himself."

The Serpens snarled and followed his orders. They shoved the three of them down on their knees and shackled their wrists. Once they had done so, they shoved them to the center of the room and collected their weapons. Drago paced over to the far wall of the chamber. He placed his black hand upon the wall, and it began to rumble. A bright green light shone out from the wall, forming a square silhouette, and when it vanished, a stone door slid open.

"Orion, remember that door," Chiron whispered.

Orion nodded silently as the three watched every Serpen pass through it, laughing gleefully as they passed through, taunting them. After his last man passed through, Drago looked back to the three of them.

"You three should know, you are not alone down here. She will be here any minute now,"

"She?" Ulysses asked.

"The Leviathan," Drago said, "The one who protects our city and our people from filth like you. It has been many years since she has fed on humans. The Arachnibats are enough to keep her fed, but she hungers for human flesh above all others."

Orion looked up at Drago, "Even with us dead, Oberon will not give you what you want," Drago stepped forward to Orion and pushed him back down to the floor with a snarl.

Orion did not flinch. He glared up at Drago, refusing to show even a hint of fear.

"You do not fear me," Drago said, looking upon Orion from head to toe, "You are the most foolish human I have ever met."

"You're the most foolish Serpen I've ever met," Orion said, "Just hear me out, for the sake of your people."

Chiron's eyes were wide open as Orion spoke, as were Ulysses'. Chiron watched for any need to intervene, and Ulysses was shocked that Orion even had the stomach to address the beast, much less demand that he listens to him.

"I will not listen to a weakling like you," Drago snarled.

"If I am a weakling, then what does that make your men?" Orion asked, "You're so quick to underestimate us even though we killed half your men on our way here."

Drago snorted, "You are capable warriors," he admitted reluctantly, "But that only makes you dangerous, inclined to incite chaos."

"And Oberon isn't?" Orion asked, "I'm sure that if you could have killed him, you wouldn't be following him."

Drago chuckled, "What makes you so certain that I cannot kill him? You know nothing about me, human."

"I know who Oberon is," Orion said, "He is a murderer, and he has taken everything he has by force, or destroyed it. Are you telling me that you and your people are exceptions?"

Drago clenched his fists, "Our agreement assures the survival and glory of my kind," he growled, "My men and I will serve his cause, and we will regain the seat of power our ancestors once held. That is worth ten times what my father has won us with his politics."

"What assurance do you have he will deliver on his end of the bargain?" Orion asked, "His word? The word of a man who has killed thousands for nothing? How do you not see that he intends to destroy you all?"

Drago turned away and did not answer, but before he stepped through the hidden doorway, he glanced back over his shoulder, "You do not know what is coming," he said quietly, "He will bring order to the cosmos in a way that the High Council never could. He will make the cosmos clean, and pure. But if you do not stand with him, you stand against him, and he will destroy you. That is the choice we all must face now. Even you…little human."

Orion nodded his head, "I know," he said, "But no one else has to die. Take your people and escape before it's too late to save them."

Drago paused for a moment longer, then stepped through the doorway, and it slid shut, leaving them in the chamber, with the feeling that they were not alone and that something even more dangerous than even him was approaching.

# Chapter Fifteen: The Chancellor

Triton, Ulysses' crewman, called out from his cage the moment the great door shut, "Who are you?" he asked.

Orion turned to face him and opened his mouth to speak but froze. He locked eyes with Triton, seeing the same hope Ulysses had in him the moment they met. Orion looked around and saw the same expression from almost every member of Ulysses' crew. He thought about what had just happened and felt embarrassed for what he had said.

"No one," he answered.

"Come on," Triton groaned, "Not just anyone could have made it this close to the city, and why say all that to Drago?"

Orion could feel Chiron's eyes glaring at the side of his face, "Don't Chiron," he groaned,

"So, this is it then? We're all going to lay down and die here?" Chiron whispered, "These men never even get the chance to know that their prince has returned?"

'I'm not a prince,' he thought to himself, 'They should see that I'm no different than any of them. I'm just one man.' That thought repeated itself over and over again until he looked over to Chiron. His grey eyes bored through to his soul. He did not have to say a single word for Orion to know what he wanted him to say.

'I can't say it,' Orion thought, 'I can't let them put their faith in me.'

Chiron raised his eyebrows up at Orion. It was as if he could read his mind. Orion let his head hang for a moment, then removed the hood from his head. He slowly raised his head up and looked around the room as Chiron whispered in his ear,

"You never needed to be anything more than what you are, Orion. Your parents, Rowan, Ulysses, me…we all see this greatness in you, just as you are. All you ever had to do is make the choice to act on it. None of us wanted to turn you into something that you aren't and even if we did, we could not. Not even Oberon could do such a thing. If he could, don't you think he would have done that instead of banishing you here? Why would he leave the greatest challenge to his rule alive on a distant planet if he could have just made you his slave?"

Orion sighed with shaking breath and ran his fingers through his thick black hair, and turned to look at Chiron, with tears streaming from his eyes, "But Rowan, I'm too late to save him Chiron."

Chiron leaned in closer to him and placed his hand on his shoulder, "Remember what he told Oberon, remember his defiance, even after everything that has been done to him, remember what he told him!"

Orion shook his head, "What do you mean? What are you talking about?"

Chiron's grey eyes blazed, "He said that you would avenge us all! He is willing to sacrifice himself because he believes that you can do this Orion. He bet his life that you could beat him, no matter what the war would cost. He bet his life that you, his friend, would honor his dying wish…the same wish your mother and father had when they fought to save you."

Tears fell freely down Orion's face, onto the stone floor. Chiron sat beside him, keeping his hand on his shoulder. Orion looked around the room at the faces of every man trapped behind a cage, the way they looked at him, with the same glimmer of hope Rowan had.

'I can't be the prince of their legends,' he thought, 'But Chiron is right, Rowan is right, my parents were right, they still need someone they can look to for courage. I just hope that I will be enough for now.'

His lips quivered as he finally forced himself onto his feet and pushed the words out of his throat, "My name is Orion Castus," he said, "I came here to help you,"

Orion could hear some of them gasp, and some of them laugh softly with joy, "So the prophecy is true!" Triton said, "You're making a stand against Oberon!" Orion shook his head, "I'm not what your legends say I am, I'm just a man like you, and I do not know anything about leading anyone. We came to help you escape, but also because we need your help. We were exiled here, and we need passage off world."

Another prisoner spoke out, "I don't know if you noticed, your highness, but we are not exactly able to help you at the moment."

Ulysses whirled around with a smile, "Ares!" he shouted with a chuckle, "I was beginning to worry you did not make it!"

Ares' voice sent a chill up Orion's spine. He could not see his face or understand how Ulysses could greet such a voice so warmly.

"I'm surprised you were able to find us," Ares said, "But I suppose you did have help,"

"Indeed," Ulysses said, "Orion and his companion, the wise Chiron have saved my life many times already, if it were not for them, I would not be here."

"Gratitude," Ares sneered, "I wonder where that was when you decided to observe the operation that got us stuck here instead of fighting alongside us."

"We all agreed to the plan," Ulysses said, "Every man here, including you. I am sorry for the outcome, and if I have lost your trust, but we have more pressing matters at hand."

"Agreed," Chiron said, "We have no weapons or anything to break open these cages. Have any of you seen a guard with a key?"

"No guards," Ares said, "No keys. The cages do not have doors or keyholes anyway."

Orion looked around at all of them and observed exactly what Ares told them. There were no hinges for doors or any gap big enough for any of them to squeeze themselves through.

"Do you know where they're keeping our weapons?" Orion asked.

"Somewhere on the other side of the door," Ares answered, "Since you three are the only ones who aren't stuck in a cage, I'd say we finally have a chance to get them back, but the only way out is that magic door, and only a Serpen can open it from this side."

"Doors open both ways," Orion said, "We just have to give them enough reason to come back in here."

Chiron raised an eyebrow and looked at Orion with concern, "What's your plan?"

"Actually," Orion said, "I think you're going to like this one."

A Serpen was standing guard on the other side of the hidden door with a sword in hand. He yawned and leaned back against the wall, grumbling to himself, then he heard a muffled grunt and a rattle against metal bars on the other side of the wall. He turned and pressed his leathery ear to the wall, hearing a voice shouting at the top of its lungs.

"You insolent little slime!" the gruff voice shouted, "I'm going to kill you myself!" Another whimpering voice cried out, "Wait! If the dark lord comes and I'm already dead, he'll kill you all!"

"I don't give a damn what he wants!" The gruff voice shouted, "He can have what's left of you!"

The Serpen looked nervously to his left and right and called his comrade over, "Hey! Listen to this!"

His companion rolled his green eyes and pressed his ear to the wall, trying to hear what was concerning the guard. They heard punches landing and rattling metal amongst unruly shouts from several voices, all of them chanting, "Fight! Fight! Fight! Fight! Fight…"

"I'm opening the door," the Serpen said nervously.

"Wait, we should…." He did not listen to his companion, he pressed his hand against the stone door, and it began to slide open. As soon as he could, he shoved his way through, and his companion followed. When they entered, they saw the oldest of the three humans striking one of the younger ones while the prisoners in cages shouted gleefully. They immediately rushed to break up the brawl, pulling them apart.

"Yeah, that's right, old man, sit down!" the younger one shouted with blood dripping down his chin.

"Come here!" the older one growled, "I'm not done with you!"

They both pushed against the two guards, who hissed and shouted in frustration, unable to stop the scuffle. Then, they heard the sound of stone scraping and a heavy thud.

One of them looked back and saw that the door to the other side had been shut. The two humans stopped shouting and struggling with smug smiles on their faces. Then, before the Serpens could react, the humans turned on them, striking them on the back of the head, and they fell to the floor.

"Well done Ulysses," Chiron said.

Ulysses rubbed his head and pinched his nostrils shut, "I think you broke my nose," he whined.

The crew joined Chiron in a laugh as he took one of the Serpens' swords and handed the other to Ulysses.

"How long do you think it will take him to get back?"

"We need to buy him whatever time as he needs, and keep these men safe until he comes back with our weapons,"

Orion stood on the other side of the stone doorway and looked over the city. It was covered in a thick haze and scattered with the light of torches running along the dirt roads. He saw countless Serpens moving back and forth in every direction, trading goods, holding their children's hands as they walked, living freely without fear, ignorant of the danger that was coming. He envied them but also saw clearly that their culture was unique and beautiful in its own way, and a part of him admired it and wanted nothing more than to see this prosperity restored to Archon Prime. Then, he saw Drago pushing through the crowd.

He pulled the cloak as far over his face as he could, concealing himself as much as possible, and began following loosely behind him, searching the street around him for any sign of their weapons. As the crowd of Serpens cleared in front of him, he saw that Drago was walking beside a pale Serpen dressed in a fine scarlet robe. He noticed that as the two strolled down the dirt street, the citizens stopped what they were doing and bowed to them both.

'That must be the chancellor,' Orion thought. He crept faster down the street, putting himself in earshot, and as he snuck behind them, he listened closely.

"Tell me, my son," the chancellor said, "Where have you been the past few days?"

"I do not need to tell you that, father," Drago said, "You know where I was."

"I assume you are satisfied then?"

"Satisfied?" Drago asked.

"Yes. You would not have returned to the city unless you got what you wanted."

Drago looked down, "Yes," he said, but not confidently, "The humans were dealt with,"

"Is there any evidence of their trespass?"

"None father, no one will ever know they were here."

"And still something troubles you," the chancellor observed.

Drago stopped and looked down into his father's sunken eyes, "Your prying is the only thing troubling me," he snarled.

The chancellor shook his head and sighed, "Please, my son, for pity's sake, let me help you, let down your guard enough for me to know what is really in your heart."

"You could not even if you truly wanted to, old man, because you will never understand,"

"Understand what, Drago?"

Drago did not answer. He turned his gaze away from his father with clenched fists. The chancellor sighed, then he placed his shaking hands up onto his son's shoulders.

"I am your father, Drago, but I am also your Chancellor. Both these callings demand that I look after you, but also to know if you are endangering our people. Please…"

Drago turned away and walked off into the city, and his father stood there alone, rubbing his eyes with his pale, bony hand. Orion snuck to a nearby alleyway. He hid behind a crate and tried to calm himself from the shock of what he had just witnessed.

'The chancellor never cared about the hunt,' he realized, 'He doesn't even know why Drago came after us. Could Chiron really be right? Would he hear us out?'

He shook his head and tried to banish these thoughts, standing up to resume his search for their weapons, but he couldn't walk away.

'Could I really turn away when there is even a small chance to save these people?' he wondered, 'If I say nothing, then I would be just as responsible for their destruction as Drago.'

Orion peeked around the corner of the alleyway. The chancellor was still there, unguarded.

There was nothing stopping him from approaching him. Nothing except for himself. Orion turned back and pressed his back against the wall of the ally, and let out a deep, long breath. Then, he ducked down and turned back around the corner.

He crept up as close as he could to the Chancellor, sneaking up to the edge of his scarlet robe, and whispered, "Chancellor."

The white Serpen whirled around but did not see anyone. Orion whispered again, "Please, I know that you can't see me, but I must speak with you."

"What is this?" he demanded, "Who are you? How are you doing this?" he turned round and round in place, searching for the owner of the whispers.

"Please, this is about your son," Orion said, "You do not know what he is involved in, but I do, and you need to know before it is too late to save your people."

The chancellor stopped and looked down at the ground. He knelt down and ran his claws through the loose dirt. "These are human tracks," he said.

Orion's heart dropped; he cursed under his breath, trying to stay as still as he could. "You are a human," the chancellor said, "How are you hiding?"

"Please, your excellency," Orion said, "I know that your kind hates mine above all others, but I promise that if you just put our differences aside for a moment, you will appreciate what I have to tell you."

The chancellor looked all around him, ensuring that none of his citizens heard any part of their conversation.

"Tell me what is happening to my son now or I will have you arrested here and now," he hissed.

"This won't be on your terms, your excellency," Orion said, "If you want to know, then you will meet me at the wall at the end of this street, by the hidden door."

"You insolent little retch," the chancellor snarled, "Who do you think you are?"

He heard no response, but he saw the dust kick up in front of him and more footprints from one in front of the other, heading down the dirt road in front of him. He grumbled and shook his head and folded his arms as he contemplated Orion's offer.

Orion rushed back to the wall with the hidden door and waited. He stared into the crowd of Serpens rushing back and forth, hoping he would see the chancellor follow him. He wondered if he had made a grave mistake and if he should have just let him be and searched for their weapons instead. His heart raced, and he started searching frantically around him, looking for anything he could use to defend himself in case the Serpen guards came searching for him, but then, he saw a bony white hand holding his bow out from the corner of his eye.

"This cloak is a rare tool," the chancellor said, "One I have not seen for many years,"

Orion sighed with relief, "Thank you, your excellency," he said.

"I presume you will want this back," the chancellor said, "Along with the rest of your weapons in exchange for this information you have."

"If you hear what I have to say, then we might not need them," Orion said,

"'We'?" the chancellor asked.

"Yes, your excellency. On the other side of this wall are eleven other humans that have been imprisoned there by your son."

"No," he said, "There can't be, my son would not deceive me, he said that he dealt with the humans."

"I would not be standing here if that were true," Orion said softly, "Open the door and see for yourself that everything I'm telling you is the truth."

The Chancellor hesitated but slowly approached the wall and sighed the way a distraught father would. Orion did not understand. his exact dilemma, but he understood that even the possibility of being betrayed by his own son had to be weighing heavily upon his heart. Looking upon his withered white face made him remember how he felt when Chiron told him the truth of his past. He remembered how he would have given anything for even the slightest comfort.

Orion pulled his arm out of the cloak and rested his hand on the chancellor's shoulder. The chancellor flinched as he placed his hand upon him.

"It's alright," Orion said.

The chancellor looked down at Orion's hand and then up to the wall. He raised his hand and placed it on the wall, and opened the door.

They entered the room, and as they did, Orion deactivated his cloak. The chancellor stood still in disbelief at what he saw.

As the hidden door closed behind them, he whispered, "Why has he done this?"

Orion stood beside the Chancellor, "Your son has imprisoned us here because he has been conscripted by someone very dangerous, someone who sent us here, then sent him to hunt us down and kill us."

The chancellor shakily looked back to Orion, "Who?"

"My brother, your excellency, Oberon Castus, of Archon Prime."

"I do not know this Oberon," the chancellor said, "but I know of your family…Castus…you and your brother must be the sons of your fallen king."

"Yes," Orion said, "Oberon murdered our father and enslaved our people. I was hidden from him when I was very young, and it was not until he found me and banished me here that I learned the truth of who I came from."

"So you are the rightful heir to the throne of your people," the chancellor said, "But that still does not explain how my son is complicit in your brother's affairs."

"When I was banished here, your son came after me in the forest, and again after I encountered Chiron, who was also banished here. We managed to escape him, but he pursued us through the forest to the caverns that lead here. He has mentioned my brother many times, and freely admitted that he is in his service, calling him 'the dark lord'. Now that he has us, he will summon him here so that he can ensure that we are executed."

"You lie," the chancellor said, "You are trespassing on our world, that is why he hunted you, there is nothing wrong with him doing so, and he would never invite more of your kind here."

"We know your laws," Orion said, "And we know that our presence here is not welcome, so why would we choose to come here? We were banished here by Oberon because no one would question Serpens killing humans. He wants be certain we were killed so he would have no one to interfere with his plans."

"But my son would never serve a human, not even if his life depended on it."

"Your excellency. All your lives depend upon it. Oberon told your son that he would restore power and glory to your people. He is using Drago's greed to serve his own ends, and we are certain that no matter what he has promised he will destroy your people, just as he destroyed ours."

The Serpen chancellor's hands quivered, as did his bottom jaw. He rose his quivering hands to his snout, and Orion could see tears stream from the corners of his sunken eyes.

"I'm sorry," Orion said.

"This is all my doing," the chancellor quivered, "I failed my son."

"It's not too late," Orion said, "You can set this right and protect your people before it's too late."

"How?"

"If you set us free, I give you my word that we will help you defend your city against Oberon and his followers."

"And what is your word worth?" the chancellor asked, "What makes you so different from your brother?"

Orion hesitated and looked around at all the eyes that watched him in a way he had never been watched before. They still gleamed with hope, unspoken trust in his words, it made his heart swell, and his fist clenched with resolve. He looked to the chancellor and answered.

"I know that you think all humans crave power, your excellency, but I promise you that if it was up to me, I would have never had this birth right. I wish I wasn't born the son of a king. I just want the suffering to end, and for there to finally be peace. But if I stand by, and I do not stand against Oberon, all the blood he sheds will be on my hands, including yours."

The chancellor ran his bony finger along the chin of his snout, "Your brother has already accomplished what the High Council has deemed impossible. No human has ever penetrated our defences on our world, much less incited treason within the alliance against the chancellors. What if you cannot stop him?"

Orion's chin fell to his chest, and his own doubts resurfaced, but he looked up into the chancellor's sunken eyes with a quivering lip, "Even if I can't, I will die trying, because everyone I ever loved gave everything so that I could finish what they started, and I will do it with or without your help if I must, and I think you would do the same."

The chancellor folded his arms across his chest, "You are… different… from any other human I have met, Orion Castus."

Orion just nodded, he could not force another word out of his mouth, and he felt himself shake all over his body as the chancellor spoke to him.

"Your courage to inform me of my own son's treachery at the risk of your own life," the chancellor said, "has earned my respect."

Orion's eyes widened. He could not believe what he had just heard. He watched, stunned, as the chancellor walked around the circle and placed his clawed forefinger on each of the cages. As he touched them, the cages dissolved into dust and fell to the stone floor. After freeing Ulysses' men, he stood beside Orion with a weary grin. The crew stepped forward to the center of the circle, and one by one, they all bowed their heads and lowered themselves to their knees. Orion opened his mouth to protest, but he also saw Ulysses and Chiron bow, and then, out of the corner of his eye, he saw the chancellor wave his arm to his side, and he, too, bowed.

Orion felt more guilty than he ever had in his entire life. He wanted nothing more than to beg them all to rise, but he could not bring himself to say the words. He saw with his own eyes that everything Chiron had told him was the truth. A strange peace washed over his shoulders, and something surged within his heart that he had never felt before. He finally saw, without a doubt in his heart, that despite his uncertainty, despite how badly he wished his responsibility was anyone else's, all the faith in him may not have been misplaced after all.

"My prince," Chiron said, rising to his feet, "What are your orders?"

The rest of the crew rose to their feet and looked eagerly at Orion with the same question shining in their eyes.

Orion looked to the Serpen chancellor, "Your excellency," he said, "Can you could send a message to the High Council to inform them of what is happening?"

"I can communicate with them, but my testimony alone may not be enough to sway them, your highness," he said, "They would likely want to hear directly from you as well,"

"What about Drago?" Ulysses said, "If he finds out what you are doing, he will kill you, your excellency."

"I have my royal guards," the chancellor said, "They are loyal to me alone, once we send the message, I will send them with you and your men to arrest him."

"We will also be facing Oberon when he arrives," Chiron said, "Your people will be in grave danger if he comes, and there are too few of us to protect them here."

"When the prince and I reach the palace, I will order a city-wide evacuation into the forest, my people will be safe there."

Chiron nodded, "A wise plan, however we need to move quickly, we are running out of time."

# Chapter Sixteen: Drago's Confession

The chancellor walked outside the hidden door and closed it behind him. He spotted a Serpen soldier walking along the wall. He glanced quickly to his left and right, then approached.

"Soldier!" he shouted.

The Serpen startled and turned to face him, "Your excellency," he said nervously, "What is it?"

"Bring me the weapons of the prisoners being held behind this wall," he ordered.

The Serpen looked to his left and right nervously, "Why, sir?" he asked.

The chancellor glared at the Serpen, "Because I told you to."

The Serpen immediately bowed and rushed away to do as he was ordered. After a short while, he returned, pushing a small hover cart filled with a quiver, swords, and many other weapons. The chancellor placed his hand on the soldier's back and looked him in the eye, "This never happened," he whispered.

"Yes, your excilency," the Serpen said, quickly bowing his head. The chancellor nodded and pushed the cart into the hidden room, and the crew eagerly recovered their weapons. As they did, Orion examined each one of them and felt increasingly confident in their ability to carry out the task at hand. Two of the men were nearly as large as Drago, both had braided hair that fell down to their backs, and their arms were covered in strange tattoos and brands. If one did not have a beard, the two would have been indistinguishable. Orion approached them as they recovered their broadswords and asked the bearded one.

"What is your name?"

The man smiled and spoke with a deep, hearty voice, "I am Jax, your highness," he said, this is my brother Brutus."

"Half-brother," Brutus grumbled.

"All the same," Jax said, "We're always up for a good fight, and we are with you to the end,"

"It will take more than brawn to beat this Drago," another member of the crew said. Orion turned to see who spoke, finding a slender man in a long coat with very little hair on his head and wide, bird-like eyes carrying a sword in his hand. "Forgive me, your highness. I am Cosmo, the navigator of our crew."

Jax chuckled and leaned into Orion's ear, "Watch out for this one. He thinks he's smarter than the rest of us, even though he makes and diffuses bombs for fun."

Cosmo simply nodded proudly, "It's difficult to find problems worthy of my intellect, but this task should prove most interesting."

Orion chuckled and looked over the rest of the crew and then back to Cosmo, "Tell me about the rest of the crew," he said.

"Well, you have already been acquainted with our Captain, Ulysses," He said, "And I suspect his next in command, Ares, the first mate."

Orion looked at Ares and felt a shiver crawl up his spine. His clothes were the same shade of black as his greasy hair and neatly trimmed beard. His dark eyes seemed to never blink, and Orion had a troubling sense that he was watching him from the moment they entered the room.

"Why is he his first mate?" Orion asked.

"Ares has travelled the cosmos four times over. He is the most experienced out of any of us, including Ulysses," Cosmo answered, "In fact, he was the captain of our ship before Nicodemus replaced him with Ulysses."

"He seems like he took that well," Orion said.

"Oh, not at all," Cosmo said, "But he is a cunning warrior and a good man to have, so Ulysses keeps him around."

Orion pointed to a young man with the same shade of hair as Ulysses, "Who is Triton to Ulysses?"

"Triton is the youngest member of our crew, and Ulysses' nephew."

"And who are those three next to Ares? The ones who look just as happy as he is."

"Those are Hanssen, Aldrich, and Benedict," Cosmo answered, "Hanssen is our pilot. Benedict is Ares' brother, and Aldrich is the son of Sirius, our weapons master,"

"Which one is Sirius?" Orion asked.

Cosmo pointed to the far wall of the room, where a man with dishevelled brown hair was carefully sharpening his sword.

"He seems-"

"Alone?" Cosmo finished, "That's because he is. He's kept to himself since his son came aboard."

"Why?"

"No one knows, but the two are quite estranged now. They hardly ever speak to one another."

"Do you think he'll be ready for this?" Orion asked.

"Oh, you need not worry about him, your highness, we are all fighters here, but Sirius makes fighting with a sword look like art."

Orion nodded gratefully for what Cosmo told him, recovered his quiver and sword from the hover crate, and walked back to Chiron, who watched over the crew with a careful eye.

"What do you see?" Orion asked.

"It's troubling," Chiron said, "It looks like a strong crew, but they are clearly pulled in two different directions."

"Ares," Orion said, "He was captain of their ship before Ulysses, and I don't think he appreciated the demotion."

"Some of them seem to respect him more than their own captain," Chiron observed, "Do you think that we can trust him?"

"Long enough to face the coming battle," Orion said, "his motivations are unclear, but we can't afford to sow distrust amongst ourselves now,"

Chiron nodded in agreement, and then the two turned towards the wall.

"How do you plan to take on Drago?" Orion asked.

"We will have to draw him out, away from his men," Chiron said, "Otherwise, he will wreak havoc upon the city and regroup with Oberon when he arrives, and then we will have no chance of capturing him."

"How do you plan to do that?"

"That part is easy. His pride consumes him. He'll meet us if we call for a fight, but we must ensure that we keep him away from you and the chancellor."

Orion felt worry grip his heart, "I should go with you. You're going to need my help," he said.

"No," Chiron said, placing his arm around him, "You know where you are needed. The high council needs to hear your voice. Without you, they will not intervene."

"I just…don't want to lose you too, Chiron. You've done nothing but try to help me from the moment you found me…I'm sorry that I didn't listen to you,"

Chiron tightened his grip on Orion's shoulder and smiled warmly, "None of us know when our time comes, Orion," he said, "But I would be just as proud as this crew to die fighting for you and when this battle is won, I would be honoured to keep trying to get through that thick head of yours, if you'll let me. "

Orion smiled. He opened his mouth to speak, but the chancellor approached him, "We must leave now your highness," he said.

Orion nodded and followed him to the threshold of the doorway. He paused, glancing over his shoulder to Chiron, who had a full, proud smile upon his grizzled face. Orion felt a small smile turn the corner of his lips up. He did not want to turn away, but he felt warmness fill his heart as Chiron's grey eyes looked at him, as always, with unspoken understanding.

"Good luck, my prince," Chiron said.

Orion nodded, pulled his hood over his head, and closed his eyes as he turned away, back into the city as the door closed behind him.

"No matter what happens," the chancellor said, "You must stay close to me and do not take the cloak off until I give you the word."

Orion nodded and activated the clasp. He held his bow tight in one hand, and with the other, he held the cloak over his chest. He crouched down so the hem of the coat concealed the bottom of his boots and walked as carefully as he could behind the chancellor, placing his feet in the footprints the chancellor left behind.

The crowd parted on the road as the chancellor strolled. There seemed to be no suspicions raised until the chancellor stepped onto the path toward his fortress. Several squads of soldiers marching in formation passed by them, armed and ready for battle. Orion could see the concern in the chancellor's sunken eyes. There was no way for him to know what Drago's orders were without raising suspicions, so he continued to press forward, holding his head up high and keeping his wits about him.

Orion's heart was thundering in his chest as they approached the threshold of his fortress. He snuck as close to the chancellor's red cloak as he could but skidded to a stop as the chancellor was stopped by one of the sentries,

"Your excellency."

"Not now," the chancellor said, "stand aside."

"It's your son, your excellency," the guard said, "he wishes to speak with you,"

Orion's yes widened. 'Say something!' he thought, trying to stifle his quickening breath.

"Tell him…if he wishes to speak with me, he will have to meet me in the city," the chancellor said.

"But sir, you just came from the city. He is waiting for you in your chambers."

"I know where I was," the chancellor snapped, "I have pressing matters to attend to, and I will return to the city once they are finished."

The guard's face twisted, fighting a scowl as he responded, "I will let him know…your excellency."

The chancellor swept past him, and Orion ducked down lower, keeping his eyes fixed on the chancellor's heels as he led him through the dark tunnels of the fortress. There were guards posted at every door, and they all watched the chancellor as he quickly paced past them. Orion felt as if their eyes were fixed upon him, even though they could not see him. Their eyes glared with malice, the way Drago's did, following the chancellor down the hallways as if they were poised to strike him down at any moment.

'Something is wrong,' Orion thought.

His heart raced as the Chancellor led him down one long, final hallway leading to a doorway covered by a dark red curtain. The chancellor grasped the curtain with one hand and looked behind him with a worried shine in his eyes as if he was sensing the same impending danger Orion was. He looked down at his heels, where Orion was crouched. Orion raised his head up just enough for his chin to shine in the dim light beneath his hood; so the chancellor could see his mouth.

"They're watching you."

The chancellor nodded very slightly, then pushed through the curtain, holding it open behind him so the guards would not see it stir as Orion entered behind him. He stepped to the side and watched the dirt floor, following the footprints as they indented the dirt one in front of the other, rounding around him until they came to rest against the wall beside the doorway. The chancellor dropped the curtain and nodded down at Orion's footprints.

Orion deactivated the cloak and walked beside the chancellor as he approached a circular metal table at the center of his chamber. The chancellor flipped a switch, and a tiny white light activated in the middle of the table.

"The aide to the chancellors will answer our communication," the chancellor whispered, "Once he does, it is imperative that you speak only when asked to speak."

Orion nodded and watched as the space above the white light began to flicker with a strange silhouette, slowly forming a humanoid shape as garbling sounds began to speak out from the table. Then, the image became clear. The chancellor's aide was a tall, slender being with a neck so thin Orion could see the veins running beneath his grey skin. He wore a black robe and a gold medallion with the high council's seal upon his chest, a star with ten rays representing the ten worlds of the Atlas Alliance. Above all other features of his appearance, Orion found his head most unsettling. It was hairless, and his eyes were the largest and darkest he had ever seen on any creature, with no pupils of any kind, a flat face with no nose and a frowning mouth.

"Chancellor Kobra," the aide said in a deep, garbled voice, "I am surprised to hear from you. Chancellor Jafar made no request to speak with you."

"He did not," the chancellor said nervously, "But it is imperative that I speak to him immediately."

The aide looked over to Orion, and his frown sank lower, "What are you doing with this creature?" he asked.

The chancellor looked over to Orion and held his hand out to him, "This is Prince Orion Castus of Archon Prime. He has come to me with a warning that Chancellor Jafar must hear himself. There is a danger that will affect all the Atlas worlds if we do not act swiftly to stop it."

The aide scowled at Orion, "Is this true, human?"

Orion gulped and answered, "Yes, sir. I am aware that my presence on this world is unwelcome, but I did not come here willingly. I was exiled here by the self-appointed regent of my world, who has enslaved my people and conspired with a faction of Chancellor Kobra's soldiers to have me, and my companions murdered."

"And what proof do you have to substantiate your claims?"

"A confession," Kobra answered, "From my own son, Drago. He is…the one who conspired with the tyrant who sent the prince here."

The aide shook his head, "No citizen of our alliance, much less an heir to a chancellorship, would dare conspire with humans."

"I do not believe that Drago joined him willingly," Orion said, "The man he is conspiring with is a dangerous warrior. He has destroyed armies of men single-handedly without your knowledge, and now that he has recruited Drago, he now has a foothold to make a move against the high council."

"No one human could pose such a threat," the aide said, "Archon Prime has no ships, no means of interstellar travel whatsoever."

"He does, sir, but it is not a ship," Orion said, "He has a machine that can send someone to any planet faster than any ship could. That is how he banished me here."

The aide scoffed but did not smile, "These are incredible claims," he said, "But you have no evidence. I will not pass this on to the Council unless you can provide some tangible proof."

"I have ordered my son's arrest," Chancellor Kobra said, "I beg you, pass on our warning. By nightfall, you will have his confession and more than enough reason to intervene!"

This intrigued the aide. He turned his head slightly to the left, "You are so certain that this human speaks the truth that you would have your own son arrested?"

"I do. Yes, there is more than enough reason to prejudge his people for their violent history, but I assure you, this one is different; his intent is to restore peace and nothing more,"

Orion lowered his head, feeling his cheeks blush with discomfort at the chancellor's vote of confidence.

The aide folded his arms over his chest, "I cannot go to the council," he said firmly, "However, if you hail me again with the confession of your son, I will alert them immediately."

Orion and the chancellor bowed gratefully, "Thank you," the chancellor sighed.

The aide turned to walk away, but he stopped, taking one last look at Orion, "You are…different, human," he said, "I will remember you, Orion Castus."

His image flickered and vanished, and Orion smiled, relieved by this unexpected and unlikely small victory. That moment quickly ended, as he heard stomping footsteps approaching the chancellor's chamber.

"Hide yourself!" the chancellor hissed.

Orion threw the hood of his cloak over him, rushed to the corner of the room, and pressed the clasp. The cloak flickered until it was invisible, as a large shadow cast itself along the floor.

A deep, rumbling voice called out, "Father!"

The chancellor gulped and stood tall, "Enter my son," he said.

The curtains were thrown open, and Drago's dark head emerged through them. "I must speak with you, and it cannot wait," he growled.

"I told the guards that I would return to the city to meet you," the chancellor said, "Did they not inform you?"

Drago nodded slowly, "They mentioned that you had 'pressing matters' to attend to," he said, "I'm curious, what exactly are these pressing matters?"

"If they concerned you, I would have let you know,"

"Is that so?" Drago snarled.

The chancellor backed up and placed his hands on the table behind him. Orion watched as he discretely pressed another switch and looked worriedly at his son's scowling face.

"I assume that what you have to tell me is just as important?" the chancellor said.

"You seem…bolder than usual, father," Drago said.

"I could say the same of you. The last several weeks, I have hardly been able to recognize you."

Drago chuckled slowly, "I suppose you would not. I have discovered my destiny, father. I have grown beyond ancient limitations and traditions," he snarled.

"You have spoken in riddles for too long now, Drago," the chancellor said, "I now tell you, as your chancellor, speak freely!"

Drago raised his head up and snorted. His dark pupils contracted, and he lowered his snout into a cruel stare, "Someone came to me some time ago, a warrior who…understands the true nature of power and order."

"Who, Drago?"

"He came to me during a great storm, in the cover of darkness. As I walked through the jungle, a great flash of lightning, larger than any I have ever seen, struck down from the sky before me, and when it passed, he appeared. I did not know who or what he was. He wore black armor and a dark hood over a mask with the jaws of a Banshee upon it, an ancient symbol of death.

He drew his sword and attacked me. I have never faced or heard tales of a greater warrior. He defeated me, but as he held the tip of his black blade upon me, he said that he did not come to shed blood. He said that he had come to enlighten me, to free our people, and that if I listened, he would show me how.

He took me deep into the forest and proved his wisdom to me. He understood the slights against our people and believed, as I do, that we could be conquerors again. He believed that there would be no need for us to abide by the will of any other species. I begged his help, asking him what I must do.

He drew a circle on the ground with his sword and drew blood from his hand into its center. He bid me do the same. It was a blood oath, one of the most ancient traditions of warriors. I found respect for him that I never found for any of our kind…even you, father."

The chancellor wheezed in despair, and pain shone in his sunken eyes, "Drago," he said, "What have you done?"

Drago stepped forward sinisterly, "I have sworn fealty to the Dark Lord Oberon, and by his hand, the cosmos will witness who truly holds power."

Drago snarled and gripped his father by the throat. The chancellor gasped and struggled against his hand as his breath was slowly choked from him. Orion flinched to intervene, but the chancellor held his palm out to him, silently begging for him to stop. Orion did not understand,

'What is he doing? Why is he letting this happen?'

Then, the chancellor shakily pointed behind him, and when Orion looked at what he was pointing at, his heart sank.

The button the chancellor pressed as Drago spoke reactivated the light at the center of the table, and the button was flashing red. The chancellor was recording every word Drago spoke, capturing his confession and his own murder.

Orion's mind erupted with conflict. Drago's confession would be enough for the High Council to order Drago's official arrest, but the murder of his own father would be an act they would respond to without question.

'Why would he do this for me?' Orion wondered, 'I can't let this happen.'

Orion stood up and silently drew a black arrow. He took aim at Drago's bright green eye and slowly emptied his lungs of their breath. He fired. The tip of the arrow pierced the center of the monster's dark pupil, and the shaft broke the bright green eye apart. Drago roared in agony and dropped his father onto the floor. Blinded by both rage and the arrow, he swung his claws widely around him, searching for his attacker, but could not find Orion. Amid his writhing, Orion drew his short sword and slowly crept toward Drago. When he was just a few paces from his scaly back, he took a deep breath. He leaped onto the raging beast. He thrust his sword into the back of his head. Drago's rabid bellows ceased, and the dark Serpen fell to the floor, with his last breath hissing from his fanged mouth.

Orion rushed to the side of the chancellor and propped him up against his knee. His pale eyes were bloodshot, and he was barely breathing.

"Why did you do that?" Orion asked.

The old Serpen wheezed, "It is the price that had to be paid...for my failure,"

"You didn't fail," Orion said, "We have his confession."

"I failed...as a father," he gasped, "L-listen...to me," he said, grasping the hem of Orion's cloak with all his strength, "Do...do not fail...your brother."

"Stop. We can still get you some help," Orion begged.

"Your brother!" the chancellor wheezed, "He fell to the darkness...but perhaps he has only lost his way...like Drago...Kill him if you must, but do not forget that no one is ever born good or evil...that is...a choice...."

He raised a shaking, bony finger to the button, and Orion quickly pressed it, and a small device was ejected. Orion took it and held it tight in his hand as if it was the most valuable thing in the universe, but when he glanced back at the chancellor, he had fallen still.

Orion felt tears well in his eyes, guilt for being the cause of his sacrifice.

"I'm so sorry," he whispered, "But I promise, I will avenge you. I will avenge us all,"

"The chancellor!" a Serpen called from the hallway, "The chancellor has been murdered!"

Orion snapped his head to the doorway, hearing growling Serpen guards approaching. He rushed to Drago's body and pulled his sword from his head and prepared himself for battle.

# Chapter Seventeen: The Leviathan

As Orion and the Chancellor departed from the secret room, Chiron turned to Ulysses and his crew.

"Our objective is simple. We must draw Drago and his men out into the city as much as possible, keep them engaged with us and only us, long enough for them to get their message to the High Council."

"We are hilariously outnumbered," Ares sneered, "How do you plan to sustain the fight?"

"We have to give them more than just a fight," Chiron answered, "Ulysses, you and your crew will divide yourselves and cover as much ground as you can, keep the battle spread to every corner of the city so they will be forced to expend all their manpower."

"What will you do?" Ulysses asked.

Chiron sighed, "Something that will likely get me killed in the process. You will know when you see it."

"Wait," Jax interrupted, "All we have to do is go out there and pick a fight?"

Chiron smirked, "Yes," he said, "Go out there and do what pirates do."

The crew looked at each other with grins and a gleeful smile washed over Jax's face, "Well, what are we waiting for?!" he shouted, "Time for some payback, lads!"

The crew erupted with war cries, and Jax pulled his sword off his back, charging through the doorway.

Chiron could hear Jax's shouting above all the others, even amid the ringing of swords and the sudden chaos.

"Come on, you reptile scum!" Jax shouted, "You have a riot on your hands!"

Ulysses ran through the city streets with his nephew Triton by his side. The Serpen civilians gasped and scrambled out of the way, calling for their soldiers.

"Humans!" they shouted, "There are humans in the city!"

The guards walking along the streets responded as they heard their cries, rushing to the commotion. Ulysses and Triton stood back-to-back and engaged them as they came, cutting them down, then continuing to run the chase through the streets.

Above them, Ares, Aldrich, and Benedict ran along the rooftops of the Serpens' homes and threw stones at the guards as they ran towards the sounds of battle. The Serpens clambered onto the rooftops and gave chase until they ran the three of them to the ledge of a rooftop that was too far from another to jump.

"We have you now," one of them snarled.

Ares simply smirked at the Serpen and pulled his coat back to reveal a coiled chain whip clipped to his belt. He unclipped it and let the end of the whip drop onto the roof. The Serpens charged. Ares snapped his whip. The chain rattled and rang as it twisted and flew towards them. A sharp clang sounded as it found its mark against one of the Serpens' necks. The soldier fell to the ground, and the others looked to Ares with shock, then rushed to avenge him. They all met the same demise.

Along the perimeter streets of the city, running in opposite directions, Jax and Brutus wreaked havoc wherever they could start it. Squads of Serpens surrounded them, but all their numbers could not get past their broadswords or match their strength.

Cosmo and Hanssen dashed along the streets, tossing small explosives from a pack Cosmo carried on his back.

"Do you ever go anywhere without carrying a bomb?" Hanssen asked.

"Nope!" Cosmo shouted maniacally, laughing as he tossed explosive after explosive into groups of charging Serpens.

Amid all the skirmishes that spread like wildfire across the dusty streets, the Serpens devoted the bulk of their manpower to one member of the crew, as they were constantly alerted that he was dispatching every squad sent his way. That crewmember was Sirius.

He was only armed with his freshly sharpened sword, and he took on no less than three Serpens at once, wielding his blade with a precision that they could not hope to match. Unlike the rest of the men, he never made a sound. It was not long before the Serpens abandoned their efforts to overwhelm him, and it was he who was chasing them.

Chiron looked over the city as the chaos of the battle erupted, pleased with the efforts of Ulysses and his crew. However, he was forced to turn to his own dreaded task. He examined every corner of the circular room, searching for anything that he did not see when they first arrived.

"Where are you?" he whispered to himself. He scratched his head and paced frustratedly around the room. Then, he finally noticed something. He stamped his foot onto the stone.

'Hollow,' he thought. He stamped again. He stamped once more. He looked where he was standing, at the exact center of the room, where a single round stone was laid. He brushed the dust from it and saw that there was an indent in the shape of a clawed hand.

Chiron rushed towards one of the unconscious Serpens he and Ulysses had dispatched and dragged him to the center of the room, then placed his scaly hand into the indent. The cracks around the circular tile began to glow, and he felt the floor begin to sink. He looked around him and saw that the entire floor of the circular room began to lower itself like an elevator. It descended faster and faster, and dust blew freely around him.

The floor rumbled and shook as it came to rest twenty feet below the doorway. Chiron cursed under his breath and looked all around him for some way for him to climb out of the hidden shaft. He tried climbing up the walls, but they were too smooth. He was trapped. Then, he heard a loud hiss and felt a hot burst of air blow against his back.

"Well, shit," he said. He turned around slowly, seeing the entrance to yet another tunnel, spanning wider than the arm span of three men and standing just as tall, but this one was not empty. Chiron cautiously stepped towards the tunnel and peered into the darkness. He saw nothing, but he still heard the hissing and felt more waves of the hot air blowing out from the tunnel.

Then, a pair of glowing red eyes with dark, slitted pupils opened, shining through the dark tunnel. Chiron felt his heart drop into his gut as he slowly backed into the wall behind him. The fiery red eyes grew larger, and an enormous, black forked tongue flickered into the light. A head as wide as the cave it came form emerged. Its scales were as white as the chancellor's, and its massive head was layered with sharp horns. The space between its crusted lips revealed rows of fangs, salivating so heavily it dragged along the ground as the creature emerged.

"So this…is the Leviathan," Chiron grumbled.

The Leviathan pressed its snout up to Chiron and growled ravenously. He could feel the force of its inhale as it absorbed his scent, and the stench of its breath made him retch as if it carried the odors of a thousand corpses. Chiron remained as still as he possibly could, watching the creature carefully. After what felt like an eternity, waiting to be eaten, Chiron heard a voice call out from above.

"Where are the others?!" the voice shouted, "The other prisoners, where are they?!"

The Leviathan looked up and saw a Serpen on all fours, looking down into the hole. It flicked its tongue, and its scaly eyelids tightened. Chiron had never seen terror like what washed over that Serpen's face. It was too late for him to call out. The monster lunged its head up, revealing a long, winding body with rows of horns running along its spine. It opened its jaws with a deafening bellow and devoured the Serpen whole. Chiron could only watch as it crashed through the wall hiding the secret room and slithered out into the city.

He sighed with relief that he had been spared but quickly spotted his escape. The horned tip of the leviathan's tail was still slithering up the wall. He leaped up and wrapped his arms around it and let the creature carry him back to the top.

As Chiron rose to the ledge, the Leviathan's tail snapped, and he was thrown to the edge of the room. He snapped to his feet and rushed to the now toppled wall and looked out to the city. The beast was crushing everything in its path, shaking the entire city with its horrifying bellow.

Orion could hear that roar from the Chancellor's chamber, he did not know what it was, but it made the guards that were rushing towards the curtain stop.

"What was that?" one of them asked. Another gasped, "Was it-?"

"Come on! We need to stop it before it destroys the city!"

Orion heard their footsteps turn in the opposite direction and heard no other sounds coming from the nearby rooms of the palace. He peeked his head out and looked in every direction. He was alone. He pulled another arrow out of his quiver and held it at the ready in front of him. He snapped around every corner, prepared to meet the Serpens as they came, but they never did.

As he approached the entrance to the fortress, Orion began to hear the calamity breaking across the city. He sprinted until he stood in the courtyard just outside the entrance, and that was when he saw it.

The entire city was crumbling. The inhabitants were running along the streets in terror as Ulysses' crew fought their soldiers, and an enormous reptilian beast ripped through the structures of the city, devouring every living thing in its path.

Orion sprinted through the front gates of the fortress, down the path, and into the crumbling city. He climbed up onto a nearby rooftop and searched all around him for Chiron or Ulysses. He heard someone call out to him.

"Orion!"

Orion turned. It was Ulysses' voice,

"I'm here!" he answered.

He rushed to the side of the rooftop and looked one street over. He spotted Ulysses standing back-to-back with his nephew, fighting against a large group of Serpens. Orion jumped from the rooftop and scrambled from building to building, running to reach them. As he flew from the last one and into the street, he fired his arrow into the Serpens. The entire group was thrown to the ground and electrified. Once the Serpens fell to the ground, Orion rushed towards Ulysses, who was covered in scrapes and dust.

"Ulysses!" he shouted, "What happened?"

"We created a diversion!" he answered, "Did it work?"

"No, I mean, how did that get here?!" Orion shouted, pointing at the Leviathan.

Ulysses shook his head, "That must be what Chiron did!"

"Where is he?"

"I don't know, we've been busy!"

Orion groaned and took off down the street, trying to find his way back to Chiron. The entire city was in shambles.

Every building Orion passed had been toppled, and the Serpen families were running in terror, unable to do anything to stop it. It reminded him of Luma City. It reminded him of everything Oberon had said.

'This is all my fault,' he thought, 'This was their home, and I destroyed it,' He watched as women held their children tight and fathers wrapped their arms around their families, 'I have to stop this,' he thought, 'I can't let them be destroyed.'

Orion slid to a stop and grabbed a fleeing Serpen by the arm, "Wait!" he shouted.

The Serpen pulled against him, "Let me go!" he begged, "We've done nothing to you!"

"I know!" Orion shouted, "Please! Let me help you! Where is the nearest tunnel to the surface?"

The Serpen froze, looking dumbfoundedly at Orion, "It's...down this street. That's where I am taking my family," he answered.

"Take them and meet me back here!" Orion said, "I need you and the other men to help me lead everyone else out of here!"

The Serpen nodded and stepped back, shaking as he looked at him, "Why are you doing this?" he asked, "You're the ones who started this!"

"I know!" Orion shouted, "I know! But not everything has to be lost. You can still save your people! We can help you save what matters!"

The Serpen looked around, then nodded again. Orion rushed down the street and began calling out to the fleeing citizens.

"This way! The tunnel is this way. Come on!"

The dust clouded the path, and the Serpens could no longer see the way out. Orion pulled a white arrow from his quiver and fired it just above the street. It struck the cavern wall and erupted with bright white light.

"This way!" Orion shouted, "Follow the light. That's the way out!"

"Orion!"

Orion turned and smiled in the direction that voice came from, "Chiron!" he shouted.

"Orion!" From the dust emerged his grizzled companion, with his sword in hand. Orion sprinted towards him with relief washing over his heart. He threw his arm around him and sighed as he held him tight.

"Alright, I'm not dead yet," Chiron groaned.

"You should be!" Orion snapped, "You released the Leviathan?!"

Chiron shrugged and rolled his eyes, "Yes, and a band of pirates. Today has not been my finest hour."

Orion pointed out to the cavern wall, "The Serpens are heading towards the flare. That's the way out!"

"Then we need to get the beast's attention. Keep it off their backs!"

Orion grinned and turned to look into his grey eyes, "You ready, old man?" "Ready as you are, my boy."

The pair rushed down the street to the heart of the city, and as they ran past the crew, they finished their skirmishes and joined them, regrouping at a square in the heart of the city; in the path of the rampaging Leviathan.

"We have to stop it from attacking the people!" Orion shouted.

"Do you see that thing?" Triton cried, "It's tearing this whole place apart. There's nothing we can do to stop it!"

"Steady boys," Ulysses said, "The prince has a plan. Just follow his lead."

The crew looked at Orion, but he was frozen. Every man was bruised, cut, and heaving with exhaustion. Even together, they were in no shape to take on the beast. It had been ravaging the entire city without suffering so much as a scratch.

"We don't have to fight it," Orion said, "We just have to keep it here and seal the exit before it can follow us. Ulysses, how many men are fit to fight?"

Ulysses looked around, mouthing to himself as he assessed his men, "Six, if you count yourself, me, and Chiron."

"No, Captain, we're fine," Brutus groaned, clutching his side. We're not going to leave you here."

"I can't afford to lose you or anyone else, Brutus," Ulysses said, "Chiron is going to give you each a blue flower, break it and squeeze what's inside over your wounds. Triton, you and the rest of the wounded are going to make a break for the tunnel once we get its attention."

"Uncle, I-"

"That's an order!" Ulysses snapped, "Find my skiff and come back to pick us up. Can you do that?"

Triton stood tall and nodded eagerly, "Yes, sir."

Chiron passed the blue flowers to every member of the crew except for Jax, Sirius, Ares, and Ulysses, then turned to Orion and handed the last flower to him.

"Just in case," he whispered.

Orion nodded and tucked the flower into his tunic, and Ulysses' men did as they were instructed. Once their wounds were tended, they stood ready for Orion's command.

Ulysses looked to Orion and grinned, "You're right, you know," he said warmly, "You're not the prince me and the lads wanted. You're the prince we needed."

Orion grinned and pulled a white arrow from the quiver. He pulled it back as far as he could.

"Once he fires, run like hell, boys!" Ulysses cried. Orion pulled the arrow tighter.

"Hold!" Ulysses urged.

Orion aligned the tip of the arrow with the Leviathan's fiery eye, "Hold!"

Orion fired.

"Run for it!"

The arrow flew across the rooftops of the city, igniting with white fire as it struck the red eye of the beast. It turned towards them with a shrieking roar.

"Split up!" Ulysses shouted.

The six of them scattered in different directions as the monster glared at Orion. It winded its body faster and flicked its black tongue, looking down on Orion as he sprinted away. Orion knew that he could not outrun it. Dirt flew out from beneath its massive body and peppered the back of Orion's neck as he ran. He could hear the monster rumbling as it slid against the road, growing louder and louder behind him. He had not even made it halfway down the street before he started to feel the monster's hot, rancid breath blow against the back of his head.

The leviathan shrieked and drove its snout down towards Orion. Orion leaped to his left, narrowly escaping its snapping jaws, and immediately ran in the opposite direction.

Seeing this, Chiron shouted at the top of his lungs from an intersecting street, "Hey! Over here!"

The beast turned and snarled. Chiron plucked a stone from the dust and threw it at the beast's snout. The stone found its mark, but it only irritated the leviathan even more. It sounded out with an even louder shriek and winded its body faster than ever. The sides of its horned spine crashed into the toppling buildings, scattering more stones onto the neighboring streets. Chiron sprinted as hard as he could, running through the narrow alleyways to slow its pursuit. His efforts were futile. The ravenous monster growled and thrust its heavy head like a battering ram into the buildings and destroyed them. Chiron rounded around one of the larger buildings, thinking the beast would finally be forced to make a wide turn.

The Leviathan did not even slightly slow itself. It reared itself up and dropped the horns on its head into the walls and crashed through. The stones flew towards Chiron, and one flew directly into the back of his head. He fell to the ground, and the monster flicked its salivating tongue.

Orion saw Chiron fall to the ground and quickly drew two blue arrows. He fired them as he sprinted towards the monster, watching them strike it in the side of its body. The shockwave electrified it. It groaned as it writhed over itself in agony. Chiron was able to crawl just out of the way, hiding behind a toppled wall.

Jax, Ulysses, Ares, and Sirius leaped down from a rooftop onto the monster's back and began hacking at its spine with their swords. The Leviathan shrieked furiously, and hot breath steamed from its wide nostrils. It snapped its tail back and forth until it flew up and whipped them off its back. The four crewmates fell to the ground.

The only one among them still on their feet was Orion, and as the beast flicked its tongue at the fallen crew, Orion drew three white arrows. He took aim at the Leviathan's hissing jaws. He waited for the beast to turn its head just a little more; for the last possible moment, before it opened its jaws to devour Ulysses and his men.

He watched as the monster widened its jaws, revealing every fang. Then, with a long, patient exhale, he fired.

The three arrows found their mark upon the side of the creature's face, and a thunderous explosion of white fire shook every building on the street. The creature hissed and groaned, falling onto its side, throwing itself on the ground again and again to try and extinguish the flames.

Orion looked back to the streets. They were empty. Now was their chance to escape. "Let's go!" he shouted, "Run for the tunnel!"

Chiron rushed to help the others to their feet, and they all followed Orion as he led them down the streets toward the flare.

On the final street leading to the open tunnel, Orion waited for all five of them to pass, counting each of them to make sure they had every man. Ulysses passed first, then Chiron, Ares, Jax, and Sirius.

Just as he was about to follow them, he saw the Leviathan rise up and glare at them from where they had left it. It roared with its most furious bellow yet as fire smouldered against its blackened face. Orion's heart dropped as it spotted him and reared itself back to strike.

It thrust itself over the tops of the ruined city, covering more than a hundred feet of distance. Orion knew that as soon as it landed, it would either crush him or devour him. There would be no escape.

# Chapter Eighteen: The Duel

The Leviathan hurdled its massive body over the rooftops to strike down and devour Orion. Orion stood firm, separating himself from the group, and drew his two remaining blue arrows with his eyes closed.

'This is it,' he thought, 'Let it mean something.'

He released his arrows. They flew into the open jaws of the beast. The shockwave rang in his ears and sent him flying backward. He landed on his back in the dirt, completely defenceless. He did not try to jump to his feet. He kept his eyes shut, waiting for the monster's ravenous jaws to snap over him.

He heard nothing. He felt nothing. He thought that it was simply the sensation of death. But after several moments had passed, when he finally mustered the courage to open his eyes, he did not see a black oblivion.

He saw a great beam of light crashing down from the high ceiling of the cavern above the city and from the main beam, dozens of smaller flashes of lightning, striking the remaining rooftops of the city and the walls of the cave.

'Where is the Leviathan?' he wondered, sitting himself up. He saw its head lying inches in from the toes of his boots, awkwardly paralyzed as if it had seen something terrifying or that it had experienced some excruciating pain. Its jaws were partially opened, and when he looked down at the rest of its body, he saw that it had been cut in half. The other half of its length was nowhere to be seen.

Orion felt dazed, not entirely sure what was happening. Then, he felt Chiron's hands grip him tightly by the shoulders. His ears were still ringing, and his vision was blurry, but he could almost make out the muffled words Chiron shouted.

"He's here! Get up!"

Orion tried to get up, falling over in his daze. Chiron picked him up and helped him run towards the dying flare shining above the cavern. Ulysses and his crew were only a few paces from its threshold. But before they could enter, another disaster struck.

A branching beam of lightning struck the flare, and rocks came tumbling down from where it struck, falling onto the path in front of the tunnel.

"Go!" Ulysses shouted, "We can still make it!" he ushered his men to run faster with every step, but they were not fast enough. A large boulder crashed into the dirt road, and a cloud of dust billowed all around them.

"No!" Ulysses shouted in despair, "Come on! We have to make it!"

His men rushed to his side, all putting their hands upon the stone and pushing against it with all their might. It did not budge.

"Cosmo, plant another charge!" Ulysses ordered.

"I don't have anymore, captain," he said regretfully.

Ulysses looked to Orion, "Orion, your arrows! You can break the rock!"

Orion nodded tiredly, but when he reached back, he felt nothing. His heart dropped into his gut. He reached back once again but only felt two fletchings. He pulled them out. Two black arrows.

"I don't have any more…" he said, "I can't."

Ulysses' frantic breathing reflected his building panic, "Chiron, what do we do?"

The great beam of light disappeared, slowly fading down into the center of the city. Above it was the enormous circular hole it had bored into the cave, revealing the blazing red light of the sunset. Hundreds of feet above them, hundreds of feet out of reach.

Chiron looked at the men gravely, "We fight," he said, "We make our stand and keep the prince alive."

Orion's hearing was clearing, and he stood taller as he regained his balance, "Chiron, we can't ask that of them," he looked up at the face of each man, "Hide," he said, "Survive long enough until Triton comes for you. You need to tell your people what has happened here."

"Orion, we aren't leaving without you," Ulysses said, "You may not trust us, but we will lay down our lives for you without question. If Chiron says this is where we make our stand, then this is where we make it."

"This isn't about trust," Orion said, "You all have done more than I could ever ask of you already. This is about winning the war. Whether or not I live or die, this fight must go on. It can't end here."

Chiron looked at Orion with a worried glare, "Boy," he said, "What are you going to do?"

Orion looked at Chiron with a sorrowful gleam in his blue eyes, "I have to give him what he wants…me, alone. Otherwise, he'll come for you and the crew."

"No!" Chiron snapped, "If you are going, I will go with you."

"Chiron," Orion said calmly, "I know you would, but they need you too,"

"I will not break my vow," Chiron said, with his voice beginning to break.

"You aren't," Orion said, "You helped me learn everything I didn't know. You helped me see that I know so much less than I thought I did, and I finally know what I have to do."

"You are not ready to face him," Chiron said, "If you do, he will kill you."

"Not really," Orion said, "As long as the story lives, my death means just as much as my life."

Orion pulled the small device he recovered from the Chancellor's chambers and placed it into Chiron's hand.

"Drago murdered the Chancellor and confessed to his betrayal. The chancellor recorded everything here. When you get out of here, you have to make sure that everyone on every world sees this."

Chiron shook his head tearfully, "Orion, your mother, your father-"

"They did the same thing, Chiron," Orion said, "Their deaths didn't mean nothing. They died so we would avenge them, so that the fight could go on," Orion placed his hands around Chiron's fist as he clutched the small device in his hand, "Please," he begged, "Help me avenge them. Help me avenge us all."

Chiron could not force any words from his throat, and a single tear slowly fell from the corner of his eye. Orion removed his hands from Chiron's fist and turned away from the group. He started walking through the suspended dust hanging in the street.

Ulysses brushed past his men's shoulders and ran to try and stop Orion from taking another step down the street, but before he could reach him, Orion had already pulled the hood of his cloak over his head and vanished.

He looked back to Chiron, who cried as he held the device in his fist, "You can't let him do this!" Ulysses said.

"That is not our choice to make," Chiron choked,

"We can't just let him die!"

"We won't!" Chiron snapped, glaring at Ulysses, "We will protect this confession and his legend so that it is heard. We will honor his sacrifice."

"Chiron, I can't believe you are saying this!" Ulysses snarled, "You swore to protect him!"

"When the people hear of what happened here," Chiron said, "He will be more than just a man to them. Yes, I did swear to protect him, and I do not want to let him do this, but I must. We all must, Ulysses."

Ulysses shook his head, "You do what you want. I'm not going to stand by and do nothing," His crew followed him, and Chiron watched them all run down the street searching for their prince.

"You would be proud of him, Lyra," Chiron whispered to himself, "You both would."

Orion could hear Ulysses and his men calling out to him in the distance. He did not turn back. He turned around the corners of the city's ruins, walking closer and closer to the bright beam of red light shining down. He observed his surroundings. There were no more Serpens, no sounds of anyone around him. He knew that if Oberon was here, he was already waiting for him.

'Good,' he thought.

He peeked around the corner of one last building at the edge of where the red light shone into the cavern. He saw Oberon immediately, clad in black armor and draped in a tattered black cloak, sitting upon a stone in the rubble with twenty hooded sentry machines standing tall with swords on their backs.

Orion leaned against the wall of the building he hid behind and notched one of his last two arrows. He pulled it tight and pointed it around the corner. He felt his hand shake so much that he had to lower his bow. He could not slow his breath. He leaned his head against the stone wall.

"Mother, father," he whispered, "If you can hear me, please…be with me. I know that I have not honored your sacrifice, but please…be with me, and I will fight…for everything you did."

He squeezed his fist tight and took aim around the corner. He took a deep breath, let his breath out, and steadied his grip. He fired. The arrow flew towards Oberon, landing at his feet. When he saw the arrow strike the ground, he turned his head slowly and looked toward the building it flew from.

"Come, brother," he said, "I've been waiting for you."

Orion closed his eyes and took a deep breath, then walked out from the side of the building. As he stepped into the edge of the light, he deactivated the cloak and removed his hood. He stood still, glaring at the sinister mask on Oberon's face.

Oberon held his hand out to another large fallen piece of stone resting beside the one he sat upon.

"Sit down," he said.

His voice sent shivers down Orion's spine and made his hands shake with fury. He clenched them tight as he begrudgingly approached. Every sentry machine watched him with shining red eyes and made no move against him. He glared at Oberon as he sat beside him, keeping his bow held tightly in his fist.

Oberon pulled back his hood and removed his mask, resting it beside the arrow Orion had fired. He turned and looked at him, smiling cruelly with shining dark blue eyes.

"I have been looking forward to this," he said, "Though I must admit I must not have given you the best first impression."

Orion did not respond. He maintained his glare, fighting the urge to strike him down right where he was. Undeterred and amused by Orion's expression, Oberon continued.

"You have begun to realize your potential since you have arrived here," he said, "Although that is likely Chiron's doing. He tends to plant false hope in the hearts of everyone who hears him."

"Is that really what you think of him?" Orion said, "The man who loved us both more than our own father ever did?"

"Rom Castus was never our father," Oberon snarled, "He was a tyrant, a swine, hungry for power and wealth."

"Sounds a lot like you," Orion said, "You promised Drago and his men power; power only you could give them. That doesn't sound like a fair deal."

"Greed is a powerful ally, and power is a deadly sword in the proper hands, but it must be wielded against the right enemies if any good is to come from it."

"Like our own people? The Serpens? The High Council?"

Oberon scoffed, "Even now, your vision is too small to see the true evil that plagues us all,"

"Or you're just too blind to see what that you've become that evil!" Orion said, "Look around you, look at everything you've caused!"

Oberon laughed at Orion's words as he stood to his feet, holding his arms out to the city, "This is your doing, just as it is mine. You and I are exactly alike, so do not think for a moment that you are above me, little brother. We are-"

"Agents of Chaos? Who bring destruction to everything we touch?"

Oberon's smug expression vanished from his face, "Do not mock me," he snarled, "You cannot tell me that this is not clear to you as well."

Orion stood to his feet, "What's clear to me is that you are wrong, Oberon. Whatever Rom did to you was wrong, but you don't need to cause anyone else pain because of it. You killed our father, our mother, the man that raised me, and countless others. You enslaved our people, who would have welcomed you back with open arms."

Oberon did not even flinch, "You still do not know the truth," he said, "But don't worry, little brother, I will show you everything that you are," He drew his sword off his back.

Orion shook his head, "I won't fight you, Oberon. Not if I can help you,"

"Even after what I have done… to your friend?"

Orion's heart dropped when he heard those words.

"Oh yes," Oberon hissed, "You should have been there. Just imagine what I could do to a man in just one day. I'm surprised he hasn't finished himself off for me."

Orion heard chains rattling behind him, coming from inside a building. It grew louder, and Orion began to hear a hoarse yet familiar voice.

"Please, don't! Don't!" the voice begged.

Orion turned and watched a sentry emerge, dragging a long chain behind him. Shackled at the other end was a man who was stripped bare, covered in bruises. His eyes were nearly swollen shut, and fresh blood dripped down his chin as he begged the sentry to leave him alone.

"Please!" he shrieked, "No! Don't take me back to him!"

Orion knew his voice, "Rowan!" he shouted.

He rushed over to him as the sentry holding his chain stood over him. Orion wrapped his hands around his friend's bashed face and cried as he tried to reassure him.

"Rowan, Rowan, it's me. It's Orion!"

"No!" Rowan howled, "Get away from me!" he kicked against him and panicked through the dirt like a wounded, terrified animal. Orion watched in horror as he curled himself and lay on the ground, rocking back and forth. Everything he had feared most for his dearest friend had been inflicted upon him. His once bright brown eyes were now hollow beneath the swelling. All his long, blonde hair had been crudely shaved off of his head, and he was covered in more cuts and bruises than Orion had ever seen or imagined that one man could take.

"He sees now," Oberon said, "For the rest of his life when he looks upon you, it will be as if death itself is standing before him."

Orion felt tears roll freely down his face as he dropped to his knee and set his bow down next to him, "Rowan," he whispered, "Look at me."

"Please," Rowan cried, "No more…I can't,"

"Look at me. You know who I am."

Rowan rocked himself back and forth faster and began to weakly chant, "You're the Dark Lord, master of all things and me, you're the Dark Lord, master of all things and me, you're the Dark Lord, master of all things and me, you're the Dark Lord, master of all things and me…."

Orion's heart sank, then filled with rage.

"What have you done to him?" Orion said, "WHAT HAVE YOU DONE TO HIM?!" He whirled around and stared furiously at Oberon, who stood looking proudly upon his tortured friend.

Oberon simply raised his palms up, "What have *you* done to him?" he asked, "You abandoned him, and then proved that the Serpens are right to despise humans; that they are a dangerous, destructive people, who must be destroyed."

"You did this!" Orion shouted, "You sent me here to serve your ends and die!"

"And it has made you strong," Oberon said, "Like me. Now you must accept yourself for what you were made to be, surrender to your true purpose."

Orion looked back to Rowan as he chanted madly. He placed his hand on his bruised, shaved head. Rowan cowered and shivered under his touch.

"Rowan, please," he begged, "Look at me,"

Rowan shook and peeked his head above the tips of his fingers, "Don't hurt me, master," he said, "I am loyal, I swear."

"He is not your master," Orion whispered, "You are not his slave. I know that you still know who you are."

Rowan broke into a new chant, "I am the filth that will be purged in the eclipse, I am the filth that will be purged in the eclipse, I am the filth that will be purged in the eclipse…."

Orion stood to his feet and looked back to Oberon, "What is 'the eclipse'? What is he talking about?"

"The eclipse is our destiny, Orion," Oberon said, "It is what we were made for."

Orion shook his head and looked back to his tortured friend, chanting a single word as he shook in the dirt.

"Eclipse, eclipse, eclipse, eclipse, eclipse…."

"Enough!" Orion snapped, "Let him go!"

"Even if I did, he would still be mine," Oberon said, "The freedom of choice is a lie, brother. Everything within this entire cosmos is predestined. Everything that lives dies, and everything that begins ends. You and I will bring about the end… together."

"You're insane," Orion said.

"I'm the only sanity left! So are you! Your destiny is to stand with me or to be buried here with my sword in your heart!"

Orion scoffed. He stood taller and stepped closer to Oberon, holding his bow tightly in his fist, looking into his eyes as they glared with savage rage.

"You said it yourself, brother. What happens next is *my* choice. I make my own destiny." he said, "But if you have already made your choice, then I will make mine. I won't let you cause any more suffering, and if I cannot save you, then I will end you."

"So, you have chosen death," Oberon growled,

"No," Orion said, "I just promise yours."

Oberon took his stance, letting the tip of his sword graze the dirt behind him. Orion pulled the last arrow from his quiver and took aim at Oberon's head. He slowly adjusted his fingers, working them up on the grip of his bow. He stood patiently, waiting for Oberon to charge. Oberon's feet scratched against the dirt. He charged. Orion stood still. He waited until the tip of his black sword was just one pace in front of him. Then, he released his fingers from the drawstring.

Oberon whirled his sword to cut the arrow down. He would have done so… if Orion had let it go. It was still notched on the bow. Orion had it pressed between his forefinger and thumb, aimed at a now defenseless target. Oberon tried to recover, raising his blade up to defend himself, but he was only a few inches from the tip of Orion's arrow. That is when Orion fired.

The arrow flew past the edge of Oberon's sword and into his chest. Oberon groaned as his body fell limp, into Orion's lap. The two brothers fell to the ground. Orion rolled out from beneath Oberon and drew his short sword, but Oberon did not spring from the ground. He laid in the dirt, motionless.

Seeing this, the sentries around Orion finally sprung to life. Simultaneously, they drew the pairs of swords from their backs and began whirring and clanking toward Orion.

He stood ready to defend himself against them, then a voice called out from a nearby rooftop, "Hey!"

Orion's lips curled up to a full smile. It was Ulysses. He came flying into the street with his sword in hand. Sirius and Ares landed beside him, followed by Jax.

"We're here to keep the fight going, your highness!" Jax shouted.

Orion nodded, and they all turned, charging into the mechanical warriors. Orion turned back immediately to where Rowan was lying, but he was no longer there. He saw the end of the chain that was holding him sliding away in the dirt. He took off after it.

"Where are you going?" Ulysses shouted,

"I have to find Rowan!" Orion said,

"Who the hell is Rowan?"

Orion did not respond. He turned and followed the chain as it began sliding between the buildings even faster. He did not want to frighten him, so he let it run freely at his feet as he chased after his friend, calling his name.

"Rowan!"

He could hear him howl madly from the alleyways ahead, "Get away! Get away!"

Orion ran faster. He could hear Rowan's somewhat coherent ramblings become one long, horrifying howl. It made Orion's heart bleed. He had to save him.

"Rowan, stop!" Orion begged, "I'm your friend. I can protect you!"

Orion looked down and saw that the chain had stopped moving. He still heard Rowan's howls, but it was no longer fading into the distance. Orion bent down and took the chain in his hand. He followed it to an intersection with small fires scattered all over the street. That is where he found he found Rowan, frantically drawing in the dirt beneath the light of the flames.

Orion slowly paced towards him as he muttered and rambled beneath the firelight. "Rowan," he said softly, "It's alright, I can take you away from here, you're safe,"

"Safe? No, no, no, no, not safe!" he rambled, "Not safe, no one safe, no one…."

"I know you're scared," Orion said, placing his hand on his shoulder, "But you don't have to be anymore. Oberon is dead."

Rowan snapped his head and roared madly as he pushed Orion away from him. Orion looked up from the dirt as Rowan pointed and shouted down to him, "Not dead! Never dead! Can't be dead!"

"I-I killed him myself. He *is* dead. It's over!"

"No, no, no, you don't know! No one knows!"

Orion picked himself up and grabbed both of Rowan's arms to stop his trembling long enough to look him in the eye, "Please stop. You're not making any sense. What do I not know?" Rowan froze and looked at Orion with a quivering lip.

"He cannot die," Rowan whispered, "I stabbed and stabbed and stabbed, and the very next day, he came like he always comes, and he hurt me…." He broke into a childlike sob, then dropped back down to his side and curled up, rocking back and forth.

Orion could hardly recognize his friend or understand what he said. It was impossible to tell what was fact and what was madness. He racked his brain for anything that might remind his friend of who he truly was, a part of him that

Oberon could not take away from him. Anything that might snap him out of his madness.

"Rowan, do you remember the family? Their little boy that came to you asking for food?"

Rowan stopped rocking back and forth, and his sobbing quieted to a gentle moan. He turned his head over his shoulder.

"They were starving," he whispered, "We fed them, but we killed them too."

Orion shook his head and knelt, "No, Rowan. Oberon killed them. We tried to help them. You tried to help them."

"Can't help, never help, only cause more pain,"

"No. You gave them hope, Rowan."

"Hope is a lie. Hope is a lie," Rowan whimpered.

"It's not. You don't believe that. Hope is why you're still alive."

"NO!" he shouted. He flipped onto his knees and crawled frantically toward one of the drawings he had left in the dirt. He pressed his forehead into the dirt, and with one outstretched, shaking hand, he pointed to it. Orion walked slowly toward what he had drawn. It was a circle, nothing more.

"What does it mean?" Orion asked.

Rowan only responded with a chant, "Eclipse, Eclipse, Eclipse…."

Orion shook his head in confusion. Rowan was the third person he heard use that word, but the significance of it was still unclear.

"Which star?" Which eclipse?" Orion asked.

Rowan pounded his fist in the dirt, "No, no, no, no," he groaned, "No one understands. No one knows what he is planning."

Orion grabbed Rowan. He flipped him onto his back and shook his shoulders, "Rowan, please! I just want to help you! Stop!"

Rowan hid his face behind his filthy hands and whimpered in terror. Orion stepped back, and his tears started to fall freely from his face. He could not believe that he felt guilty for killing Oberon. He wanted more than anything to make him undo whatever he had done to Rowan, but he could not. He could not help but feel as if he had lost his friend forever.

"I told you," a cold voice said from behind him, "He is mine forever, and he always will be."

Orion could not believe what he was hearing. He turned around, and he felt as if the wind had been kicked out of him. Oberon was standing completely unharmed in front of him.

Orion shook his head in disbelief, "I-"

"Killed me?" Oberon said, "No, little brother. Nothing can kill me, not even you."

Oberon charged towards him and drew his sword; Orion reached back to his quiver and drew his sword. He raised it to block Oberon's strike. As their swords met, Orion could feel Oberon's incredible strength as he pushed him back toward the fire. Orion planted his feet, and they scratched to a stop. Oberon swung his fist and struck Orion in the jaw, knocking him to the dirt. Orion flopped himself onto his back as Oberon raised his sword overhead.

They locked blades again, and Oberon glared down at Orion with a cruel smile. "Accept it, Orion!" Oberon grunted, "Think of all the people you've killed, all the pain you've caused. Because of you, your friend will spend what's left of his life begging to die! You are just like me. If you join me, we will be the most powerful beings in the cosmos! We would bring the cosmos to its knees!"

Orion grunted and kicked Oberon's knee. Oberon stumbled back. Orion rolled out from under him. He jumped to his feet, pulled his hood over his head, and activated the clasp of his cloak, vanishing before Oberon could turn around.

Oberon smiled as he looked around, peering through the flames, "You can't hide from the truth, Orion! Whether you can see it or not! We are what everyone refuses to acknowledge; we are inevitable!"

Orion swept to the other side of the flames so Oberon could not see his footprints in the dirt, looking for the right opportunity to strike. He crouched down next to a larger flame and shouted.

"Chiron trained you to be the best of us! He taught you to fight for peace, not cause chaos!"

Oberon stomped towards Orion's voice, and as he did, Orion rushed to hide behind another fire. Oberon swung his sword through the flames. Orion called out again, "You're the one who hides from the truth! Stop this madness!"

Oberon shouted furiously and thrust his blade through the fire toward Orion's voice. "Your tricks will not save you or your friend!" Oberon shouted, "Show yourself!"

Orion climbed up onto a rooftop and looked down from above. Oberon had turned back towards Rowan, who was still sobbing and rocking back and forth, unaware, or perhaps numb to the imminent danger walking towards him.

Orion jumped off the rooftop and swung his sword into Oberon's arm. It sliced into the meat of his shoulder, and he groaned in pain, wildly swinging his sword around him. Orion ducked beneath it and snatched Rowan's chain up from the ground, breaking it with a swift chop of his sword. He picked Rowan up from underneath the arm and dragged him back toward the center of the city.

Oberon took off after them as they ran towards the crumbling fortress. They ran past the statues of Serpen warriors, faster with every step as Oberon called out to them,

"There is no escape, Orion!"

Orion pulled Rowan behind him, running headlong across the threshold and through the hallways. All the torches had been extinguished, and after the first few turns, it became impossible for him to find his way through the dark.

Orion looked back and heard Oberon's footsteps behind them. They were slow but getting closer with every step. Orion quickly pulled the cloak off his shoulders and threw it around Rowan.

"You need to stay here," Orion whispered, "Don't move. I'll hold him off."

Rowan did not respond. He just rocked back and forth on the ground where Orion set him, muttering under his breath. As Orion was about to turn down the hallway, he felt something sharp scratch the skin underneath his tunic. He reached in and pulled out the flower Chiron gave him. He looked back down at Rowan with wide and hopeful eyes as he knelt beside him. He snapped the stem in half, then gently turned Rowan's head up and opened his mouth. He squeezed the stem over his cracked lips and watched each drop fall into his mouth.

"I don't know if this will do anything," he whispered, "But if it does, please wait for me. I promise I'll come back for you."

Rowan remained silent, still rocking back and forth on the ground. Orion clenched his fists, wishing that there was something else he could do for him, but he knew that even if there was, none of it would mean anything if they did not escape from Oberon. He activated the clasp on the cloak, and once his friend vanished, he took his sword and ran back the way he came, towards what dim light remained in the fortress.

He crept towards the sounds of Oberon's footsteps. They grew louder as he approached, but they had changed in cadence from a determined stomp to a prowling scratch in the dirt. Orion jumped out from around the hallway corners, sure that he would find him, but he was not there.

"You feel it, don't you?" Orion could hear Oberon's voice behind him, like a whisper as loud as a roar. He swung his sword behind him, but he was not there. Orion felt his hands shake as his cold voice continued to taunt him.

"You can feel it in your heart. You know this is the end. You just can't see it," Orion began to question if he was hearing him speak or if it was something else inside his mind. He was no longer sure if he could trust his own senses or if what he was seeing was real.

Then, he felt something very real. A sharp pain across the back of his leg. He reached down to clutch his leg as he groaned, feeling his blood dripping onto his hand from a large open cut. He felt it again, this time on his shoulder. He turned around, wildly swinging his sword, but could not see anything. Then, he felt a fist strike his face, then his side, his gut, and then he felt the bottom of a boot strike him in the chest. He flew backward, landing hard in the dirt.

He groaned as he struggled to get back on his feet. He backed down the hallway slowly, but after only a few careful paces, he felt a fist snatch him from behind and a blade press against his throat.

"I'm sorry, but this is the end for you, brother," Oberon whispered.

Orion felt something take hold of him as he felt the blade begin to slide against his throat. Something so powerful that it seemed to stop time itself. He shut his eyes, feeling his impending doom, but when he closed his eyes, he was shocked when he still saw the hallway and in front of him, but something else was in front of him: a full head of long, black hair. He saw that he was holding the person in front of him the same way Oberon was holding him. Orion could feel his heart beating within his chest the same way it did when he had his vision of Rowan. It felt exactly the same. He could not even move his fingers; he was frozen in place. His suspicions were confirmed. He was inside Oberon's mind.

He could feel the posture of his body as he was trapped within it. He felt the intent of the arm that held the sword, the strength of the other that held him in place, and he also felt something strange and uncomfortable, as if he was about to fall backward. That was his only chance for survival.

He opened his eyes and it was as if time resumed it's normal flow. He mustered all his strength, throwing himself onto his back. Oberon's knees buckled as Orion pushed against him. He lost his grip on Orion, and they both fell to the ground. Orion rolled away and held his sword out in front of him. He caught a glimpse of his reflection on the blade, it was blurry, but he distinguished a bright, blue glow shining in his eyes. He looked back to Oberon as he regained his footing, but he did not feel fear. He felt adrenaline coursing through him and thoughts that were not his own, Oberon's thoughts. He felt his intent to charge and strike with precision.

As those thoughts pulsed through Orion's mind, Oberon charged, raising his sword to counter whatever move Orion made. Orion sensed a flicker of fear in him, feeling his vulnerability to one particular counter. Orion sprang forward, pushing Oberon's blade against the wall and striking him in the jaw, then kicking him backward.

Orion pushed him back through the halls of the fortress, countering him again and again and striking with every opening until their brawl had been pushed to the most damaged part of the crumbling fortress. Orion kicked Oberon back again, and with every blow, Oberon's face twisted more with confused rage. He cried out as he charged with another strike. Orion countered again and fell to a knee, swiftly cutting Oberon across the thigh.

Orion felt as if his senses had doubled. His heartbeat doubled, and his awareness was at a height he had never experienced before. He could hear Oberon's confusion, his fear, even before he spoke.

"What is this?!" Oberon shouted to him, charging wildly once again.

Orion did not answer. He just countered again. Perfectly. The two brothers locked blades again. Orion could feel how much stronger Oberon was than him. He knew that he could not overpower him. But he could use his prowess against him. He pushed their blades down, holding them to his left side, forcing Oberon into an awkward, leaning position.

Oberon glared at Orion as he held his blade over his, "Whatever this is, it will not be enough to stop me or save yourself."

"I've already beaten you," Orion grunted, "You just can't see it."

"I see everything!" Oberon shouted, "What could you see that I can't?"

Orion looked at Oberon, and the glow of his eyes reflected off the darkness in Oberon's, "I learned to look beyond myself," Orion said, "You never could. That is the difference between you and me."

Orion looked to the wall next to them and saw several gaps where the stones had fallen out. He mustered all his strength and pushed Oberon into the wall. The two broke through the remaining stones, and the walls of the room came toppling down on top of them. The room beside it also crumbled, and Orion could feel more and more weight fall onto his back. He could hear Oberon's pained shouts beside him fade as half of the walls of the crumbling fortress came crashing down. Orion felt the surge of adrenaline leave him and a calm wash over him as everything faded to black.

The silence and blackness seemed to last for eternity. Orion thought he could hear voices, but he did not know whose voices they were. He felt as if he was floating above the ground but was no longer sure what he was experiencing. He could not tell if it was unconsciousness, a dream, or a glimpse into Oberon's mind.

Then, the blackness was penetrated by light. Blinding light. Orion held his hand to shield his eyes, and everything around him became a blur of grey. He heard muffled voices above him.

"Is he waking up?" one asked, "He is alive!" another said.

"We need to tell him," the first said.

Then, a grizzled voice that was familiar even through the muffle spoke out to all of them, "Let him rest. We will tell him when he is ready."

Orion felt his lips move as he gave voice to the only thought in his mind, "Rowan," he wheezed, "Where's…Rowan?"

He tried to move, to do anything to reach out and find his friend, but his strength failed him, and the blackness engulfed him again.

# Chapter Nineteen: The Prince's Arrival

"Orion?"

Orion immediately recognized Chiron's voice, hearing it clearly and close to his ear. He opened his eyes and saw his surroundings clearly. He was inside Ulysses' ship, lying on a bedroll placed on the floor. He looked down at his arms and legs and realized they were covered in bandages. He looked to his left and saw Chiron sitting above him in one of the chairs at the rear of the ship.

"Chiron," he wheezed, "Where's Rowan?"

Chiron let out a long sigh and shook his head, "Orion, you need to rest. We will have more than enough time to talk about it when you've recovered."

Orion shook his head and tried to set himself up but felt pain shoot up his leg. Chiron placed his hand on his shoulder, "You barely survived. Half of the fortress came down on top of you. It took hours for us to pull you out from under it, even when the rest of the crew came back for us."

"Chiron," Orion grunted, glaring up at him, "Where is Rowan?"

A sad glimmer shone in Chiron's eyes, "We could not find him," he said, "We pulled every bit of the wreckage apart after the battle, but we could not find him or Oberon,"

"What? What do you mean you couldn't find them?" Orion demanded, "Rowan was there. Both of them were! I wrapped the cloak around Rowan, and Oberon was right next to me when the fortress came down, so there's no way they couldn't have been there!"

"Orion, we searched everywhere. If they were there, we would have found them."

Orion's eyes welled with tears, and he let himself fall back onto his back. "Rowan's alive, Chiron, and Oberon is still out there, we have to go back."

"Orion. We've already left Serpeno."

Orion's heart dropped. He rolled onto his stomach and struggled to his feet. He leaned against the side of the ship and limped towards the cockpit. His legs ached with every step, and his knees could barely support his weight, but he did not stop. He reached out to one of the chairs in the cockpit and pulled himself into it. What he saw when he looked out the window made both his heart and tears fall freely to the floor. What he saw was not Serpeno. It was an enormous room with a long opening looking out to a White and blue planet surrounded by enormous rings. Chiron walked up behind Orion and placed his hand on his shoulder as he sat behind him.

"Ulysses took us to Diana City, just as he promised. We were not followed, so we are safe for the time being."

Orion turned to him with streaks of tears wet against his face, "Chiron, you promised me that you would do everything you could to protect Rowan."

"Orion, there was nothing I could do," he said gently.

"You didn't see him. You didn't see what Oberon did to him. He destroyed his mind, his spirit, everything that mattered! We actually had a chance to save him! He needed us, and we just left him!"

"I did as you asked," Chiron said, "I protected the chancellor's confession and the crew. None of us could have predicted that he was bringing Rowan to Serpeno with him,"

"I could have. I should have known that's what he would do," Orion sobbed.

Chiron shook his head and leaned forward, "We don't know what those dreams actually were. It could have been the toxins, the seizure-"

"It wasn't Chiron," Orion said, "It happened again when I fought him, and I was wide awake."

Chiron's eyes widened, "What?"

"It was so fast. Just for a moment, I saw everything as he was seeing it. I could feel everything he was doing, just like I could before. I was able to…feel his weaknesses, and hear his thoughts."

"Did your eyes…?" Chiron asked.

"They were glowing," Orion answered, "Just like before," Chiron rested his bearded chin on his hands.

"This connection might be our biggest advantage against him."

Orion shook his head and wiped tears off his face, "Oberon can wait, Chiron. Rowan can't."

Chiron sighed and placed his hand on Orion's, "Orion. I am sorry, but it is far more likely that he did not survive. You need to accept that no matter how badly you do not want to."

Orion shook his head again and pushed Chiron's hand away, "Chiron!" he shouted, "I am sure he is still alive! Whether or not you are!"

Chiron nodded his head, "You said he was wearing the cloak when you hid him?"

Orion nodded. Chiron's eyes shined under the light as he reached over to the chair beside him. Orion's heart dropped. His cloak was resting on the chair. Chiron picked it up and gently placed it in Orion's lap.

"I'm so sorry," Chiron said, "We did not find anyone wearing it. It was just blowing above the rubble," Chiron unfolded it and pointed to a small tear with blood dried around it, then flipped it over and revealed a much larger stain running down to the hem, "Whoever was wearing it was wounded. They lost a lot of blood, and we did not find this wound on you, Orion."

Orion's head dropped into his hands. He could feel the tears pooling in his palms and the blood rushing to his face. Chiron watched him cry with a mournful look in his own eyes as he folded the cloak, placed it back on the chair, and sat down.

"He didn't deserve this," Orion cried.

"No, he didn't," Chiron said softly, "No one deserves death, Orion, not even Oberon. It comes for us all, no matter who we are. It comes in just about every way imaginable, from anyone or anything, for any reason. The only thing that separates the tragedy of death from its inevitability is the way one chooses to live. Rowan's death is tragic because he lived as a good man would, and that is something that even death cannot take."

Orion wiped his tears and sniffed. He sat still, looking out to the beautiful, white planet before him. He knew what Chiron was saying was true, Rowan had lived the best life one could live in his circumstances, but it did not take away the ache festering inside of him.

"I don't want to let him go, too," Orion cried.

"Everything he was will never be truly gone," Chiron said, "You will carry him with you forever," Chiron pointed to the center of Orion's chest, "In here."

Orion nodded gratefully, and Chiron patted his shoulder softly, "I'll leave you to rest," he said, "Do you want anything? Food? Water?"

"Water, please," Orion said softly. Chiron nodded and retrieved a canteen. When he placed it in Orion's hands, Orion could feel how cold it was. It made him twist the cap off eagerly to feel it on his tongue. As he drank, he savored every sip and did not stop gulping until he had swallowed every drop. Once he had, he leaned back in the chair and set his feet up on the console. It was not long before his eyelids grew heavy, and he drifted into a deep, restful sleep.

As he slept, he dreamed, remembering every little moment that he shared with Rowan. Some felt as if they were a lifetime ago, others as if they had happened yesterday. Those moments made even the difficult days bearable for him. They gave him something to look forward to, someone he could look to who had not yet been taken away from him. He remembered their adventures through the dead forests, imagining that the trees were still rich with leaves and that the animals had returned. They imagined seeing free people. They imagined a life where they were not hated for being human. He also remembered everything that had happened before he had been banished. Every biting word he said. How angry he was and how unfair he had been. He thought of all the chances he had to help Rowan fight to realize their childhood dreams. Those thoughts ate away at his heart and forced him to wake from his sleep. When he looked around, he saw that he was alone, with nothing but those regretful thoughts.

When he looked back to the skiff, he saw that he was alone. He looked back out to the planet, realizing that the daylight had faded from its surface and that the night had shadowed him. He shifted himself in the chair, trying to let his mind wander, hoping to fall asleep again, but his restless thoughts kept him awake through the night.

'He really was right,' he thought, 'About everything. I never got the chance to tell him just how right he was or show him that I finally understand.'

Orion looked back over to the cloak and took it from the seat. He unfolded it and let it fall to the floor until he found the bloody cut Chiron had shown him. He felt tears fall from his eyes and watched them wet the dried blood. He squeezed the torn cloak in his hands and held it tight to his chest. He held the cloak through the night until he could see the light of a nearby star break over the edge of the planet and bring the light of a new day.

He could feel the warmth on his skin and watched it shine against the fabric of the bloodstained cloak.

"You were right, Rowan," he whispered to himself, "About me, the people, everything. I'm so sorry… But I promise I will not let you die for nothing."

Orion jumped in the chair as he heard the hatch of the skiff open and looked back to see who it was. He saw Ulysses enter first, dressed in an ornate green tunic with silver trim, then Chiron behind him. His unruly hair and beard had been neatly trimmed, and his old, tattered clothes had been exchanged for a sharp blue suit coat with gold trim and shining black boots, the typical dress of a military officer.

"Hey," Orion said tiredly.

Ulysses stepped forward with a solemn expression on his face, "Your Highness," he said, "Nicodemus and his advisors have requested an audience with you."

"Why?"

"He would not say."

Orion shook his head with annoyance, "This isn't the best time, Ulysses. I'm tired."

Ulysses sighed, "I'm sorry. I know it isn't, but it's not just him. Word has already spread to the people that the prince from the prophecy is here, and they're desperate to see you."

Chiron took a step forward beside Ulysses, "We brought you clothes more fitting for the occasion," he said as he placed a pair of fine brown leather boots on the floor beside him and a folded set of clothes in Orion's lap. As the fabric touched his hands, Orion felt an unexplainable guilt for even touching it. The dark blue fabric was seamless, softer than anything he had ever touched, and the silver trim had small glimmers of gold in its reflection.

"I'm not wearing this," Orion said.

"Orion," Chiron grumbled, "These people have certain expectations of you, and it would be far easier to sway their support if you were to meet them on their terms."

"This war won't be on their terms," Orion said, struggling to his feet, "If we are going to ask for their help, then they deserve to see that so they understand what is coming."

Orion threw his cloak over his shoulders, recovered his bow and sword, and threw them onto his back.

"Nicodemus said no weapons," Ulysses said nervously.

Orion looked over his shoulder at Ulysses, "I don't care what he wants," Then, he flipped the hood of the cloak over his head and walked down the ramp.

As soon as Orion exited the ship, he saw Ulysses' crew standing tall in two straight lines, facing a long, blue carpet running into the enormous room. All of them were dressed in the same tunic as Ulysses, and as Orion set foot onto the blue carpet, they all raised their right hands into a sharp, simultaneous salute. Orion lowered his head and felt the heat of his blushing cheeks flow to his ears.

"Stop," he groaned, looking around at the crew, "Why are you doing this?"

He felt Chiron's hand on his shoulder, a warm, desperately needed touch of comfort followed by his soothing whisper, "This is a hero's welcome, Orion. They do this because you saved their life."

Orion looked at the face of each man, their posture, their eyes; he could see their resolute, collective pride and realized that no matter what he said, they would continue this gesture.

"Chiron, I don't know how to give the people what they expect. I don't want to pretend to be something I'm not. I just want to be me. I think that's what they'd want anyway."

Chiron chuckled and nodded, "I don't disagree, Orion," Then, he whispered in his ear, "And that's exactly what you must do. No matter what they say to you, be true to who you are, and take command of your people."

Orion looked at Chiron with shock, then felt a smirk break across the corner of his mouth as Chiron patted his back with a warm smile.

Then the grizzled man cleared his throat, "But please, change your clothes. You wreak."

Orion felt himself cave in with a chuckle. He shook his head as he turned back into the ship. Chiron smiled and walked beside him, keeping his hand on his shoulder.

Orion set his bow, quiver, and sword down and looked down at the clothes Chiron had given him.

'I don't deserve this,' he thought, thinking of Rowan and all he had suffered. He picked up the shirt and held it out, letting it unfold freely. 'I could never deserve this,' Orion thought, 'So I must earn it. I must earn it every day…for Rowan, for my parents, for all of us.'

He set the shirt on the back of the chair and started to pull his clothes off his back. He slipped the fine clothing on. He fastened a new leather belt around his waist, but before he could buckle it, he heard Chiron chuckle.

"Let me help you," he said gently.

"You don't have to," Orion said, feeling foolish.

Chiron smiled as he pulled the hem of Orion's shirt down to straighten it, "As I said, I'll teach you everything you do not know."

Orion looked at Chiron as he paced around him, making adjustments, "I never really thanked you for that."

Chiron stopped, "You will never have to."

"Yes, I do," Orion said, "And I have my own vow to give you in return."

Chiron nodded and folded his hands in front of him with glistening attentive eyes.

"I will not fail you," Orion said, "I can't be everything that everyone wants me to be, but I can promise you that I will earn your trust and faith in me, and I will let you teach me everything I need to know."

Chiron smiled warmly, "I already trust you, Orion, because you are true to who you are. That is the kind of prince the people deserve."

Orion nodded, and Chiron finished his adjustments, "There is something else you will need," he said. He walked to the back of the ship and returned with a large, shining metal band. "Not long after we arrived here, Ulysses and the rest of the crew made this for you."

"What is it?"

"This is your crown," Chiron said.

Orion's mind instantly protested, but he held those thoughts within, "It's beautiful," he said.

"It's actually not worth much," Chiron said, "Each of them gave a piece of their sword to make it, and the rest came from mine, and at its center is this," Chiron held it out to Orion, and Orion reluctantly took it from his trembling hands. He looked at the center of the crown and saw an arrowhead from one of his black arrows, polished to a shine and smooth at the edges.

"You may not have chosen this birthright," Chiron said, "And whether or not you accept it is up to you, but I know the people will follow you because they will see that their prince does not just fight for one man. He fights for everyone."

Orion felt his own hands tremble as he held the crown. He looked to Chiron with grateful, glimmering blue eyes and nodded as he made his decision.

Chiron stepped out of the skiff, and as he stepped off the ramp, he took one crisp step to the right and stood tall. Then, he raised his bearded chin and shouted, "Stand tall!"

The crew stood erect, their heels stamped as they found their mark. Chiron raised his gruff voice to a proud volume, "Present arms!"

The crew raised their salute, sharper and quicker than before, as Orion walked onto the ramp. He walked as tall as he could as his heart beat faster than it ever had in his entire life. No monster, no warrior intimidated him as much as this ceremonious process. As he stepped onto the carpet and walked past Chiron, he called out again.

"Hail Orion!"

The crew dropped their salute and stood tall, resounding Chiron's call, "Hail Orion!"

Their voices thundered through the enormous room. They rang in Orion's ears. The length of the carpet he walked on seemed to never end, and his heart pounded with every echo he heard sounding off the walls. Chiron and Ulysses marched quietly behind Orion, walking side by side, and as they passed each man, they turned forward one by one until they all faced the same direction.

Orion passed the last of the crew and stepped off of the carpet. The crew began marching forward at his sides, guiding him to a large, open doorway into another room. Orion could hear more voices. Many more. As he approached, he could see the faces of who they belonged to, craning around the corner for a glimpse of him, whispering in excitement. He could barely fend off the urge to tuck his chin to his chest and hide from their gaze, but it was too late. He had already crossed the threshold.

The room was full of people with beautiful clothes and smiling faces full of healthy color who roared with a triumphant chant as he passed through the lane they created for him.

"Hail Orion! Hail Orion! Hail Orion! Hail Orion!"

Orion kept his head forward and fought to keep the sadness he felt off of his face as he looked upon the people.

'They really don't know,' he thought, 'They don't know what is coming or what it will bring upon them,' The task of rallying this joyous crowd to a warpath seemed heavier and heavier with every step he took. He glanced to the end of the room and saw a bearded man with smooth white hair dressed in a long blue robe sitting on a large bronze throne. His face was pale as if he had seen a ghost beading at the top of the brow.

'Why is he not smiling with them?' Orion wondered, 'If this Nicodemus and this is what he prophesized, he should be pleased with himself.'

The old man stood up and held his hand out to the crowd. An instant hush washed over them.

"We are indebted to the heroism of this young man," the old man declared in a deep, smooth voice, "He has returned some of our best warriors to us, and upon their return, it was revealed to me that…he is no ordinary man."

His reluctant pause troubled Orion. His fears began to fade into the back of his mind, giving way to his growing suspicions.

"This young man," the old man said, "Is a son of Archon Prime, our lost homeworld. A glimmer of hope to us all that one day…our lost prince will return to us."

An outraged woman shouted out from the crowd, "He is our prince!" she shouted, "You know he is!"

The old man snapped towards the sound of her voice and glared at the woman, "Step forward!" he roared.

Orion looked back to Chiron with worry, but he was already storming up toward him. He stepped past him and raised an angry finger at the old man.

"You insolent coward!" he shouted, "You will not withhold the truth from these people or punish them for seeing what you do not wish them to see!"

The old man's eyes widened as he took a fearful step back, "Ch-Chiron?" he said softly, "That's right, Nicodemus," Chiron grunted, "I am not dead, and neither is the prince."

Chiron held his hand out behind him, "He is here right now. You will find whatever honor you have left and not deny it."

Nicodemus rose his head from its recoil and spoke even louder, "I-I have prophesized the prince's return, but there is no proof that this young man is who says he is."

The crowd murmured as he spoke. Some cried out with the same protests as the first woman who spoke out. Ulysses stepped forward beside Chiron.

"He has done just as you said he would!" he shouted, "He will lead us to reclaim our home. This is what you promised us!"

Nicodemus scowled again, "Careful, Captain. Do not forget with whom you speak. I brought all of your fathers and mothers here and kept them hidden from the dangers that lurk beyond this city. I have loved you, watched over you, and used my divine gifts to ensure that we continue our survival!"

Orion stepped between Chiron and Ulysses and looked up at Nicodemus, "Enough!" he shouted.

Every voice in the room fell silent once again, listening earnestly, "Nicodemus," Orion said, "May I speak with you alone?"

Nicodemus scoffed, "Whatever you have to say, you can say before us all, boy."

Orion nodded and turned to the rest of the room, looking at every pair of eyes that looked at him.

"There is no time for this, and this is not why I am here," Orion removed the crown from his head and handed it to Chiron, "I do not care if any of you recognize me as a prince, and I don't care if you do either, Nicodemus. I never asked for such a birthright, and I never will. I am here because a war is coming, a war that has already spread from Archon Prime to Serpeno. It will continue to spread across the cosmos if it is not stopped. The safety Nicodemus has given will not protect you, and there will be no running from it."

"No one would attack Diana City," Nicodemus said confidently, "It is a sanctuary protected by the High Council itself."

Orion turned back to Nicodemus with a glare, "This war will come for them, too," he said. "The son of chancellor Kobra betrayed his father, swearing his allegiance to the evil that is coming. He took control of their soldiers and murdered his own father…and that we can prove to you here and now."

Chiron smirked as he reached into his pocket and pulled out the device housing the chancellor's recording. Orion took it and held it out to the crowd as they murmured and whispered amongst each other. A man stepped forward with a communication device. Orion handed it to him, looking confidently up at Nicodemus as the man connected the two devices. He placed it on the floor in front of Orion, and the image began to flicker. The shadowy likeness of Chancellor Kobra appeared above the device, facing the image of Drago.

The entirety of the murder replayed before them. As the image of Drago choked the life from the image of his father, the life seemed to leave Nicodemus's face. He fell into his throne and gasped as the image of an arrow flew into Drago's eye, and the crowd's eyes widened when they watched Orion's image leap upon his back and plunge his sword into Drago's head.

When the recording ended, the man handed it back to Orion, who gave it back to Chiron. "There is your proof," Orion said to Nicodemus, "What prophesy do you have to deny that?"

The air in the room was thick with whispers and doubt. Nicodemus's lips quivered, and his eyes darted from left to right as the people's whispers turned to shouts of outrage against him. Orion looked around the room, letting all their disgruntled murmurings build to a roar, and then, he raised both his hands out to them. Seeing his gesture, the crowd turned from Nicodemus back to Orion with their full, silent attention.

"You can't doubt what you see for yourself," he said, "And the high council will not be able to deny this either. They need to see this for themselves, and we must prepare to fight!"

Nicodemus rose from his throne and stepped towards Orion.

"Give me the recording," he said, "I will see to it personally that it is transmitted."

Orion smirked, "That's alright, Nicodemus. Your finest warriors and I are more than capable of…acting on your behalf."

Before Nicodemus could further protest, Orion turned his back to him and walked back the way he came. Nicodemus's face twisted with anger, and he shouted out.

"Stop him! These are lies! Illusions! I assure you all you are safe! He will lead you all to death if you follow him!"

Chiron walked beside his old captain and grumbled, "For your own sake, you should hold your tongue. The truth will have its day, Nicodemus and the people will see through your lies," But before he could turn away, Nicodemus grabbed Chiron's wrist with a quivering grip, and he craned his head down with a whisper of his own.

"I am the one who gives you and the boy sanctuary here in respect for bringing my men back to me, do not forget that. These people are mine, and you will not take them from me."

"You sound like our king," Chiron said gravely, "Remember what happened to him?" Chiron jerked his wrist out of Nicodemus's grip and turned to follow Orion as Ulysses and the rest of the crew marched out of the room.

Just before Orion was about to step onto the ramp of the skiff, he heard Ulysses' voice call out to him.

"Your Highness?"

Orion turned to face him, "Don't need to call me that, Ulysses," he said.

Ulysses took a deep breath and sighed, "Orion, what happened in there…I'm sorry, I don't know why Nicodemus said those things."

"Well, he's been the leader of your people for a long time. It makes sense that he'd feel threatened."

"Not just that," Ulysses said, "It didn't sound like he wanted to help us at all. He promised all of us that any human that comes to him for refuge would be protected, so I don't think he means to do you harm, but the very mention of giving this recording to the High Council seemed to terrify him. I don't think he'll help you do it, no matter what the people say."

Orion nodded, then turned to the crew, "Cosmo!" Cosmo stepped forward and faced Orion, "Yes, sir?"

"Is there a way we can send a mass communication from here?"

Cosmo shook his head, "Not from the skiff or anywhere else Nicodemus oversees," "But you could go somewhere else within the city?"

Cosmo chuckled, "Your Highness, all the planetary rings are the city. That's a very large area to canvass."

Orion shook his head as he explained, then raised his hand, "Cosmo, I just need to know if it is possible."

Cosmo took a deep breath, "Yes, it is, and the best place to do it would be from the main communication tower."

"How far is it?"

"It's on the other side of the city," he said, "Nicodemus has no influence there, but it is heavily populated with Japrans and High Council security."

"How wide can you spread the message?"

Cosmo turned his chin upward and blinked rapidly, mouthing to himself, Orion craned his head forward, "Cosmo?"

Cosmo blinked and snapped his eyes back to Orion, "Theoretically, I can send it to every communication device in the Cosmos."

Orion looked at Ulysses with a grin and then turned back to Cosmo. "And how long would this take you?"

"Sending the message would take only a few seconds for me. I just need to get inside the tower,"

"It's impossible," Ulysses said, shaking his head, "No one could get in without being seen, and we'd be arrested on sight."

"I could," Orion said, "I can take the cloak, and Cosmo can walk me through what to do," A gruff voice spoke out behind him, "Are you sure you want to take that risk?"

Orion turned around and saw Chiron standing behind him, "Yes," he said, "But before we do this, we need to add a message to this recording."

# Chapter Twenty: The Beginning of a Beautiful End

As the sun broke over the horizon of Archon Prime, the people stopped, staring in amazement as thin rays of light broke through a small gap in the clouds, casting a rare but welcome warmth and light upon the dismal city. The routine of the slaves, however, continued as it always had. The workers answered the summons of the sentries and moved quietly to their respective stations. It was not until the sun rose to its height at midday that this routine would finally be broken. The interruption began with a small boy serving foul rations to the hungry workers when he heard a ringing from the communication device within the ration house. He gasped as he heard it. He stepped cautiously past an overwatching sentry to answer it. Every other slave within the ration house turned and faced the communication device, quivering as the boy's tiny, stained finger pressed the button to answer the communication.

Within the dark palace, a woman who was scrubbing the black tile heard the same trilling ring from a communication device in the main hall. She rushed to answer it, as she had always been ordered to, and the other servants working within the palace huddled around her.

Out in the black agro fields, the workers were ordered to stop and assemble as the sentry taskmaster summoned them, holding a communication device in its metal palm.

Each device received the same message. First, the image above the device flickered, then sharpened, and the shadowy silhouette of a tall young man in a cloak with long, curly black hair and striking blue eyes appeared before them,

His voice echoed throughout the city, "My name is Orion Castus," he said, "I am the last son of Rom Castus, the fallen King of Archon Prime. As I speak, this message is being sent to every corner of the Cosmos, and I beg you all to hear it because a great danger is coming for us all. The Regent of Archon Prime, my brother, Oberon Castus, who has enslaved, tortured, and murdered hundreds of my people, is the author of this danger, and he is not to be underestimated by anyone.

Despite the fact that Archon Prime no longer has the means for conventional interstellar travel, Oberon possesses a device capable of transporting himself and his forces to any planet long before any ship would arrive. He has used this device to banish many of my people, including me, and also to recruit followers to his cause. I do not know how many followers he has recruited, and I do not know where they are hiding, but I assure you, they are out there, waiting for their Dark Lord's command to strike. For those of you who doubt this warning, I have undeniable proof that what I say is nothing but the truth.”

The image flickered and disappeared, and a new one replaced it, an image of the Serpen Chancellor, and his son Drago. Every month that watched gasped and whispered as they watched and heard Drago’s confession. Sentries moved to intervene, but the slaves pushed them back, swarming desperately around them, bringing them to the ground and pulling them apart piece by piece.

More sentries rushed to their counterparts’ aid, silently cutting down the slaves as they tried to fight them off. Those who were able to crawl and push through the erupting chaos, protecting the communication as their friends, brothers, fathers, mothers, and children were slaughtered all around them.

Once the entirety of the chancellor’s murder had been broadcast, Orion’s image reappeared above every communication device.

“This threat is real,” he said, his voice echoing throughout the entire city, “But it is not too late. I call upon the Chancellors of the High Council and every willing soul who would fight to defend their homes from this terror, to prepare their warriors and intervene immediately. But if I am alone in this war, I will leave you all and my brother with a promise: I will not rest, I will not surrender, and I will stand to defend all worlds against this Dark Lord. I will avenge both the living and the dead, and when we face each other again, I will end his reign once and for all."

Orion's image vanished, and every communication device fell silent. There were no further protests around any of the devices after the message ended. All that remained of the uproar were fallen bodies over pools of blood, next to the fallen tears of the survivors, who had been forced to their knees by the sentries. The hands of each slave shook with rage, and their tired, sullen eyes gleamed.

One man in the fields spoke out to the sentries, glaring up at him with a filthy face and tearful eyes, "You've lost," he said in a wheezing voice."

"Silence," the android demanded.

"You can kill as many of us as you would like," the man said, "But it will not change this. Finally, after all these years, the war has begun again, and no matter what your master thinks, one day he will lose,"

The sentry raised his sword and decapitated the man for his outburst. Another man stood up and tackled the sentry, knocking its sword out of its hand. He crawled across the black dirt and snatched it up from the soil, and before the sentry could retaliate, he thrust the blade into its blazing red eye.

"Come on!" the man cried, "The prince needs us! The war has begun!" The remaining men from the field leaped to their feet and took whatever they could get their hands on, farming tools, stones, and fallen branches, and they charged into the city.

As their cries and the sounds of commotion resurged, everyone within the city heard them. Those who could not deny their newfound courage charged the sentries holding them on their knees and freed the others. Many sacrificed their lives, but none of their efforts were in vain. The sentries were not prepared for the riot that ensued. The inhabitants of Luma city began to burn down their homes and every structure they could set ablaze to slow the sentry army's advance. Families held each other tight and followed the cries of men shouting,

"Come on! This way! Into the forest!"

Hundreds were lost, but hundreds were saved, and the only structure they left standing in their desperate escape was the dark tower. Within its walls, watching from the window in the high chamber, was Oberon. He did not stir, even after what had transpired. He stood still, holding his hands behind his back.

A sentry rushed in, droning, "Master, the slaves are escaping. Shall we pursue them?" Oberon did not answer. The sentry repeated itself, "Master, the slaves are escaping. Shall we pursue them?"

Oberon turned and faced the machine, "No," he whispered, "Let them go."

"This is illogical," the sentry said, "I recommend we pursue them before-" Oberon drew his sword and sliced the machine's head from its shoulders. As its heavy body dropped to the floor, he turned to the center of his chamber with a horrifying scowl. His dark blue eyes blazed with rage as he spoke.

"This changes nothing. This small victory will not save any of them from what is coming."

"Eclipse, Eclipse, Eclipse, Eclipse," a frail voice chanted from the center of the room.

Oberon nodded as the frail voice continued to chant, "There is so much beauty in the cosmos that no one seems to ponder, Rowan," Oberon said, "Particularly, the beauty of an eclipse," Oberon walked to a fireplace at the edge of the chamber, picking up a metal prod and examined its glowing end. "An eclipse is the natural end to light. Unavoidable, impenetrable darkness that no light can penetrate. It is what death is to live. The end…pure…natural…perfect. Don't you agree?"

Chains rattled as Rowan quivered, "Yes, master, yes, the eclipse will come for all."

Oberon paced back to the center of the room and looked at Rowan with a smile. He had chained him and suspended him from the ceiling high enough for only the tips of his toes to graze the shining black tile on the floor. Rowan mouthed madly with wide, tearful eyes, staring down to the floor.

"Look at me," Oberon whispered.

Rowan quivered as he turned his head towards him, "Please," he whispered, "Just finish me. Find someone else. You don't need me…."

Oberon nodded his head, "I will. Once you have fulfilled your purpose, and believe me, Rowan, your purpose…is a great one."

Oberon thrust the end of the prod into the center of Rowan's chest, and he screamed out in agony as the red-hot prod seared his skin. After the agonizing moment, Oberon dropped the prod on the floor and stared proudly at what he had done. A steaming brand simmered upon his prisoner's chest. A thin, red circle of burnt flesh, and within it, another full, red circle.

"This is only the beginning," Oberon whispered, "of a beautiful end."